SALLY O'KEEF

Every Breath

First edition

This book was professionally typeset on Reedsy.
Find out more at reedsy.com

To my wonderful husband, Daniel.

Contents

Acknowledgement

Where to start? Firstly, thank you to God. Without Him and the talents He has given me, this book wouldn't exist. I want to thank my six children for their patience as I worked on just one more chapter; or put off dinner for an extra half hour to finish one last scene. My incredible husband for picking up the slack. My beta readers, ARC readers, proof readers, and editors; you all really put the time it to help this thing shine. Riley Moore for the lyrics for Every Breath and Whiskey's like love. And a special thank you to my friend, Kim, for reminding me what matters. I love you all and am so grateful for your friendships.

One - Dylan

How could Mom do that to me? I stormed into the pawn shop and stopped just inside the door. I took a deep breath as I saw the man who had knowingly ripped her off. The middle-aged jerk wore a dingy wife-beater and what looked like a sweater, but was actually a thick layer of body hair. He was sorting through a water stained box, and paused when he saw me.

"Can I help you?" He sucked something from between his teeth and chewed on it as his gaze crawled over me.

Gross. I straightened and tried to channel my best friend, Jenny's, confidence. "I'm here to buy back the 48' Chevy 3800 in your lot." I crossed my fingers behind my back. *Just sell it to me you Jabba the Hutt stunt double.*

His eyes flashed with recognition. "You Tom Kennedy's kid, then?"

How dare he even speak Dad's name as he was ripping off his widow. It sent a pang through me, but I stiffened my spine and forced a smile. "Yes, sir." It got on my last nerve to be nice to this man, but he had what I wanted, and he'd paid a pittance of what it was worth.

"Twenty-five grand."

My mouth dropped open, and a knot formed in my stomach. "You bought it from my mom for twelve!" I knew it was worth more than that, but Mom had stupidly sold it to a pawn shop.

He had the audacity to grin. "Inflation."

"Since yesterday?"

He shrugged his furry shoulders. "I had a buyer in mind when I got it. He's offering twenty-five grand. He's out of the country for a couple months, so if you can come up with it before then, I'd be happy to sell it back to you." He turned back to the box he'd been rummaging through. "But you understand, missy, I can't just sell it for what I paid. I wouldn't be able to keep the lights on."

I reached into my purse and fingered the envelope of money. I'd taken it from Mom last night when she told me she'd sold the truck. And I'd come down first thing this morning to get it back. But to pay double that? "I'll see what I can do. Don't sell it to anyone else while I come up with the money, okay?"

Skeeze ball shrugged. "Can't promise anything."

My shoulders slumped as I left the pawn shop, and I swallowed back tears. There was no way I could come up with that amount of money in time. Despair threatened to overwhelm me. I took a shaky breath as I walked through the lot to the truck and ran a finger along the camo-green paint near the rear tire.

Memories flashed through my mind. *Handing Dad tools as he worked on it. Helping him sand it down before painting. Spending hours doing homework in the shop while he worked. The soundtrack of his tools clinking and clanking as he finally brought the thing back to life. Going on daddy-daughter dates and eating ice cream in the bed of his truck.*

Then finally, his casket being lifted into the bed, and driving it the two blocks to the cemetery and his final resting place.

I swallowed the lump in my throat and blinked away the tears that were threatening to fall. I couldn't let it go.

But what were my options? I'd applied for a summer job at the grocers between semesters at Montana State, but nothing had come of it. They said they'd keep my resume *"on file." Whatever that meant.*

I could sell a kidney on the black market.

Yeah, probably not.

I could ask Jenny. She won the reality TV show, *Singing Sensation,* a couple years ago and was rolling in the dough. But, no. I shook my head. I couldn't do that to her. I never wanted her to think I was using her for her money.

After a couple minutes, Jenny walked up beside me. She'd been waiting in the car for me. "He say no?" Her tone was tentative, and she placed a hand on my wrist.

The tears fell in earnest, and I dashed them away. "He wants twenty-five grand for it."

"What? You said your mom sold it for twelve."

"Inflation." I clenched my fists and visualized myself punching the smug smile off of the dude's face.

Jenny started marching toward the building, and I grabbed her arm.

She spun and glared up at me. "No! He ripped you off! He ripped your mom off! He's ripping your dad's memory off! I won't sit by and just let him."

"What are you gonna do?" I released her arm but stayed close in case I needed to grab it again.

"I'm gonna shove my boot up his butt! He can't just get away with this."

"He has a buyer offering him twenty-five grand. My mom signed the paperwork. There's really not much I can do." A pit formed in my stomach and I considered for the first time that I might actually not get the truck back. Get those memories back. *Get Dad back.* I closed my eyes and exhaled a few deep breaths.

She huffed, tossing a lock of dark hair over her shoulder. "At least let me lend you the money."

Borrowing the money still didn't sit right, but it felt good knowing she was willing to help. "I'll think on it. He said I had a few months until the buyer was going to be in town. If I can't come up with the money by then…" My voice trembled, and I shook my head. "I can't think like that. I've gotta find the money."

"It's there if you need it, Dyl."

We got into the convertible that Jenny drove when she was in town visiting her mom. It was extremely impractical in the farming community of Clearview, Montana. But it was fun, nonetheless.

Jenny cranked the engine and we drove back to my place.

"Tell Evan I said hi." I got out and closed the door, then stood, looking at her.

"If my mama hasn't scared him off yet." Jenny threw her hands in the air and half-laughed. "She won't leave him alone. Next time we come, we'll stay at the Clearview Inn. Then he can get some privacy." She shook her head, her nose wrinkled like she'd smelled something sour. "I shouldn't have let her guilt me into staying with her."

Jenny hitting it big and getting out of this town was the best thing she could have done. Occasionally, I looked in on her mom when Jen was gone, just to make sure she was taking care of herself.

"See ya tomorrow, then."

"See ya!" Jenny waved and sped away.

I pulled my purse tight and trudged up the walk to our house. My little brother, Colby, and his "band" banged on drums and played their guitars in the garage. Jenny had given Colby an electric guitar for his fourteenth birthday, and he'd thought himself some sort of rock god ever since. I had to admit, he was getting better, though.

When I got to the door, a piece of paper was taped to it. *Notice of Foreclosure.* It was worse than I thought. I ripped the paper from the door and looked down the street in either direction, making sure no one had seen it. *Why wasn't Mom telling me about this stuff? If she needed help, she just had to ask.* I clenched my teeth and stalked inside. Mom sat at the kitchen table sorting through a stack of papers. I pulled the envelope of money out of my purse and dropped it, along with the foreclosure notice, on top of the pile.

She looked at the notice and closed her eyes. "I didn't want to worry you."

My jaw worked as I bit back my hurt and anger. I shook my head. We couldn't lose the house, too. It was the last thing we had of Dad.

Mom's brow creased and she looked up at me. "He wouldn't sell it back?"

"He ripped you off," I said flatly.

I left her at the table and took the stairs two-at-a-time to my second-story bedroom. It faced the back of the house, and my window overlooked the fields. The fields I'd spent countless hours planting, harvesting, and fertilizing with Dad. We'd already parceled them off, they weren't ours anymore. Just one more memory of Dad, gone.

Maybe I should drop out of school and go to work full-time. Help pay the bills here. Heaven knew mom needed the help. I was still a year away from graduating with my bachelor's in education. It would be an extra two years to get my master's. That was too long.

Mom tapped on the door and cracked it open. "Can I talk to you for a second?"

I nodded.

"That twelve-grand will pull the house out of foreclosure. That's why I sold the truck." She grabbed my pillow from my bed, and perched on the edge, putting the pillow onto her lap. "I'm doing the best I can."

"I know." I sat on the bench in the bay window and grabbed a pillow, mirroring Mom.

"I just don't have any more answers, Dylan. I don't know what else to do." Tears gathered in her eyes, and she hugged the pillow to her chest. She sniffed as she tried to gain control of her emotions.

I nodded. It was my fault. I shouldn't have left her with all this while I went to school. I should have stayed and helped her after Dad's death. I'd failed as a daughter. After I saw Jenny off on her next reality TV journey, I'd drop out and find a job.

Colby and a stampede of boys appeared in the open doorway. "Mom, we're hungry!"

Mom plastered on a smile and stood, tossing the pillow at the head of the bed. "Let's go find you boys some snacks."

I laid back on the padded bench and closed my eyes. One by one my dreams were slipping through my fingers. If Mom couldn't make it on a teacher's salary, there was no way I'd be able to either.

My phone dinged, and with my eyes closed, I pulled it from my back pocket.

I read Jenny's text:

I have the solution to all of your problems.

Two - Aiden

I stared at the empty spot on the wall. Rachel had stolen my platinum record plaque, too? I was done. *Done.* I pulled my phone from my pocket and dialed my manager's number.

"Hey, Aiden."

I dropped onto the barstool at my kitchen counter. "Cancel *Couple's Cruise.*"

Peggy half-laughed, probably thinking I was joking. "What? Why?"

"Rachel's gone." I squeezed my phone too tight and the insides creaked.

"What'd you do? Did you scare her away?" She tsked, and it took everything in me not to fire her on the spot.

"She robbed me, Peggy," I said between clenched teeth.

Her laughing stopped abruptly. "What?"

"She freakin' stole a bunch of my crap, includin' my platinum record!" I picked up a piece of plastic fruit from the bowl in front of me and launched it at the cabinet.

"We'll sue her for breach of contract. She can't do that." I could picture her standing at her desk, furiously picking at her fingernails. Something she did when she was pissed.

I stood and paced back and forth across the tile. "I don't care about her contract. I want my record back." *Stuff was just stuff. But that record meant something to me. I'd earned it.*

"I'll find her. But keep your options open, Aiden. You need this publicity. If you don't take that spot, the show will find someone who doesn't deserve to be there." There was urgency in Peggy's voice.

"Find my record, Peggy," I growled.

She ignored my anger and plowed on. "You don't know anyone who would be your girlfriend for the show? You promised you'd give me at least two weeks on this cruise."

"Not that I'd trust." *Sad truth.*

"Aiden, *they'll* sue *you* for breach of contract. This is the opposite of what your image needs." I heard a slamming in the background and pictured her shoving a filing cabinet drawer closed.

"I don't have anyone to go on it with, Peggy! Am I supposed to go on the cruise alone? You wanna be my fake girlfriend?" She was about double my age, and more like a second mother than a manager.

She laughed. *Laughed.*

"What's so funny? I told you not to put me on the stupid show anyway. You've booked me on this cruise and I'm not sorry I'm not going to be able to go. My next album is coming out in twelve weeks, and I don't have a single song for it."

"I sent you demos, Aiden. Listen to them. They're good."

They could've been greatest hits, but they weren't *mine.* "You know I only sing my own songs."

"There's no shame in singing someone else's song. You just gotta connect with it, honey. If the emotion is there, then it'll do well." It was something she'd said multiple times over the past twelve months, but I still hadn't listened to any of them.

I wanted to sing songs that *I* wrote.

The phone beeped in my ear, and I pulled it away from my face to look at the caller ID. "Evan's callin'. I gotta go." I swapped the calls without waiting for a response. "Hey, Evan."

"Hey, bro. How's it going?"

"I'm alright."

"Hi, Aiden!" Jenny's voice called in the background.

"Jenny says hi," Evan said.

I paced to the couch. "Hi, Jenny."

"Can't wait to see you tomorrow!" Jenny shouted.

My jaw ticked. "Can you go somewhere private?"

"Just a sec." The sound of a door closing came through the phone. "What's up?"

"I'm not goin' on *Couple's Cruise.*"

Evan scoffed. "Why not?"

I didn't want to get into too much detail. "Rachel and I broke up."

"Shoot, man. I guess it's better to do it now than on the ship."

"Peggy still wants me to go. And apparently, I'm gonna get sued if I back out now." I shook my head and pushed a hand through my hair. "I think it would be good for my image, but I don't have anyone I'd trust."

"What about Dylan?"

"Who's Dylan?"

"Jenny's friend. Jenny's been begging me to set you two up."

I stifled a laugh. "No offense bro, Jenny isn't my type." *Whatever friend she had probably wouldn't be either.*

"Nah. Dylan's cool. You'd like her. She's down-to-earth. Country through and through."

"No. I'm good."

"I'm contacting Peggy. I'll have her set the whole thing up."

I shook my head, but smiled. It was just like Evan to bully me into it. "I'm not goin', man."

"I'm hopping on a plane right now. I'll be there to pick you up in a few hours."

"You suck."

~

As promised, Evan showed up at my house that night.

I opened the door and stepped back to let him in. "I told Brad to keep you out."

"Guess he likes Benjamin Franklin more than he likes you." Evan held up a bottle of Jack. "Straight outta the bottle, or do you want glasses?"

I took the bottle from his hands, and we walked to the kitchen. I snagged glasses from the cupboard and put a couple of ice cubes in each.

"So what happened with Rachel?" He perched on the stool across the bar from me.

I gestured to my empty wall. "She robbed me."

"Holy crap. Wasn't that where your platinum record was?"

"Yup." I poured some Jack into each of our cups, then slid Evan's across to him. We both lifted them in a toast to each other and drank.

Evan exhaled and placed his cup on the counter, then turned his pleading gaze on me. "You gotta come, man. I can't go on that cruise with a bunch of dudes I don't know."

"I'll probably get kicked off the first week." I took another swallow.

Evan shrugged. "Then I'll get kicked off week two." He grabbed the bottle and refilled his glass. "Jenny already contacted Peggy. And she told Dylan. You have to come."

"Fine." It had nothing to do with Dylan. I'd been everywhere looking for inspiration. But a cruise wasn't one of them.

Three - Dylan

If someone told me yesterday I'd be sitting in a production trailer near the beach, preparing to be a contestant on a reality TV show, I would have laughed in their face.

"I'm Raymond Dexter, pleased to meet you." The lawyer put his fancy briefcase on the table and popped it open, producing a small stack of papers. "Now, I understand we're here to make sure everything with this contract is on the up-and-up."

I sat on my hands to stop their fidgeting and nodded.

"I looked it over this morning, and I would say it's a fairly standard contract, as far as things of this nature go." He wiped his bald head with a handkerchief and tucked it into his back pocket. "Miss Gentry had some excellent suggestions that have been implemented."

Nerves bundled in my stomach, like a diet soda with a Mentos inside. Jenny refused to tell me who my boyfriend would be. She just grinned like a Cheshire Cat and said, "You'll see."

Mr. Dexter pushed the stack in front of me, and I forced myself to focus.

"The duration of the contract is six weeks, or until you're voted off of *Couple's Cruise—Celebrity Edition* by the viewers. Sign here." He pointed to a pre-labeled spot, marked with a sticky tab and extended a pen.

I pulled my hand from under my butt and took it. After skimming the section, I took a deep breath and signed on the line.

"And date."

I scrawled the date.

He moved his finger to the next line. "This explains how the show works.

10

I'm required to read it to you. 'The First week three couples are voted off by the viewers. Week two, three, and four, two couples will be voted off by the viewers. In week five, one couple gets voted off, then the winner is crowned in week six." He shifted his finger down to the next sticky tab. "Sign here if you understand."

I did.

"The next line explains the compensation. This is where Miss Gentry worked her magic." He smiled and wiped his forehead again. "You are being given ten-thousand dollars for your appearance on the show."

Ice flowed through my veins, and I stared at the paper, unseeing. "Jenny said it would be more." That wasn't enough to get Dad's truck back.

"I'm not finished." He cleared his throat. "It's tiered. At week four and each subsequent week, you'll receive an additional five-thousand dollars. For a total of twenty-five thousand dollars. Sign here."

My hands trembled as I scrawled my name. *Holy crap. I was being* paid *to go on a cruise.*

Mr. Dexter turned the page. "This next one states the recipient of the prize money. Please verify this is the charity of your choice and sign here."

I did.

"Look through the next section, then sign and date at the bottom."

I murmured, "I, Dylan Kennedy, agree to be cast in the unscripted-role as the girlfriend of Aiden Miller for the duration of this contract, or until voted off *Couple's Cruise—Celebrity Edition* by the viewers." I re-read the name, thinking I had dreamed it. *Aiden Miller.* I laughed and looked up at Mr. Dexter. "Is this a joke?"

"What?" He pulled the contract toward him and pushed his glasses to the end of his nose as he read it. "I don't see anything out of order."

I leaned back in the seat and dropped the pen on the table. "Aiden Miller? Aiden *Freaking* Miller? The country singer?" *There's no way.* Jenny was pranking me. "Where's the real contract? Who is it really?" I had a crush on Aiden Miller. *Had.* Past tense. When his first album came out five years ago, I was a little bit obsessed, reading anything I could get my hands on, from interviews to gossip magazines. I hadn't kept up with those in years, though.

Aiden was the reason I'd started listening to country music. His deep voice, and the way he could hold a note sent my heart a-flutter.

Mr. Dexter pulled his glasses off and scowled at me. "I assure you, this isn't a joke." He placed the contract back in front of me and pointed to the line. "Sign, please."

I picked up the pen, but hesitated. Kissing a stranger was one thing. Kissing and pretending to be Aiden Miller's girlfriend? That was an entirely different matter. I didn't know if I could keep my heart intact.

"Miss Kennedy?" Mr. Dexter tapped the paper. "You're almost finished."

But still, I hesitated. "Can we come back to it? If I don't sign that one, the contract is void, right?"

He cleared his throat and straightened his tie. "The rest is a code of conduct. You agree to act in a manner that wouldn't harm Aiden Miller or his image in a negative way. If you'll just scan the list and sign at the bottom."

I looked at the list. It included drunkenness, lewd conduct, slandering him or any other contestant... *Wow.* It was quite extensive. I felt confident that if I decided to go on the cruise, I wouldn't have any problem keeping his image clean. I signed that one, then flipped the page back to the final signature required.

Holy crap. I'd have to kiss Aiden Miller.

Have to? Like it was a chore.

I turned the page back to the compensation. To make it worth it, I had to get to the finals. I needed that twenty-five grand.

Flipping the page one final time, I scrawled my name on the line.

"Thank you, Miss Kennedy. If you'll come with me, we'll get you ready for the cruise." Mr. Dexter led me out of the trailer.

As we walked toward our destination, I caught glimpses of *The Callistus*, the *Couple's Cruise* ship between tents and production trailers.

Mr. Dexter knocked on a trailer door, then opened the handle without waiting for a response. "They're waiting for you."

When I walked in, Jenny gasped and ran to me.

"Aiden Miller?" I accused, swatting her arm.

She beamed and bounced on her toes. "I thought you'd be happy."

A blond man in light blue pants with whales on them and a white linen, button-up shirt came around the clothing rack. "Ahh. You must be the bestie." He glanced at Jenny, who nodded.

"Fabian! This is Dylan. Dylan, this is your new personal stylist Fabian." She dragged me to him by the arm.

I held out my hand to shake his.

Instead he lifted it to his lips, kissing my knuckles. *"Mademoiselle."* Fabian took a step back and looked me over head to toe. "You *are* a tall glass of water, aren't you?"

He linked my arm with his and led me to an area partitioned off with screens. "This is your dressing room. Just try on everything, and we'll pick what's best for your hair and eyes. Oh, I just love blondes with brown eyes. It says, 'I'm deep, not ditzy.'"

"And what do your blue eyes say?"

He swatted at me and tsked. "My eyes say all sorts of things." He turned his back to me, then struck a pose, and gave me a smoldering look over one shoulder. "This one is my— 'Trust me, I'm a stylist' look. Now get your beautiful butt in that room, and I'll start handing in clothes." He pushed me toward the screen.

Two hours later, I was like Malibu Barbie—after she'd gone five rounds with a personal stylist. At least I'd have something to wear, though. Fabian bustled out, leaving us to find our way to the styling trailer.

If I was having second thoughts before walking into this trailer, eight hours later, I was having an existential crisis. Every inch of my body had been waxed, tweezed, dyed, polished or painted.

The stylists did a wonderful job, but I hardly recognized the California blonde staring at me in the mirror.

Jenny grabbed my arm and hauled me outside. Fans screamed as we emerged, and as we disappeared into another trailer with Aiden's name on it, their cheers faded.

We stopped inside. It was just like the kind you'd camp in, with a table and benches. Bunk beds were built into one wall, and a door partitioned off what was probably a bedroom.

Jenny twisted a strand of my hair around her finger. "Oh my gosh. He's going to fall in love with you."

I pulled on the hem of the miniskirt that barely covered my rear end. "How do people wear clothes this short? What if I drop something? What if I have to sit?"

"Don't cross your legs. Angle them one direction, and keep your knees together. If you have to cross, cross at the ankles. You'll be fine." Jenny smacked my hand away from my hem and pulled her ringing, pink jeweled phone from her purse. "Hey, baby. Are you here? We're in Aiden's trailer." She glanced at me, her eyes dancing. "Of course. See you soon." She put the phone in her bag and said, "Aiden's almost here."

I blinked slowly, letting her words sink in. It was almost time. My insides decided now was the best time to do an Irish jig, and I grabbed the dining table to keep myself up.

She nodded. "So, how are you playing this?"

"Playing what?" I turned and sat on the edge of the table.

"Dating Aiden Miller."

What? "Um. I'm not? I was just planning on being myself."

She shook her head. "Think of all the girls Aiden has dated. They all wear makeup and take time doing their hair in the morning. And while you know how to straighten your hair and put on lipgloss… I just don't want you to get cut right off the bat because the viewers don't like you. You have to fit a certain mold to date a guy like Aiden."

I pointed to myself. "I just spent all day getting made up."

"I'm just saying, you need to *act* the part as well as look it." She grabbed my shoulders and shook me. "Guys like Aiden don't change their taste overnight and the viewers know it. I just don't want you to get cut before you reach your goal."

She had a point, didn't she? "Fine." I clenched my jaw.

Fans screamed in the parking lot and Jenny pulled back the curtain.

"They're here." She turned to the mirror and primped her hair, then applied lip gloss and adjusted her boobs. "Ready."

Awkwardly, I tugged on the hem of my skirt. The contrast between Jenny and me was comical. She was barely pushing five-feet, and I was almost six. She had dark, voluminous hair, and mine was blonde.

We watched from the window as girls near the set perimeter clustered together, their hands reaching past the tape toward a black SUV in the parking lot. Security guards spread their arms wide, keeping any daring fans out. Some held up signs with Aiden's name and others with Evan's. "Evan! Marry me!", "I love you, Aiden!"

Two figures emerged from the back of the SUV wearing sunglasses, and my heart leapt into my throat. Both men waved to their fans and strode toward the trailer.

Holy, Mama. Aiden Freaking *Miller.*

He pulled off his cowboy hat and ran his fingers through his dark hair. His blue T-shirt was pulled tight over his muscular chest, and he wore his signature black cowboy boots. *His jaw was so chiseled.* It wasn't fair to the remainder of the male population.

Evan's hair was a shade lighter. His black T-shirt and ripped skinny jeans looked painted on. Black combat boots and a cocky smile completed his ensemble.

As they reached the trailer, I backed against the bunk beds.

Jenny opened the door and threw herself into Evan's arms.

I stood frozen, unwilling to go out into the sun. I needed more time. I hadn't adjusted to the fact that Aiden was the guy. I wasn't ready. My hands shook and I clasped them behind my back, and did my best to control my breathing.

Aiden stepped into the trailer and pulled off his sunglasses. "Hi."

A knot formed in my stomach. "Hi." Was that raspy dying rat my voice?

He glanced over his shoulder. "Give us some privacy, will ya?" The door slammed, and he held his hand out to me. "I'm Aiden Miller."

I shook it. It wasn't often I could wear high-heels around a guy and not tower over him. Aiden and I were nearly eye-to-eye. "You're tall." *Way to go brain. Way to freaking go.*

A dimple flashed in his cheek, nearly disguised by the scruff that darkened his jaw. "So are you."

"I'm Dylan Kennedy."

"It's nice to meet ya. Thanks for fillin' in on such short notice." He released my hand and stepped back, gesturing to the table.

His southern drawl was real too? I was fan-girling just a smidge.

"Yeah, no problem," I said belatedly, sliding into the bench across from him and holding the hem of my skirt. *Please don't let me flash him.*

There was no chance we'd be anything more than friends. I didn't want to be a number. He was on the cover of magazines with a new girl every week. *What? I didn't buy them. I just saw them in the grocery store.* But I couldn't get my body on the same page as my brain.

Besides, I'd seen what fame did to people. Jenny had survived it pretty intact, but her relationship with both of her parents was... Not ideal.

The trailer door opened, and a blonde woman stepped in, aiming her smile right at Aiden. "I'm Desiree, your producer. We'll start filming in a half-hour, but in the meantime, I thought we should just make sure we have our ducks in a row." She glanced at me for the first time. "The three of us, and, I assume Evan and Jenny, are the only ones on the ship who will know about this charade. We need to keep it that way. That means in interviews, or any time anyone is speaking to you, you must assume you're being filmed. No slip ups. We don't want a scandal."

"Understood." Aiden nodded and turned his gaze to me. "We've got this."

Desiree clapped her hands once and inhaled deeply. "Great. We need you over in the production tent in about ten minutes. You need to come up with a story about how you met. I'll leave you to it." She spun and sauntered out the door.

"We should set some ground rules, too." I twisted my hands in my lap, unsure of how much to say. I wanted him to stay. Wanted to make it to the finals, and blurting, "I'm not going to sleep with you," probably wouldn't accomplish that.

He laughed. "What?"

Oh shoot. I blurted it. "Was that out loud?" I blew out a breath and covered my face. "I mean, I'm not. I just didn't want to say it like that. Is all…"

Silence stretched between us, and I peeked at him from between my fingers.

"Fair enough. What other rules should we set?" He was gracious enough to let it slide.

No kissing. Kissing Aiden Miller might make me forget why it was such a bad idea. "No touching in private." My cheeks flamed, but I forced myself to watch for his reaction.

He nodded, his lips pulled down thoughtfully. "So only for the cameras. Okay."

"No tongue." I knew not kissing was impossible. TV viewers would expect it. Most on-screen kisses were just actors and actresses smashing their mouths together anyway. We could do that.

"No tongue. Anything else?" Amusement played across his features, his lips twitching as he struggled to keep the smile from them.

I thought for a minute. "No, but I reserve the right to add to the list at any time."

His dimple flashed again. "Agreed. The producer said we should talk about how we met, too."

"Well." I licked my lips, and his gaze tracked the movement. *What did that mean?* I was over-analyzing everything. *Maybe no kissing was a good rule.* "We were both at Evan's birthday party. I said hi, but almost passed out from the excitement of meeting Aiden Miller. I'd been a fan of yours for years, after all." I forced myself to look at him.

Aiden studied me with interest, and my heart kicked up its rhythm.

"You caught me before I fell and carried me to the couch," I finished, my mouth suddenly dry.

He grinned, drawing my gaze to the crinkles around his eyes. "After the party, I called Jenny and demanded she give me your number. She was very protective of her best friend, but I wore her down with my persistence and charm."

I laughed, nerves momentarily forgotten. I loved that he jumped in to finish the story. *Dylan! Stop it.* I couldn't let myself get wrapped up. Guys like Aiden Miller could have any girl they wanted, and monogamy was a myth in Hollywood.

Aiden glanced at his watch and stood. "It's almost time. We should get out there."

My stomach leapt. *Holy crap, it was actually happening.*

Aiden held a hand out to me.

I stood and smoothed my skirt.

As we walked, Aiden grabbed my hand and leaned in close, whispering in my ear over the screaming fans. "Do you have a preference for terms of endearment?"

"Hmm?" I pulled back to look into his eyes.

He shrugged, and his dimple winked at me. "Pet names, like sexy, or kitten, or anything like that?"

I snorted and put a hand to my mouth, trying to cover it with a cough. *Did anyone actually want to be called stupid nicknames like that?* "I'm sure whatever you come up with will be fine."

He threw his head back and laughed, the sound warming me to my toes. *Great, what was he going to come up with?*

The production tent was on the beach between the parking lot and the ocean. I clutched Aiden's arm as we trudged through the sand. *Note to self: high-heels and sand do not mix.*

When we entered, people were scrambling everywhere, and I stopped in my tracks as I took it all in. The set and lighting crew bustled around the stage messing with equipment. The back wall had been removed, leaving the ocean and the white *Couple's Cruise* ship as the stage's backdrop.

People swarmed us, and Aiden released my hand.

"They need you in makeup, Aiden," someone said, and he was whisked away to who knew where.

Desiree fished a wire with a microphone up my tank-top with cool efficiency and clipped it on the neckline. I jumped, but forced myself to stay still. *Celebrities didn't flinch at this type of stuff.* A battery pack or something was shoved into the back of my skirt. *Apparently, personal space was no longer a thing.* "The seats all have names embroidered on the backs. As soon as you're done, go find yours," she said.

They got a seat with my name on it? Wow, that was fast. I looked around for Aiden. He must've been still in makeup because he was nowhere to be seen.

I walked to the stage and stared at the mostly-empty white producer's chairs. It was surreal. There were people I recognized from TV, or movies, and one girl whose dad was a famous singer back in the 90s, which had catapulted her own auto-tune-assisted singing career. Actors, other musicians. *It was a trip.*

Jenny waved to a few people and sauntered over to stand in front of me. She'd changed since I'd seen her last. She wore a cute white linen romper and leather sandals. "I'll block the view while you sit so you don't flash anyone."

Bless her. She always knew what I needed. We took the steps up the stage together. I clutched her hand to keep from falling over. Were four inch heels really necessary? I was going to break an ankle.

We found my chair near the center. I glanced around. No one was watching so I sank into it, tugging at the hem of the skirt. "You and Fabian are evil."

She smiled with glee. "Trust me. You look so hot." She looked at the chairs on either side of me. "Which one is Aiden's?"

I glanced at the chair backs and pointed to my right.

"Angle your legs toward him, and remember to keep them closed. We don't want any wardrobe malfunctions." She patted my hand.

Evan climbed the steps to the stage and Jenny ditched me to go kiss him. *Crap on a cracker. Was I supposed to stand when Aiden got here?* I was gonna flash the whole crew.

Someone planted a kiss on my cheek from behind. "Hey, beautiful."

I jumped and pressed a hand to my heart, a blush climbing up my neck. I put on my best adoring face and turned to Aiden. "Hey, handsome." *How weird was that?*

He came around the chair and sat beside me, pulling my hand into his lap. *Please don't let my hand be clammy and gross.*

19

The other seats filled quickly. A football player whose face I recognized, but name escaped my memory, and his girlfriend sat on our right. And a hotel heiress with her fiancé on our left. The host took her position on stage. Someone with one of those clapper thingies counted down, and snapped it closed.

My heart was racing faster than a pack of hyenas.

A slew of red lights flashed on all the cameras around the room.

"I'm Trisha Thames, and welcome to this special season of *Couple's Cruise—Celebrity Edition.*"

Four - Aiden

I was gonna kill Evan. He promised me a down-to-earth country girl, someone with substance. Dylan... was not that. *Don't get me wrong, she was pretty in that spend-all-day-at-a-spa kinda way, but she wasn't what I expected.* I'd dated enough of her type, leeching onto me for money or fame.

For once, I wanted someone real, someone who saw beyond the spotlights to the man beneath their artificial glow. A girl who appreciated me more than my music, who would stick by me once my fingers quit strumming the chords on my guitar. *Which might be sooner rather than later, if my comeback album flopped as bad as I feared.*

What did it really matter? With only twelve weeks until the album release, if I didn't find inspiration and get some of my own songs on there, I'd be a sell-out. This stupid reality show was a waste of time. Two episodes, three at most, then I could go back to focusing on my writing.

Dylan nailed the opening interview, using our story about meeting at Evan's birthday party. Which was probable, but not true. If it were, I had a feeling I would have noticed her. She would have made sure I did. There was no way I'd been in the same room as that woman and missed it. Her lying skills would come in handy for the show. I didn't know whether to be impressed with the ease with which she'd come up with the story, or frightened by it.

After they unwired us, we were directed to a boat that would take us out to the cruise ship. Loud music drowned out most of the screaming fans.

Dylan grasped my hand and pulled me to a stop. "I forgot something."

She made a beeline for the wardrobe trailer and I followed along like the dutiful boyfriend I was supposed to be. Though watching her walk in that mini skirt wasn't a hardship. Just cause I wasn't buying the car, didn't mean I couldn't enjoy the upholstery.

"Be right back." She disappeared into the trailer and came back a second later, wheeling a bright pink suitcase.

The wheels made a terrible racket and set my teeth on edge. That grinding was gonna get on my last nerve. I forced a smile and took the suitcase from her, retracted the handle into the bag, and lifted it.

She wrapped a hand around my elbow. "Thanks, Aiden."

Momma didn't raise me to be rude. "Absolutely." And she also wouldn't want me to snap at a woman in public for annoying me.

"I can't believe you deal with this all the time." She glanced around at the screaming fans as we approached the ferry.

Here it comes, the star envy. The gold-digger must-have. Next would be the pageant wave she spent her free time practicing in the mirror.

"It must be annoying. Never any privacy."

My jaw dropped. *Well, I'll be.* "Yeah, but it's the price you pay for bein' famous."

But was it worth it? Security guards 24/7, never being able to run to the store for a beer without getting recognized. But, then there was the music. To play my songs to a crowd of fans, to stop singing and hold the mic out and have them finish the stanza. To turn on the radio and hear something I wrote. *Yeah, It was all worth it.*

I'd give her credit, Dylan handled herself well on the dock and boarding the ferry. No squeals that some of the other girls made. No clinging to my arm for dear life. She didn't say a word. Just stood at the rail, closed her eyes with a contented smile, and let the ocean wind whip her perfectly styled hair. A gust caught a wave, spraying the boat with water. She cringed back, but laughed, and not a tittering giggle or a tinkling snicker. She laughed, a real, full throaty sound. Part of me wanted to be the one to make her laugh like that, but I tamped it down.

Was there more to this girl? She *was* being paid to be my girlfriend, just like Rachel had been, til yesterday. *I had to keep my priorities straight: music first, then women.* With the album on the horizon, I couldn't afford to get distracted.

As we boarded the ship, she teetered on her heels, and I wrapped my arm around her waist to steady her.

She regained her balance and nudged my hand off her waist. "Thanks, that would have been really embarrassing."

What kind of high-maintenance chick couldn't walk in heels? Maybe she *didn't* tote around in heels like I thought. Rachel could've walked a tightrope in her heels. Any falling on her part would have been intentional. She would have milked it for all it was worth, plastering herself against my chest and stealing a kiss.

We'd been given a schedule and a list of rules, one of which was no cellphones. We had the afternoon to settle in, and first thing that evening, we'd film an interview. Mondays were interviews. Competitions or outings on Wednesday and a live elimination on Thursday. We'd still be filmed throughout the week. They couldn't afford to miss a juicy fight or a "wardrobe malfunction," but it would give me time to focus on my music.

On board the ship, a concierge led us to our suite and opened the door.

"Wait. We share a room?" Dylan stopped, her eyes wide as saucers.

I tipped the concierge and sent him on his way. Dylan stood at the threshold, seemingly undecided.

"We're datin', Dylan. This is the entire premise of the show." I walked past the bathroom and set her suitcase on the king sized bed. A sliding door with a small private balcony was on the wall between the bed and a chaise lounge. On the far wall was a television, and next to that, a table and two chairs.

Dylan took a small step into the room, letting the door close behind her. "Sorry. I just didn't think about all the logistics. We can ask for an extra blanket and stuff, and I'll sleep on that couch thingy." She gestured to the chaise lounge.

My mouth hung open. *Who is this girl?* "We can work all that out later." I pulled up a chair and sat at the table. "Have a seat."

She glanced around the room as if looking for an escape. Her shoulders sagged, and she plunked herself on the chair next to mine. Dylan stretched down and unstrapped her sandals, then pushed them off her feet.

"Ugh. It feels so good to have those off." She tugged at the hem of her skirt. "But beauty is pain, as they say."

I put my palms on the table and leaned forward. "Let's cut to the chase. I promised my manager I'd make it to week two. That's the goal. After that, we can have an argument and make it as clean or as messy as you like." *There, I gave it to her straight. Maybe she'd quit trying so hard.*

Dylan's mouth dropped open, and she gaped like a beautiful cod fish. Her brows drew down and hurt flashed across her face before she pulled the mask back on.

The briefest moment of guilt ate at the edges of my resolve, but I swatted that sucker then smashed it with my boot. I had to get back to my music.

"Okay." She sat up straight, and she looked everywhere but at me.

I nodded. "You bipolar or somethin'?" *I was trying to consolidate these oddities in my mind. Watching her on the boat vs. Pain is beauty? What a crock of crap.*

"What? No. Why?"

"Evan said you were a down-to-earth country girl. But that's not what I'm seein' in front of me." *Hope I didn't hurt her feelings.*

She opened her mouth, looking like she was about to protest, then her shoulders sagged. "Jenny said you liked high-maintenance women."

I burst out laughing, slapping my knee and holding my belly.

"What's so funny? Look at all your past girlfriends!" She shot to her feet and pointed in the direction of land, as if that was proof. I must've looked confused, because she glared at me. "Do I have to name them all?" She lifted a finger as if she were about to start.

I held my hands up in surrender. "Likin' a woman that takes care of herself, isn't the same as likin' high-maintenance women. I assure you, I don't." I thought back on my previous girlfriends for a moment. *Okay, maybe she had a point.*

"Jenny said your tastes wouldn't change over-night, and that if we wanted to stay for as long as possible, the public needs to buy into our relationship. Which means, they need to be able to picture us as a couple, I guess."

"You can act however you want. We're only going to be here a couple of weeks. At most." I folded my arms over my chest. *Discussion ended.*

Tears shimmered in her eyes, and she set her jaw. "I need the money," she whispered.

"Ask Jenny for it." *Simple solution.* She had a best friend worth millions. Why wasn't she taking it? I knew Jenny well enough to know she wouldn't hesitate to help.

"I can't. If I did, I'd be letting myself, and Jenny, down."

"How so?"

Dylan lowered herself onto the chair. "Jenny and I have been friends forever. Like, since preschool. We've been there for each other through thick and thin. I don't know how much she's told you or Evan, but she's been through a lot. Her dad has been in and out of her life, only showing up when he needed cash for drugs. Her mom is a lot better, but she quit working and relies on Jenny for everything. Jenny resents that. If I accepted money from her, it would change our friendship. Irrevocably. If I took money from her, I'd be no better than her parents, and she'd question my motives. She'd think I was only sticking around because of what she could *do* for me."

I was speechless. I couldn't even fathom that kind of loyalty or friendship. "Wow."

She shrugged. "So I can't ask her for the money."

"How much do you need?" I drummed my fingers on the table, considering my options. I needed to be here for my image, and to get my name back out there. But I also needed time to write my songs.

Dylan swallowed and met my gaze. "Twenty-five thousand dollars."

"How far do we have to go for you to get it?" If we could get away with leaving after a week or two, our goals would align, and it would be fine.

"The finals."

Shoot. "I can't promise the finals." I needed to get back home and get to writing my album.

"I know." She dropped her head onto the table.

"But." I was going to regret this. "We can try." I hoped something on this cruise would break the lyrical dry spell I was in. If I didn't feel inspired soon, we'd have to reevaluate.

She looked up at me. "Seriously?"

"Seriously." I had no idea why I'd agreed. She just seemed genuine, and she deserved a break. If I could be the one to give it to her, all the better.

She squealed and balled her hands into fists as she pumped them in the air. "Thank you, thank you. You won't regret it! I promise."

That remained to be seen. "Now, Trisha's gonna ask us a lot of questions to see how well we know each other. We've gotta really sell this couple thing. Tell me about you. Brothers and sisters? How old are you? Your parents still around? Where'd you grow up?" I leaned forward, bracing my elbows on the glass table. Time to get down to business.

She smiled, but it was tinged with sadness. "I have one brother, Colby. He's fourteen. No sisters. I just turned twenty-two, and my dad passed, but my Mom is still around. She's in Clearview, Montana, the tiny town where I grew up."

Hmm. Tears shimmered in her eyes, and she blinked them away.

"Sorry to hear about your dad."

She waved away my condolences. "If I sit and think about it I'll cry. Keep going."

Fair enough. "What's your favorite color?"

"Purple. My turn." She tapped her lip and started to cross her legs, her skirt sliding dangerously high. She grabbed the hem and dropped her feet. "Where did you grow up? Do you have brothers and sisters? What about your parents?"

"I grew up in Middleton, Tennessee. I have one sister and no brothers. Brin is sixteen." A smile tilted my lips, thinking about my baby sister. "My parents are still living in Middleton."

"And your favorite color?" She lifted a brow.

"Blue." I shrugged.

"Cause of your eyes. You look really good in blue." Her cheeks flushed. She was real pretty when she blushed.

Dylan cleared her throat. "What made you want to be a musician?" She

26

leaned back and crossed her ankles.

"I've always loved to sing, and I guess songwritin' just came natural to me. Til recently." Now I couldn't write a song to save my life. Couldn't find inspiration anywhere. It wasn't in the crystalline lakes of the Rockies, the orange sunsets over the Utah desert, or the acres of cornfields in Nebraska. It wasn't even in my tranquil cabin on Tahoe. No, I'd searched everywhere to find my muse. It was gone.

Dylan dropped her feet and leaned forward. "What happened recently? Your girlfriend?" Concern laced her voice.

I scoffed. That last "relationship" was Peggy's idea, too. Lasted all of two weeks, and Rachel made out like a bandit. Peggy was hunting auction sites for my platinum record plaque. *Wonder if she found it.*

"It wasn't real. My album comes out in twelve weeks, and my manager says I've gotta get my name back into the forefront of people's minds before it does. I needed the publicity, so she set up the relationship."

"Sucky timing for a break-up." She shrugged. "Her loss, I guess. Why does a guy like Aiden Miller need his manager to line up fake girlfriends for him, anyway?"

It wasn't that I couldn't get a girl to date me, it was just... What? I was going through a dry spell? That didn't sound right. "I'm tryin' to focus on my music. I don't need any distractions."

Now if only I could write a song, my album wouldn't be a total sham. As it was, I had exactly zero of the fourteen I needed for my next release. Peggy had been sending me demos for months, trying to get me to sing someone else's songs. She was even pushing for a single to put out as a teaser beforehand. Don't get me wrong, there were plenty of talented songwriters, but I had to sing my own songs. My fans expected it. Heck, I expected it of myself.

But I had nothing.

She glanced at the digital clock on the wall by the door. "We're supposed to head to the pool. There's a mixer there." She bit her bottom lip and shrugged a shoulder.

Dylan really was quite beautiful, her eyes the same deep brown as the leather strap on my guitar. Her mascara was a little thick around her lashes, but at least they looked real. The tarantula eye that many girls favored was a little too much for me.

"Let's get ready." I stood and pulled her to her feet. "Do you need help with anythin'?"

"I've got it. Thanks."

Our stuff had been brought in and hung in the walk-in closet. Dylan rummaged through the drawers and found a royal blue swimming suit, then left me sorting through my drawers for a pair of swim trunks.

I dressed quickly and found Dylan sitting at the table wrapped in a white cover-up.

Why was she wearing a cover-up? She had nothing to hide. "Ready?"

She stood, and the wrap gaped open. She had absolutely nothing to be ashamed of. Her legs were toned and sunkissed, curves in all the right places. I squeezed my eyes closed.

That image would be burned in the back of my mind for a while to come. "Wow."

"Thanks." Her voice came out a whisper as she tugged the wrap around herself once more, eyes glued to the floor.

I offered her my arm. "Let's go show those losers what a power couple really looks like."

Five - Dylan

I was on the arm of Aiden Freaking Miller.

I slipped my feet into a pair of flip-flops that Fabian had made me fight tooth-and-nail for. It was these or my one dollar flips from Old Navy. He'd made gagging noises but agreed to them. They weren't as comfy, but they'd do. Little tiny jewels lined the straps and sparkled as we made our way to the Lido deck.

Jenny lounged on a pool-chair in her bright yellow bikini. A large sun-hat shaded her face, and sunglasses covered her eyes. "Dyl!" She waved. "I saved you guys a seat."

Let the games begin. The contestants had split into three different groups. It was like high school all over again. Jocks were in the pool. The drama nerds sat at the bar and the band geeks were on the lounge chairs. Or were we choir dorks? Either way.

Country singer, Sheena Renfro, and a guy I assumed was her boyfriend, perched on the chair next to Evan. She used her boyfriend as a backrest. The man was pure muscle. *His muscles probably had muscles.*

"Sheena, Jorge, this is my best friend Dylan, Aiden's girlfriend." Jenny leaned over and patted the seat beside her.

I pulled my gaze away from Muscles—err—Jorge and gave a small wave. "Hi."

Aiden reached over and shook Jorge's hand, then smiled at Sheena. "Good to see you again, Sheena."

Sheena's eyes glared, but her full lips were turned up into a grin. "You too, Ace."

Okay, there was obviously some backstory there. Then it hit me. Sheena was Aiden's ex-girlfriend. *My gosh. I'd be compared to that woman. Her petite little hands and feet. Her tiny perfect body. The woman was flawless. I couldn't catch a break.*

"So Dylan, are you a singer, too?" The miniature auburn goddess turned her critical gaze on me, her tone smug.

"Yes, she is!" Jenny glanced at me, her eyes full of pride. "She sang back-up for me on *Stars Align.*"

"OMG! Your harmonies were so perfect." She smacked Jorge's shoulder. "Weren't they so perfect?" Sheena's voice oozed with fake sweetness.

I was gonna get a tooth ache just listening to her.

Jorge tossed his long dark hair from his eyes and ran his fingers up her arms. "Perfect." He leaned down and placed a soft kiss on her shoulder. She looked so dainty next to him.

I, on the other hand, never looked dainty.

They were going to win. And I was going to lose my lunch. *Not that I counted cucumber water as lunch.* My stomach was currently digesting itself. *Didn't they feed us?* I returned the fake smile. "Thanks. We've had years of practice."

Aiden sat and pulled me onto his lap. I shrieked and turned it into a laugh. He scooted against the backrest, then opened his legs, dropping me between them.

Goosebumps rose all over my skin, despite the heat. So much of me had just touched so much of him. I forced my breathing to slow, and I was hyper-aware of his body so close to mine. Every move made our skin brush and my pulse quicken.

A waiter came over to get our drink order, and I really, really wanted to beg him for French fries, but stopped myself. Aiden would probably be mortified if his girlfriend ate the way I did at home. "Water, please. And do you have any kale chips?" *That's what celebrities ate, right?*

"Of course." He turned to Aiden. "And for you?"

"Beer, and can I get some fries?"

"My pleasure." The waiter spun on his heel and went to get our orders.

French fries. A man after my own heart. I barely knew Aiden, yet here I was, sitting between his legs. I wasn't comfortable enough to lie back on his chest, but watching Sheena and Jorge reminded me I was supposed to be his girlfriend. Besides, when would I ever get the chance to sit on Aiden Miller's lap again?

I relaxed into him, and our bodies stuck together with sweat. When I tried to lean forward, though, he stopped me.

"Relax." His arms rested on his knees, which bracketed me in. I mirrored his position, and his fingers caressed my forearms. *Holy crap. Was this how the whole cruise was going to go?*

The waiter came around with our drinks.

I sat up and chugged my water like it was a shot. My stomach growled and Aiden poked my side. I turned and our eyes caught.

"If you're hungry, just get real food."

I bent my legs and spun until I was facing him. Leaning in close, I whispered, "Can I just share with you?" *What did other girls do here? Puppy dog eyes or something?*

He chuckled, throwing his head back. I grabbed a tiny patch of hair on his leg and pulled on it, just enough until I had his attention. It was a move I used to use on Dad.

He rubbed his knee, his eyes playful. He pulled on my arms and leaned into me. His scruff scratched my cheek and his lips brushed my ear. "Careful. You're starting to sound like a real girlfriend."

My stomach flipped, and I inhaled his cologne, citrus and woods. *I could bathe in it. Mmm.* If he was my real boyfriend I'd bury my nose in his neck and... and my nose brushed against his warm skin.

His breath hitched.

Whoops. I sat back, my cheeks burning. "Sorry."

His fingers tightened on my arms, and his stormy eyes glanced at my lips and back. *Was he gonna kiss me?* My hands were clammy, and my heart pounded in my chest. The citrus lingered between us.

Holy Hannah, he was going to kiss me.

The waiter brought our tray, breaking the tension. He placed two plates on the small table beside us. "Can I get you anything else?"

Aiden released my arms, and I exhaled the breath I was holding.

I glanced at the small bottle of ketchup. "Can we get some mayo in a little bowl?"

"My pleasure." The waiter nodded and disappeared.

"What's the mayo for?" Aiden took a swig of his beer.

I sipped my water. "Fry sauce. I think it's a regional thing."

The waiter brought a little dish of mayo, and I squirted the ketchup with it, then used a fry to combine it. When it was mixed, I held the fry out to Aiden. He eyed it dubiously, then leaned forward slowly and took it with his teeth.

He closed his eyes as he chewed. "Mmm. That is incredible."

I laughed nervously and grabbed my plate, scooting to the foot of the lounge and sitting cross-legged.

Jenny and Evan laid on their separate lounges, eyes closed. At some point during my exchange with Aiden, Sheena and Jorge got in the pool. Aiden placed his fries between us. I grabbed a kale chip and popped it in my mouth. Ew. My gag reflex insisted I spit it out, but the camera with the red light forced me to swallow.

Aiden chomped on a fry, and I grabbed another kale chip, pretending it was a fry. *Come on, brain, just one more thing we're going to lie to ourselves about. Mmm, french fry.* I shoved the kale chip in my mouth. *Mistake. Ack.* I swallowed it without chewing and the pieces got caught in my throat. A cough exploded from my chest, and I gasped in a breath.

Aiden moved our plates and was patting my back before I'd even gotten a breath in. He flagged down our waiter and ordered another water while I continued to hack. *Please don't let them be filming.* I chanced a glance toward the camera. *Of course they were. Just what I needed. I'd never live this down. The girl who almost died on TV. My cheeks were probably bright red, too.*

The waiter brought the water, and Aiden held it to my lips.

"You okay?" He brushed the hair from my face, tucking it behind my ear.

As my coughing subsided, I realized the entire cast had circled around me. *Perfect, an audience.*

My eyes were watering, and I wiped at my tears. When I pulled my hand away, I noticed mascara smudged all over them. *Crap on a cracker.* I did my best to wipe under my eyes and not on the lashes, but I wasn't used to wearing makeup and smeared even more mascara.

Jenny pulled me up by the arm. "Let's get you cleaned up."

Oh, thank the stars.

We brushed between a couple of cast members. "Soak it up, attention whore. Your fifteen minutes of fame are almost up," a female voice spat.

Jenny stopped and spun on her heel. "Who said that?"

Felicity Black grinned like a hyena, her beady gaze darting between my face and Jenny's.

Jenny lurched forward, and I grabbed her arm.

"Stop. It's not worth it." I pulled her back.

"Say anything like that again, you no talent hack, and I'll break your nose-job. Maybe it'll straighten out that botched lump on your face." Jenny spat the words inches from the girl's face.

I dragged Jenny away, and she led me to her suite. It was nearly identical to the one Aiden and I shared. She sat me on a stool in front of a vanity in the bathroom and wet a washcloth in the sink. I rubbed the makeup from my face and finally recognized the girl staring back at me.

Evan and Aiden came through the door. Aiden saw me and stopped. *Shoot. He probably shouldn't see me without makeup on.* I turned away from him and scrambled in Jenny's makeup bag for something that looked familiar. So many brushes and bottles. Mascara! I knew how to use that. I snatched the tube and opened it, bringing the wand to my eyes.

"Wait." Aiden's voice was urgent. He stepped into the bathroom and raised a hand.

I stilled, the wand inches from my lashes. I met his gaze in the mirror. "What?"

"You're prettier without makeup." He held the door frame and stared at me. "Just leave it." The last was almost a whisper.

Jenny huffed. "She can't just leave it. She's going to be on camera. I'll fix it. Out." She shooed the men out of the room.

Aiden gave me a soft, lingering look before Jenny closed the door in his face.

What was that about?

Thirty minutes later and I was va-va-voom. Red lips and smokey eyes. I'd never be able to duplicate it, even after she gave me a tutorial. I'd probably forget it all. The girl staring back at me was fierce and confident. *And not me, at all.*

It was only the first day. There was no way I'd be able to pull this off for even an entire week, let alone six. I couldn't maintain this fake persona. The kale chips, not eating French fries. *I needed real food.*

But the money. The potential twenty-five thousand dollars. It would buy Dad's truck back. Two years of chemo, followed by Dad's accident on a catastrophic insurance plan, had left us in a really bad place financially. I stared in the mirror unseeing as I briefly considered the what if, and Aiden's words from earlier. *One week. Two at most.*

When I got back down to the pool, everyone was being wired for sound. There was a raised stage with a row of director's chairs and a slew of cameras and lighting equipment in the shade on one side of the deck.

Aiden swaggered up, carrying two drinks. He handed me a bottle of water. "You feelin' better?"

"Mmhmm." I sipped the water. He stared at me for a minute, then shook his head and walked to the stage, leaving me to stare after him.

I'm no expert on body language, but I don't think he's digging this whole relationship thing.

Desiree came over and handed me a microphone. I threaded it through my armpit and clipped the mic to the lapel of my cover-up as Desiree hooked the battery pack to the back of my suit. She dragged me onto the stage and pushed me toward a director's chair. I pulled my wrap around me and played with it for a minute until it stayed closed. Then she went to help Aiden do the same.

Crew members carrying dry-erase boards rushed across the stage, handing each contestant one. Another man handed out markers.

Aiden dropped into the seat next to mine and smiled at me.

Trisha Thames stood in front of the camera. "Welcome back to *Couple's Cruise—Celebrity Edition*. I'm your host, Trisha Thames. We've met the couples and learned the stories of how they met. And now we're going to play a game we like to call, *'Finish This Sentence.'*" She turned and walked across the stage as the closest camera panned with her.

"I'll read a sentence, and our couples will answer *as* their significant other. So they write what they think their significant other would say." She glanced around the set. "Looks like we're ready to begin."

Crap. Aiden and I knew almost nothing about each other. *This was gonna be a train wreck.*

"First question: I hate it when my significant other... blank." Trisha gave a gleeful smile.

Hmm. From my limited experience, Aiden hated it when I wore makeup. And probably when I wheeled my suitcase on sand. He'd tried to hide his cringe, but I'd seen it. I scribbled my answer on the whiteboard.

Trisha went down the line one-by-one. A group of staff stood off camera and clapped at every answer.

Jenny made adoring eyes at Evan. "He hates it when I steal the blankets."

Evan held up his sign. "Steal the blankets."

They high fived as a bunch of us clapped.

Trisha turned to Evan. "Alright Evan, how would Jenny finish this sentence? 'I hate it when my significant other...'"

Evan bit the bottom of his lip and shot a wicked grin at Jenny. "She hates it when I eat off of her plate."

"Yes!" Jenny stood and held the sign over her head like a ring girl at a UFC fight, strutting across the stage. "Eats off my plate!"

A smattering of applause followed.

Oh crap. I had to come up with how Aiden would answer for me. Something that didn't cast him in a bad light. *Jiminy Christmas! There was only one more couple before us.*

Felicia Phoenix, a tennis player, and her girlfriend, Jessica. They bickered when the first answer was revealed. *Good for me. Bad for them.* Felicia revealed the second answer. "I hate it when my significant other looks at other women." Jessica picked up her water cup and threw it in Felicia's face, then stormed off stage, and suddenly it was our turn.

"Aiden Miller, how are you?" Trisha smiled at him from off camera, and the cocky man I'd seen in interviews emerged.

"How ya doin', Trisha?" He leaned back in the chair, draping one elbow over the backrest, not even a little phased by the fight just seconds ago.

He was good.

"Doing great. Aiden, finish this sentence. I hate when my significant other…"

Aiden glanced at me and smiled. "Well. She's beautiful. She doesn't need any extra enhancement. So, I hate it when my significant other wears makeup."

Oh my word, he got it. He got it! I held up my sign, and he looked at it. A genuine smile overtook his face, and he leaned over and placed a kiss on my cheek. I was gonna pass out.

All for the cameras, Dylan. Settle down.

"Very good." Trisha applauded. "Now Dylan, I hate when my significant other…"

"Buys me flowers?" *Crap.* I panicked. We hadn't talked about anything like that.

Trisha raised an eyebrow and held up a hand to stop Aiden from revealing his answer. "Wait. You don't like flowers?" She brought her voice low in a conspiratorial tone.

I shook my head. "They only last a few days before they die. I'd rather have something like chocolates, at least *those* would live on my hips for the next few years."

Sheena's condescending titter cut through the silence. Jenny joined in and waved her hand in a circle, encouraging me to make light of it. I forced a laugh, and heat crept up my cheeks.

Aiden held up his sign and gave an exaggerated shrug, palm up. "Snores." At my fake pout, he reached over and grabbed my hand, then gave it a gentle squeeze and kept it in his lap.

For the cameras.

Trisha moved on to the final two couples on our other side.

One out of two. Not bad. Not bad at all.

Round two.

Trisha read from a card. "If my significant other were an animal, they'd be a..."

The Jeopardy theme song played over the speakers.

My eyes locked with Aiden's, I studied his features. *Wolf?* He did have those piercing blue eyes that Huskies had, and that reminded me of a wolf. According to an interview I'd read, he loved horses. After a moment to consider, I jotted down "horse."

Now what animal would he call me? Probably a chameleon, because I was being something I wasn't. I thought back to our conversation about nicknames. He *had* mentioned kitten. Maybe he'd use that because it was fresh on his mind? I was grasping at straws.

In my panic, I missed Evan's answer for Jenny, but they got the second one right. Jenny called Evan a tiger.

The tennis player's girlfriend was back, and as the first answer was revealed, tears were shed. Probably calling your celebrity a dirty dog on national TV was a sure way to end the relationship. Their breakup must have been a long time coming. *I felt bad for them. What an embarrassing way to break up.*

People off camera waved their arms, making a cutting motion across their throats.

Trisha skipped the second answer and moved directly to us. "Dylan, you're first this time. If my significant other were an animal, they'd be a...?"

I ducked my head and glanced at Aiden. "Kitten?"

He flipped the whiteboard and pulled me toward him. "Kitten." He placed a kiss on my nose.

Holy crap, he's good at this. I need to up my "couples game."

"Aww, aren't you two cute?" Trisha's eyes narrowed. "Aiden, If my significant other were an animal, they'd be a...?"

He took up his cocky position again. "She'd say a stallion."

Trisha snickered, along with a couple of the contestants. Technically, he wasn't wrong.

I flipped the card. "Horse?"

Trisha looked at a couple of men sitting off set. They both nodded. "Our panel says 'Horse' is acceptable. Good job!" She clapped, and a bunch of the film crew and staff joined in.

She moved on to the final two couples. Aiden squeezed my hand and winked at me. He was a little all over the place, and if I wasn't careful, I was going to be warm goo by the end of the cruise.

Trisha turned to the camera. "Which three couples will be eliminated Thursday night? Their fates are in your hands, America. Tweet your vote using #couplescruiseS14. Or call and text your votes to the numbers scrolling across your screen. Data and messaging rates may apply." The red light turned off, and everyone seemed to let out a breath.

One of the men who had been on the panel of judges stood and ran a hand over his bald head. "Thank you all for coming. I'm the executive producer, Walt Gregory. You'll see cameras around the boat, both manned and unmanned." His gaze zeroed in on me.

Crap, was he calling me out? I didn't mean to choke on the kale.

He continued, his tone a little softer. "Always assume the camera is rolling. The only place there aren't cameras is in the private rooms and restrooms. Tomorrow we'll be stopping at our first port. Please report here at one in the afternoon to travel ashore and participate in the activity. The viewers will eliminate three of the twelve couples at the live results show on Thursday. See ya tomorrow." He clapped twice, and we dispersed.

Six - Aiden

It was getting close to sunset. I just wanted to go back to the room, order room service, and spend the rest of the night in bed. *Sleeping.* I rubbed the bridge of my nose as members of the film crew unhooked us from sound.

Jenny wandered over and wrapped an arm around Dylan's waist. "You two up for dancing tonight?" She swayed her hips and put the other arm above her head, dancing to a silent rhythm.

No. Please, no. I glanced at Dylan, and she widened her eyes at me, then gave a tight shake of her head.

Thank heavens. "Um. Not tonight. Dylan and I need to spend some time gettin' to know each other better."

Evan laughed and nudged my arm. *The jerk.*

Dylan grinned, her cheeks tinged pink, and punched Evan's shoulder. "Not like that."

"Ouch." He rubbed the spot and gave her a dirty look. "Geez girl, that hurt."

I smirked at Evan. *Served him right.* He was always making crude innuendos. I'd have to remember her killer right hook. I linked my arm through Dylan's. "We'll see ya tomorrow."

We walked to the room, and I opened the door, gesturing for her to enter first.

"I need to shower. Do you have to use the restroom before I do?" She pulled off her wrap and draped it over one of the chairs by the table. Her blue one piece didn't leave much to the imagination, and my gaze roamed her body.

"Aiden? The bathroom?" She raised an eyebrow.

"No. Go ahead." *Pretend nothing happened.* I peeled off my boots and socks, grabbed my writing notebook from the nightstand and collapsed onto the bed, then picked up the remote. One of the channels was dedicated to recaps and edited portions of today's interviews before they went on the air. The camera zoomed in on Dylan's arm draped over the back of my chair, her hand lazily running through the hair at the nape of my neck. I had a smile plastered on my face.

Who was this girl? She practically read my mind. Her answers today were brilliant. How much did she already know from magazines and tabloids? I couldn't figure her out. One minute she seemed super cool, asking if she could steal my french fries, the next she was running off to fix her makeup.

The shower turned off in the bathroom, and I checked the clock. It hadn't even been fifteen minutes. The footage cut off and less than five minutes later, Dylan emerged, her hair wet and wavy. She had a toothbrush sticking out of her mouth and her face was makeup free. She wore a ratty t-shirt and a pair of boxer shorts. *Again—who was this girl?*

"Do you have any floss?" She cupped a hand under her chin and spoke around the toothbrush, muffling her words.

I stood and slipped past her into the bathroom and dug through my toiletry bag. I pulled out the floss and handed it to her.

"Thanks." She leaned over the sink and spit a big wad of white foam into it, then brushed her tongue.

"Yup." I watched her a minute longer as she rinsed her mouth and smoothed lotion over her face. Our gazes met in the mirror.

"Everything okay?"

Well, darn if I wasn't more attracted to her without makeup on and hair all done. "Yup." I spun on my heel, then retreated to the bedroom and dropped back onto the bed.

She came out a minute later and glanced around the room.

"You can sit by me. The bed is big enough for the both of us." I patted the spot beside me and adjusted the pillow.

Her eyes widened, and she gave me a horrified look.

Well, shoot. "That wasn't what I meant." As I stared at her, it struck me. No girl had ever brushed her teeth in front of me before. I didn't know why it seemed so monumental. Other girls felt self-conscious about it? It was an oxymoron with what I knew of her. I didn't care what it meant; I liked it.

"I'll just sit on this thing." She stumbled through her words as she sat on the chaise lounge, bringing her long legs to her chest. She wrapped her arms around her knees and rested her chin on them. "So. We have more getting to know you to do."

Definitely not the typical girl. Any other girl would've jumped at the chance to be in bed with The *Aiden Miller.*

I muted the TV and dropped my notebook onto the bed. The blank page mocked me, just like all the other blank pages over the months. "Sounds like it."

"You wanna go first?" She gnawed on her bottom lip. *Man, she was beautiful.*

"What do you want to know?" Everything about me was basically plastered all over the internet. Really, I could just hand her a magazine, and she'd get the gist. Or at least the version people cared to see.

She shrugged one shoulder. "Something I can't find online."

"Okay." *That's specific.* "After high school, I moved down to Nashville. I was discovered while doing a performance at a club. Toured with Evan and my first album went platinum. I was incredibly blessed."

The side of her mouth tipped up into a smile. "I already knew that. Tell me about your childhood."

I blew out a breath. "Well, my dad's a mechanic and has his own shop."

"Did you spend a lot of time with him there?" She shifted in her seat and dropped a foot to the floor.

"He restores old cars. My favorite is a sixty-two, orange Plymouth Road Runner. A lot of my childhood was spent in his shop, either handing him tools, or messin' around on my guitar." I could almost hear the crank of the ratchet, smell the motor oil, feel the grittiness of old grease on my fingers.

"My dad had a fifty-eight army-green Chevy 3800. He loved that thing." Her brown eyes went distant. "We used to joke that it was his third child.

41

When I finally got my license, he took me to the church and let me drive it around the parking lot." She laughed. "I wasn't allowed to go over fifteen miles an hour."

That was familiar. "My dad wouldn't even let me drive his. Some day, I'll get my own. When I've got some time on my hands, I'll rebuild it." *Maybe with my own son, whenever I had kids.* "What about your family? Tell me about your little brother."

"Colby. He wants to be a rockstar. He plays the guitar and is lead singer in an awful band. They practice in our basement sometimes." She closed one eye and twisted her mouth like she'd tasted something sour. "Not good."

"Jenny said that you sang backup for her?" *Just a little fishing line to see how quick she self-promoted.*

Dylan's cheeks flamed. "Yeah, I love singing. I just never pursued it. I co-wrote her last album. She's still trying to force money on me from it."

Interesting. "Why won't you take it? You earned it." *How could she co-write an entire album, and I couldn't even come up with a single lyric?*

She shrugged. "I don't know. Partly it's because of what we talked about earlier. But partly because it just doesn't feel right. It was fun. If I get paid, it'll take the fun out of it."

I knew exactly what she meant. I loved singing, but now I had a contract and deadlines… The pressure robbed me of my creativity.

"So, where have you traveled?" *I didn't know what to expect. Her best friend was a superstar with three platinum albums. She oughta have been somewhere extravagant.*

"Um." She studied her nails for a minute. "This is my first time out of the country. I only have a passport because Jenny's threatening to drag me to Europe on her next tour."

The more I learned about her, the more intrigued I became. "And where do you live?" If I hadn't known about her financial troubles, I would've expected an apartment in LA or NYC.

"I still live with my mom while I go to school." She slumped her shoulders and stared at the floor.

"In Montana?"

She picked at her nail polish. "Yeah."

"What's your major?" I reserved judgement this time. She had surprised me so far. No need to build on my misconceptions.

"Elementary Education. I want to be a teacher like my mom." She hesitated a moment, then added, "Or, I did."

"What changed?"

She glanced up at me, then went back to picking at her nail polish. "I dunno."

"That's a non-answer." Peggy had called me out on that multiple times, so I knew it when I saw it.

Our gazes caught, and hers bounced back and forth between my eyes, searching for something. I nodded my encouragement.

"It doesn't pay the bills."

My heart lurched for her mom. Losing her husband, then having to do it all on her own. I couldn't imagine.

"Anyway." She shook herself, literally shaking out her hands and feet. "Blegh. Let's change the subject."

I picked up the remote and held it up for her to see. "What's your favorite TV show?"

"Promise not to make fun of me?" Her eyebrow quirked.

Oh, now we're getting somewhere. "I promise nothing." I held back a grin.

Her eyes danced. "Have you ever seen Forged in Fire?" A blush bloomed on her cheeks. I really liked how easily she blushed.

"The knife show, right? I've heard of it."

She nodded.

"Is it streaming?" I unmuted the TV and pressed the button for the streaming service.

Another nod. She dropped her other foot and turned on the chaise to look at the TV behind her.

A quick search, and I turned on the show.

We spent the next hour watching it together. It was cool. And by the end of the episode, I added weapon forging to my bucket list. I stopped the next episode from playing and turned to her. "Do you have a bucket list?"

43

"Yeah." Her smile didn't quite reach her eyes.

"Have you done anything on it?" I sat up and adjusted the pillows behind me.

She stood and walked the few steps to the bed and perched on the edge. "I swam with dolphins when I was seventeen."

That was cool. "Awesome. Was it all you hoped it would be?" I'd have to add that one to my list, too.

"It was fun, but I think it was funner to see Colby swim with them. He was only eight." She leaned back on one hand. "He was scared at first, thought their dorsal fins were sharks. He didn't come in until after we'd all been in for a few minutes and hadn't been eaten alive." She grinned, and her eyes seemed to focus. "What about you? Any bucket list items?"

"That's an understatement." *It's miles long.* I was using bungee jumping as a reward for my album release.

"So, you have a lot?" She raised her eyebrows and darned if that wasn't adorable, too.

I pulled my legs back to give her more room, in case she wanted to get more comfortable. "Skydiving, swimming with sharks. There's an extensive list."

Dylan tilted her head to the side, her hair falling over her face. She blew some of the strands away. "Have you done any of them?"

"One." I rubbed my chest. It didn't hurt anymore, but if I thought about it long enough, I could still feel the sting of the needle. "A tattoo."

"The tribal tattoo on your peck?" Her delicious blush reappeared.

Ahh. She knew about it. "That's the one." I lifted the edge of my shirt, flexing my abs as I did. A habit I'd picked up from all the photo shoots.

She leaned closer, her eyes drinking in my chest. "Does it mean anything?"

"Courage. I got it after I released my first album."

"That's cool. I always thought that if I got a tattoo, it'd be because it really meant something to me." She stifled a yawn, and I tossed her a pillow. She adjusted it and laid across the foot of the bed, her legs still dangling over the edge. "Thanks."

"What would you get?" I adjusted my pillows again and laid sideways on the bed, our faces across from each other.

Her mouth twitched. "A Reeses bar, probably."

"Ahh, I love Reeses. I could be convinced to get a matching one. Where should we get them?" *And this is where most girls would offer to show me.*

She shrugged and yawned again.

It was refreshing to be wrong, for once. "Should we order dinner before you fall asleep?" I sat and looked for the menus.

"We can do that?" She propped herself up on her elbow.

"Dylan, we're celebrities. We can do anything we want." I held her gaze, then winked.

She gestured toward me. "You're a celebrity. I'm a fish out of water." Her words were matter-of-fact. No pouting or awkwardness.

I found the menus and spread them on the bed between us. "You are, too. You've been on the radio, and after today, TV."

She flipped through the stack and held up a Chinese menu.

Yes! My last girlfriend would have asked for a salad, or looked through each of the menus until she found one with a low calorie option. "What'll ya have?"

"Egg rolls." She flopped back onto the bed and grinned. "And Sweet and Sour Chicken with fried rice."

I picked up the phone and placed her order, adding dumplings and Beef with Broccoli. They told me it would be ready in twenty minutes, and I hung up.

She sat up, a grin on her face. "What did you say?"

"What?" I shot her a confused look.

"What did you order?" She leaned forward on her hands.

"Sweet and Sour chicken, like you wanted."

"And what else?"

"Beef and Broccoli, and an order of dumplin's."

She looked like she was holding back a laugh. "Say that again?"

"Beef—"

She waved her hands dramatically, cutting me off. "No. The other thing."

"Dumplin's?"

45

She fell back on the bed, laughing. "Maybe it's just because I'm tired, but I love the way you say dumplings with your drawl."

I grinned.

After Dylan had laughed herself out, she laid back on the bed, one hand beneath the pillow and the other curled under her chin. I draped the blanket over her.

"Hmm?" Her eyes fluttered. "I'm not sleeping, just resting my eyes," she mumbled.

The Dylan laying without makeup, asleep at the foot of my bed, was the Dylan that Evan told me about. The Dylan for the cameras was a completely different person. *I definitely prefer this one.*

I pulled out my notebook and stared at the blank page, then back at Dylan. Then I scribbled a line of lyrics.

For the first time in over a year.

Seven - Dylan

A knock startled me awake, and I discreetly wiped the drool from my face. There was nothing to be done about the dark spot on the pillow, though. I flipped it over as Aiden went to answer the door.

Guys wearing white wheeled a cart into the room. One offered to light candles, and Aiden declined.

I stood, smoothed the blanket over the bed, and tossed the pillow back up to the head.

Aiden handed the men a tip, and they nodded, then left. He pulled the table over by the lounger thingy. "Let's watch another episode of Forged in Fire while we eat." He placed the plates side by side on the table facing the TV.

"Be right back." I slipped into the bathroom and cringed at the reflection in the mirror. My hair was frizzy and matted, but that wasn't even the worst of it. Along one side of my face was the red imprint of the pillow I'd lain on. *Ugh. That's crap.* I rubbed my face. *Please fade, please. Nope.*

When I came out, Aiden was already eating with the next episode cued up. *Bonus. He was even sitting on the right side, so he'd get the perfect view of the pillow imprint on my face.*

I walked behind the lounger thing and sat next to him. The smell of the plastic cover over our food brought bile to my throat. It reminded me too much of the hospital stays, and spoon-feeding Dad after his surgery. Other memories tried to surface, but I forced them down.

Alden lifted my lid and hit play on the remote. The tangy sweetness and spices hit my nose, making my mouth water.

The Sweet and Sour chicken was still crisp on the outside; just how I liked it. I dipped it into the rice, coating it like a little porcupine, and popped it into my mouth. The bite was probably bigger than I should have taken, and the sauce was scalding hot. I did the reverse blow, sucking air into my mouth. I didn't know which was better: spitting it out, or fanning my face as I sucked in air.

"Hot?" Aiden's mouth tilted up into a half-smile.

He must think I'm a total spaz.

"Uhn hunh." I nodded and continued fanning my mouth while I chewed. I guzzled water then watched a few minutes of Forged in Fire while I waited for it to cool.

"You're not what I was expectin.'"

"You already said that." My gut twisted. *Of course I wasn't.* He was expecting Malibu Barbie. *Why did it matter if he liked me? Yes, he was hot, and he had a voice that made me melt, but I didn't want to be a number. It mattered that he liked me.*

"You okay?" He muted the volume and turned to look at me.

I yawned. "Yep, just tired." I coated another bite of chicken in rice. As I brought it to my lips, Aiden grabbed my wrist and brought the bite to his mouth. I thought he'd steal it right off the fork, but he gently blew on it to cool it off.

Warm goo. I'd be warm goo by the end of this.

When he deemed it sufficiently cool, he released my hand and nodded. "Now try it."

I popped the bite into my mouth.

"Care if I try a bite?"

"Go ahead?"

He stabbed a piece of chicken with his fork, then rolled it around in the rice. "That enough?"

"Yeah." For some reason, watching him get a bite felt really intimate. I shifted uncomfortably, putting a little space between us.

Aiden brought it to his mouth and blew on it a few times, then placed the entire thing in his mouth. "Oh, that's delicious."

I smiled. "I know, right?"

He pulled the lid from his plate, revealing his food.

"Potstickers," I said.

"What?"

"What you call dumplin's," I pronounced it like him, with an exaggerated southern drawl, "I call potstickers."

"I don't care what you call 'em. I call 'em heaven." He speared one, dipped it in soy sauce, then popped it in his mouth. "We had this Chinese restaurant growin' up. Man, they had the best dumplin's. I haven't been in years, but every time I have one, I'm teleported back home."

He ate another, then held the third out to me on the end of his fork.

Holy crap. Aiden Miller was feeding me dumplings. Tentatively, I leaned forward and used my teeth to pull it off his fork.

Aiden watched me chew, and I tried to be as lady-like as possible.

The flavors exploded on my tongue. "It's good," I said around the bite.

We ate in silence for a couple minutes, and I glanced at his dumplings again. I'd forever think of them as dumplings now, thanks to Aiden.

He grinned. "You want another?"

I nodded.

"They're addictive, huh?"

Instead of answering, I stole one from his plate with my fork.

He laughed and pushed his plate back, then pulled mine toward him, putting them between us. He raised a brow as if asking for permission, and I nodded. Aiden unmuted the TV, and we took turns coating our chicken in rice and eating dumplings as we watched the rest of the episode.

When it was over, Aiden looked at me. "Another episode?"

"I'm so tired. I can sleep through it, though. Feel free to keep watching." I stood and went over to the bed and pulled back the blankets. *He wouldn't try to get in bed with me, right? Did security confiscate my mace?* I slid between the sheets and pulled the blanket up to my chin. "Sorry, the sun takes it out of me." Not to mention the hours of trying on clothes, getting every hair ripped from my body, and having my makeup done. *Oh, and let's not forget trying to be someone I wasn't.* A few minutes later, I was asleep.

49

~

The next morning, I was alone in bed. Relief mixed with disappointment. *Crap on a cracker. I liked him.* Not just the media's version of him. He seemed like a genuinely nice guy. His sleeping form on the lounger was proof of that. But liking Aiden Miller brought a slew of consequences I wasn't ready to deal with.

Jenny's room was down the hall, and I snuck out and tapped on her door.

Evan answered in nothing but a pair of boxers. "Hey, Dyl. She's in the shower." His chest was covered in tattoos, including a tribal tattoo on one peck that matched Aiden's.

"I'll wait." I fidgeted with the frayed hem of my shirt.

He looked me up and down. "That's what you wore to bed?" Evan ran a hand down his face.

"Mmhmm."

His lips puckered, and he shook his head.

"What?"

He shrugged. "You're just not doing yourself any favors, is all."

Any favors? I wasn't trying to get Aiden in bed. I looked down at my clothes. Okay, they were old, but they were comfy—my main requirement.

He stepped back and let me in.

Their king-sized bed was stripped, and the sheets were piled on the floor. "What happened to the bed?"

"Jen puked." He yawned and shuffled to the lounge, dropped onto it and threw an arm over his eyes. I pulled out a chair and sank into it.

Jenny emerged from the bathroom, her hair wrapped in a towel. She was cocooned in a robe and had pink fuzzy slippers on her feet. "Hey, Dyl."

"You feeling okay?" I stood and went over to her and put a hand on her forehead. "You don't have a fever."

She brushed my hand away. "I'm fine. It was just something I ate. What's up?"

I pushed her back into the bathroom. "Fix my face. Please."

She sat me in front of the vanity and perched on the counter in front of me. "Alright, let's beautify you for your man."

My hair was straightened and smoothed into a sleek style, and my face had been contoured and painted until I was nearly unrecognizable.

"You wanna borrow some clothes?"

I scoffed. "I'm good. I'll find something." Jenny could represent the lollipop guild; she was so short. Her clothes never fit me right. I slipped back down the hall to our room. *The room I shared with Aiden Freaking Miller.* I stood outside the door. My stomach did a few cartwheels. *Relax, Max. Cool as a cucumber.* I took a few deep breaths and entered.

He was still sleeping, and I crept into the closet to find something to wear. *Wonder what they have in store for us today?* I slipped on a black swimming suit, pulled a pink tank top over it and paired it with some cut-offs and a pair of white tennis shoes—the only tennies Fabian allowed me.

It was already noon. *How late had Aiden stayed up after I crashed last night?* I sat on the edge of the lounger and shook his bare shoulder. A notebook lay beside him, and words were written, then scribbled out and written again. "Aiden?"

He cracked his eyes open, then rubbed a hand down his face. "What time is it?" He stretched, and the blanket slid down to his waist, revealing a whole lotta muscly hotness. *Holy mother, he was... Yum.*

"Noon." My voice was a little breathless. Heat crept up my neck, and I stood, putting some distance between us. If I wasn't careful, my body would jump him before my mind had a chance to catch up.

He stood and stretched his arms above his head.

I averted my gaze.

"Wow. You look good. How long have you been awake?"

"Thanks. A little while." I smoothed my hands down my hair. "We better get going if you want to eat." The ship swayed slightly, then vibrated.

"We must be at port. I'll be out in a few." He retreated into the bathroom and the shower turned on. I folded his blankets, then placed them at the foot of the lounger. While I waited, I slid out onto our private balcony. The wind blew my hair and the fresh salt air felt amazing. Our balcony faced the ocean, and the sun glinted off the water. *Wow.*

I leaned my elbows on the rail and searched the blues of the ocean. Every wave, every ripple, could be a sea creature. The hum of the engine was louder out here, and water swirled near the rear of the boat.

Aiden snaked his arms around my waist from behind, and I gasped. He placed a kiss on my neck, then rested his face on my shoulder next to mine. My stomach fluttered, and my heart worked double time.

"There are cameras on the balconies." He spoke so quietly I barely heard him over the engines.

Of course there were.

He straightened and spun me to face him. I caught myself on his waist, my hands touching the bare skin above his shorts. The wind whipped my hair into my face, hiding my blush. Aiden smoothed it down, then placed a kiss on my forehead. His gaze searched mine, and he leaned in and kissed my nose.

Don't stop now.

His hands cupped my face, and he brought his lips to one cheek. He paused, his eyes dark and stormy, then planted a kiss on the other.

My breaths shuddered out. *Kiss me, Aiden.*

He released my hair and wrapped his arms around my waist, pulling me into him. "You're so beautiful." He lifted my chin and placed a kiss at the corner of my mouth.

When was the last time a man had to lift my chin? I never felt dainty, but with Aiden, I did. I melted into him and wrapped my arms around his shoulders, tangling my hands in his hair. The black lens of the camera above the door caught my gaze. My stomach soured, and I pulled back. *He's doing it for the cameras, Dylan, simmer.*

He leaned down and kissed my shoulder. "Let's go get some food." He grabbed my hand, then linked our fingers, and we walked down to the Lido deck where most of the casual restaurants were. *No Chinese for this girl.* We found Jenny and Evan at a table with a deck of cards.

"We're gonna grab lunch. Be right back," Aiden said.

We split, and I grabbed the saddest salad I'd ever seen. Not a piece of lettuce anywhere, all mixed greens and veggies. I ate while Aiden had a burger. *I'd kill for a burger right now.* After skipping breakfast this morning, my stomach was growling. Ugh. I attacked my salad with new gusto. *I should have bathed it in Ranch instead of this low-fat Italian.*

Unseen speakers crackled to life. "Please head to the pool on the Lido deck. The ferries depart in ten minutes."

Aiden twined our fingers, and we walked to the pool. There was a balcony that ran around the upper level of the Lido deck, and lights and equipment were strapped to every square inch. The producers, directors, and whoever else made a film crew ran around getting the set ready.

Desiree approached us. "You guys are doing great. Just remember to sell the relationship."

Trisha Thames stood on a small platform, and we all gathered around it. *Holy crow.* Actress, Laura Gilchrest, and her fiancé were beside us. I loved her in her last movie. What was that called again? Last Rodeo? Rodeo something? I couldn't remember. I squeezed Aiden's hand, and he bumped me with his shoulder as if he'd seen my starstruck moment.

He leaned down and put his lips to my ear. "What's really weird is when a celebrity comes up to you as a fan."

I pulled back and met his gaze. "That would be so weird."

He winked.

"If I can have everyone's attention." Trisha spoke into a megaphone. "Today's activity will be deep sea fishing."

Yes! I love fishing. I'd never been *deep sea* fishing, but how different could it be?

Whines and moans went up from more than one person. Guess this was the plan, put us in situations we didn't want to be in and see who cracked. Aiden rubbed his hands together, his bottom lip between his teeth. We shared a look, and he grinned at me.

"Now, if you'll follow me." Trisha waved and led us down a hallway and several flights of stairs. In front of us, Laura Gilchrest teetered on her heels and clutched her fiancé's arm. We walked out of a hatch on the side of the ship and down a ramp to a waiting boat. Camera men were already in position and capturing every moment. The boat had rows of benches covered by an awning.

Jenny kept up a constant stream of chatter as we loaded onto the boat and waited for the stragglers.

Aiden squeezed my hand and leaned down to whisper in my ear. "Have you ever been fishing?"

My knee jerk reaction was to nod and say yes. My head bobbed, and I opened my mouth and then clamped it shut. "What?" *Play dumb. That always works.*

His brows drew down. "Have you ever been fishing?"

Oh my gosh, I'm such an idiot. "No." The word squeaked out, high pitched. It was painful, even to my own ears. "Yes." I couldn't do it.

He scrutinized me for way longer than was comfortable. "Which is it?"

"I have."

Aiden shook his head and faced forward, effectively ending the conversation.

Jenny said Aiden wouldn't change his tastes overnight. She said his fans and the viewers would expect me to fit a certain mold. A mold that I obviously didn't fit. Apparently, Aiden didn't like that mold.

The boat bumped along the waves as we motored toward the shore. There, they assigned us spots in four different boats. Jenny and Evan weren't on ours.

We got paired with hotel heiress Kourtney Fieldgate and her boyfriend Blake. And Trojan's quarterback Jake Donahue and his cheerleader girlfriend—and I wish I were kidding—Barbie.

Our film crew was four people. The boat crew, another four guys. We all shuffled onto the boat, and our captain gave us a quick safety speech. He used more creative language that would have to be bleeped for prime-time television. But to paraphrase: don't jump overboard, let the boat crew do all the casting, and for heaven sakes, don't drown. We were ushered to some tables near the front of the boat and wired for sound during the ten-minute ride.

During which, Kourtney had a panic attack. Someone brought her one of those orange life jackets, which she pulled over her head, destroying her hair. And they gave her alcohol. Plenty of alcohol. Blake sat beside her, face pinched, rubbing her back. But his attention was on the crew setting up the fishing rods.

I wasn't sure if I felt more sorry for him, for not being able to participate like he wanted to, or her for having a boyfriend more interested in fishing than making sure she was all right.

"Aiden Miller and his girlfriend." One of the boat crew signaled for us to come and man a couple of fishing rods near the back of the boat. "Just watch these rods, and if you get a bite, let me know." He walked toward the front of the boat.

Oh good. I was just some random girl, no name, just Aiden's girlfriend. I shook my head and stood at the rail, staring down into the water directly below us. "Have *you* ever been fishing?" I picked up our dropped conversation from the ferry.

"Yeah. I used to go every weekend with my dad and grandpa." He came and stood beside me, our shoulders touching.

"Then you moved to Nashville." I glanced at him.

His face was drawn, and his mouth pulled into a frown. "Yep." He met my gaze and something over my shoulder caught his eyes. "Don't look now. The cameras are on us."

I froze. The tip of the fishing pole beside him dipped and reflex kicked in. I grabbed the rod from the holder and jerked, setting the hook. "We caught something!" I grinned and reeled.

He came up beside me and held onto the rod while I reeled. The first few seconds were easy; then the fish thrashed, nearly yanking the rod from my hands.

Good thing Aiden was there. The cameraman came closer.

"I'm gonna wrap my arms around you." Aiden's words were so low that I barely heard him.

My head bobbed in a quick nod, and my heart forgot to beat for a minute.

His arm held the rod, and the other wrapped around my waist. He positioned himself behind me, his face next to mine, and our bodies pressed together. *Holy Moley.* My heart resumed its beating, but at a more spazzed pace. I forced myself to relax into him. *You're a couple, Dylan.* How many

55

times would I have to remind myself?

There was commotion around us, and our crewman made his way to our side. Each spin of the reel was a struggle, the fish fought, pulling the line out farther, and the tension release clicked. A splash out in the water caught my eye.

"A marlin!" The crewman exclaimed.

I twisted until I could see Aiden's face. He grinned from ear to ear as he studied the water. I'd missed the first jump. I wouldn't miss it again. Dad would've been so jealous! *I hope you're up there watching, old man.* The marlin leapt into the air, and a chorus of cheers followed.

My arms ached from the effort of reeling, and Aiden took over, but kept his arms around me.

I gripped the rod high, and he reeled low.

The film crew was all up in our faces. *Would they let us keep our fish? Or would this be catch-and-release because of television?*

It took over half-an-hour. *Which I'm sure was riveting television.* Sweat dripped down my face and back, and Aiden's shirt was damp with it... His or mine, I couldn't be sure.

Our crewman held a long pole with a hook on the end, and as the marlin got close enough, he hefted it up into the boat. *Oh my gosh. It was the coolest thing.* I mentally checked deep sea fishing off my bucket list.

Someone handed me a towel. I wiped my face and cringed at the amount of makeup on it. Then Aiden and I posed with the fish and one of the camera crew snapped a couple of Polaroids. He fanned the pictures in the air and handed one to me and the other to Aiden. In the picture, Aiden held his arm up, flexing his muscles, his face bright with sweat and pride. I matched him smile for smile. But I'd wiped most of my makeup during our sweaty struggle. This would be a hard memory to top. At least I'd have a souvenir once the show was over. Something just for me.

Eight - Aiden

The kisses that morning were for the camera. But, as I watched Dylan help the fishermen release the marlin back into the ocean, I wanted to do it again.

For me.

She hadn't even balked; she just wrapped her arms around the middle of the fish and helped hoist it. The boat coasted for a moment to allow the fish to get its bearings before they released it back into the wild.

The crowd cheered, and she grinned up at me. Her smile had my heart racing. I held my arms out, and she wrapped hers around my neck.

"Good job." The words were spoken directly into her ear, sending a thrill up my spine.

"Thanks." She pulled back and her smile faltered. "It was so slimy."

She wiped her hands on what was left of her shorts. No girl I'd ever dated before would have done that. It would have been a shower and sanitizer for days.

"We got a bite!" a male voice shouted from the other side of the boat. Dylan gasped and grabbed my hand, her excitement palpable as she towed me toward the other side of the boat. I didn't even mind that the floral scent of her shampoo was mixed with the fishy smell of marlin.

The heiress's boyfriend worked on reeling in the fish. Kourtney sat beside him in her sunhat, a disgusted look on her face and gulping a frou-frou drink of some sort. She crossed her legs and one kicked with increasing speed. Her lips were pursed, and she shook her head.

"This is ridiculous. Why would they have us do something so stupid?" Kourtney inspected her fingernails, then threw back the rest of her drink.

The boyfriend glanced at her. "It's not stupid. A lot of people go deep sea fishing." His fish must have tugged because he grunted and shifted as the tension meter clicked.

"Yeah, but a lot of people don't want to waste their day waiting for a fish to bite a string."

"Just go below deck. No one wants to hear you whine anymore, babe." He glanced at the group of people gathered around them.

Awkward. Props to the dude for growing a pair and telling her to take a hike, though.

She huffed and stomped to the steps, her heels clicking on the deck. "Find me when you decide I'm more interesting than a fish." Her voice was near screeching volume, and she chucked her empty glass at him. It hit his shoulder and bounced harmlessly on the deck. *Musta been made of plastic.*

I wrapped my arms around Dylan's waist from behind and propped my chin on her shoulder. "Thanks for not bein' crazy."

She turned her head to the side and planted a kiss on my temple. "Any time."

My heart lurched, and I tamped it down. Physical attraction was not the same as caring. She was an attractive girl, even better when she didn't cake her face in makeup.

The workings of a song began in my head, a sequence of chords playing in my mind. *When was the last time that happened? Lyrics last night, and now a tune?*

I released Dylan and linked our hands, pulling her behind me toward the front of the ship. "We'll head back over in a bit if you want. I need to find some paper and write somethin' down."

"What are you writing?"

Hopefully, the start of my next album. "Just a couple chords that came to me and a line of lyrics."

"Awesome." She smiled, and my gut tightened.

A cameraman followed us to the front of the boat. We found a crewmember, and I asked him for a piece of paper and pen. I hid my smile. No need to get fans excited about a song if it didn't take shape. The chords and lyrics came easily.

You laughed when the ocean kissed your face

And it caught me by surprise

'Cause then I wanted to be the waves

And bring that smile to your eyes.

I folded the paper and stuffed it into my pocket with the Polaroid.

"Do I get to know what you wrote?" Dylan's voice lilted at the end, and she turned her body to the side, looking at me over her shoulder.

Darn, she was cute. I grinned. "Nope, I can't tell you all my secrets. Maybe it'll be on the radio some day."

"Did you bring your guitar?" Her face was so hopeful I was glad I didn't have to disappoint her.

"Yeah."

She beamed and clapped her hands. "Yay! I'll have to play you something."

"You play?" Maybe I shouldn't sound so surprised, since we're supposed to be dating. Her playing my guitar didn't sit well with me. *It was my baby. Sacred. I couldn't just let some chick play it, regardless of how she affected me.*

I glanced at the cameraman. His camera was pointed right at us. *Great, I'd just revealed to the world I didn't know my girlfriend played guitar.* I reached out and flipped him off. *There. Problem solved.*

Dylan swatted my arm. "Why'd you do that?" Her mouth was part smile—part dropped open in shock.

"Now it'll be harder for them to use the footage." I shrugged, and she burst out laughing. *Man, her laugh was a breath of fresh air.* When she really let her guard down and just laughed, it got me more than anything else she did.

"To answer your question, yes, I play." She flicked her eyebrows up and bit her bottom lip.

Hope she brought her own guitar, 'cause mine was off limits. It was my first purchase after hitting it big. She went with me everywhere. No one touched her but me.

~

My guitar didn't come up for the rest of the afternoon. By the time we made it back to the ship, we were worn out and collapsed in our room. With

59

any luck, we'd eat dinner and go to bed, the guitar forgotten.

"Favorite thing you've ever done?" She forked a bite of shrimp and shoved it into her mouth. I really enjoyed the Dylan I got when no one was around. She showered as soon as we got home and put on another pair of pajamas, this one flannel. It was adorable.

"Well." *That was a hard one.* "I went to Kuwait and sang for the troops last year. I think that was my favorite experience."

She cocked her head to the side. "Elaborate."

How to describe it... Hmm. "Well, before my performance, I had the opportunity to just go around and meet a bunch of the soldiers. They were so grateful to me for comin'. Some of them had been out there nearly a year, some on their second or third tour." I swallowed down the lump forming in my throat. If I hadn't pursued music, I would've joined the military. "I sat down with some of 'em and they told me some crazy stories about things I could never imagine and of some of the true heroes who died trying to make it home."

I shook my head and cleared my throat. "What about you?"

She bumped me with her shoulder, a knowing look on her face. "Florida."

"The dolphins?"

Her response was hummed around another bite of shrimp.

"If you could travel anywhere, where would you go?" I spun a bite of noodles onto my fork while I stared at her.

She swallowed and slowly swiped her bottom lip with her thumb before popping it in her mouth. *Yup, she's dangerous.* If I wasn't careful, I could *really* like her.

"I haven't thought about it. Hawaii sounds fun, but I like the mountains."

"Hawaii actually has a lot of mountains. You'd probably love it." And I'd love to take her there. *No. Album first.* "Tell me something else about you." I pushed my plate back and focused on her.

Dylan shrugged. "What else do you wanna know?" She took another bite.

"What were you like in high school?" The question popped out without much thought, but as I considered it, I really wanted to know the answer.

"Mmm. Nerdy. I was in band and choir and I loved drama club." She glanced at me and picked at her scampi. "I played volleyball and basketball. I had to, being five foot ten. Though I wasn't great at it. I hadn't quite figured out how to use my height."

How funny. "I played basketball and football, because of my height. I wasn't bad, but sports really weren't my thing. Music was my real passion. What instrument did you play?"

She held up a finger as she swallowed her bite. "Lots. I love music. Always have. I played the clarinet, learned the piano, then taught myself the guitar."

Wow. Had to admit I was impressed. "You still have your clarinet?"

"Yeah." One side of her mouth lifted in a smile.

"Still play it?" That was the real question. The nerdy side of her was incredibly attractive.

Dylan laughed her real laugh and shook her head adamantly. "No."

"How come?" My words came out with a chuckle. I could picture her in a marching band costume, complete with an awkward hat and feather, towering over the rest of the group.

She looked around the room, a smirk on her face. "Cause I can't sing and play, I guess."

Ahh, that made sense. I stood and went to the closet and grabbed my acoustic, suddenly wanting to feel the strings. If she asked to play, I'd just shut her down. I brought it out, and she bounced in her seat, rubbing her hands together.

"Any requests?" I sat and strummed a couple of chords. Her song choice would tell me a lot about her, too. I hated to keep comparing her to other girls, but when I typically asked for requests, it was always *Love, Always.* The song was great, the memories with it, not so much.

She pushed her plate back and turned to face me, shifting closer. "Do you have anything new?" Her prior excitement carried to her voice, and I had to smile.

Interesting. I played through a few chords of the song I'd started this afternoon.

"Oh, that's pretty."

"Thanks. I don't have the lyrics though." Which was partially true. I just didn't have lyrics that I was ready to sing for anyone.

After a few minutes of messing around on the guitar, I played through one of my favorite songs. I didn't sing. It was too intimate. Experience told me it was a mistake; women mistook the passion for my music as passion for them.

When I finished, I stood to take my guitar back to the closet.

"Do you mind if I play it for a minute?" She leaned forward on the chaise as if she was about to grab my arm. Her voice was soft. "Please?"

Shut her down.

Her brown eyes pleaded with me. Her expression was so open, so vulnerable. She dropped back onto her heels.

Darn it.

"I promise to be careful with your guitar." She clasped her hands in her lap and raised her eyebrows.

Double darn it.

I held the guitar out to her, and as promised, she cradled it carefully and scooted back against the arm of the chaise.

She adjusted it on her lap and played a couple of notes.

I sat on the edge of the chaise, ready to lunge forward to save my guitar in case she was careless with it.

Dylan's voice joined the music, and she sang through one of Jenny's songs. Chills raced down my body. *Wow. Her voice was angelic. Pure.* She closed her eyes, and I studied her unabashedly. The words pierced my heart; I could understand why girls mistook my passion. If I didn't know any better, I'd think she was singing directly to me.

She played the closing notes of the song, then let her hair fall over her face.

"That was beautiful." *She was too good to be true.*

Another line of lyrics popped into my head.

Nine - Dylan

Eliminations were today. Jenny dolled me up, and I slipped on a long, black, silky gown. I refused the high heels. It was enough that I towered over her. I didn't want to accentuate the difference with heels. Before the cruise, Fabian actually had me put on a green dress. I vetoed that so fast. *Dressing as the jolly green giant? Hard pass.*

Twelve white loveseats were positioned across the stage with a starlight backdrop. Aiden was already seated, and he stood as I approached. He wrapped his arms around my waist and buried his face in my neck. Citrus and woods invaded my senses. *Intoxicating. Don't let this be our last week.* I could do without the cameras, but to have Aiden at my side... It was pretty much my childhood fantasy coming true. *Only problem? It wasn't real.*

"You look beautiful." His scruff scratched my cheek, and I melted into him.

Danger Will Robinson. Most of the time, I could just forget that Aiden was a superstar. It was easy. But now and then, when I looked at him, my heart stuttered and my insides popped like popcorn. Then I had to remind myself he was doing it all for the cameras.

Desiree came and wired me for sound, her hands cold as ice-cubes. Trisha swayed onto the stage in a sparkly white evening gown. The crew finished touching everyone up and cleared out as the cameraman counted down.

"Welcome to The Results show. Live from *The Callistus*, the *Couple's Cruise* ship." Trisha paused and a large screen on the far wall played the intro. A still image flashed across the screen of Aiden and me sitting at the table on the fishing boat. He was laughing, and I was grinning at him.

It was freaking adorable. Aiden pulled me into him, then rested his arm on the back of the couch and crossed his legs man-style.

My heart fluttered a tiny bit. *Cause—hello, live TV. What if I said something stupid? What if I blew our cover? There were too many "what ifs."*

Aiden placed his hand on my bouncing knee. *When did it start doing that?*

He leaned in. "You'll be just fine, Dylan. You're gonna do great." His warm hand on my bare shoulder wasn't helping, just making me hyper aware of how close he was.

"Sorry. I'm just nervous."

His fingers grazed the back of my neck, and I shivered. *So not helping.*

Trisha picked up, and we sat through a recap where they highlighted the highs and lows of each couple. Aiden was right. They didn't use the footage of us when he flipped off the camera.

Occasionally, Aiden twisted my hair around his finger, and I sat like a love-sick puppy with a stupid smile on my face.

"Now the results. Three couples will be leaving us tonight." Trisha held an envelope in her hand and broke the seal.

Holy crap. This was it. The do or die. Or I guess, the stay or go. Get Dad's truck back, or fail spectacularly.

"The first couple voted off this week and who will be asked to leave immediately is..." She pulled the card from the envelope. "Jessica and Felicia." The light above the tennis player and her girlfriend turned off.

It wasn't a surprise. We stood and hugged the departing women as a montage of their time on the show played on the screen. They left the stage in separate directions. *Not good.*

Aiden kissed my temple and linked our hands together. We took our seats back on the couch, and I leaned into him, resting my head on his shoulder.

Trisha took her spot back at center stage. "The next couple leaving us tonight is..."

The dramatic pause was almost too much for my stomach to handle. The coughing incident could have painted me in a bad light. *What if we went home because of a stupid kale chip?*

"Martin and Celia."

Whew. I sagged in relief. Martin McDonald was a child actor who hadn't been in much since his series had gone off the air. I hadn't even met them. We repeated the goodbyes as the montage played.

We retook our seats, and Aiden wrapped an arm around me.

"I'm nervous." I twisted my hands in my lap, and he rested his head against mine. *Yup, definitely wanted to stay.*

"It was a good week. We'll be just fine." His thumb grazed the bare skin on my shoulder.

"And the final couple leaving us tonight is…"

Did she have to pause for dramatic effect every time? It only gave me time to go over all the dumb things I'd done all week. When this was over, Trisha Thames and I were gonna have words.

"Penelope and Daniel."

An invisible weight lifted from my chest, and I leaned into Aiden. We made it. *Week two, here we come.*

~

We spent the weekend swimming, hanging out in our room, and going down the deserted water slides near the front of the ship.

Monday night we had filming. The Lido deck was completely cleared except for a line of tables along each side of the stage. On top of the tables were bulging tablecloths with something hidden beneath. We gathered in a group, and someone went around separating us into couples for better camera shots. Trisha was dressed down in a t-shirt and shorts. Her normally elaborate hair had been pulled into a stylishly messy bun.

"Welcome to another episode of *Couple's Cruise—Celebrity Edition.* I'm your host, Trisha Thames." The red camera lights turned off, and the *Couple's Cruise* theme song played in the background.

"What do you think we're doing?" I leaned into Aiden and whispered. My heart was going a mile a minute. As much as I hated the cameras, I loved anything competitive.

"No clue." He wrapped an arm around my waist. *Would I ever get used to that?*

The music stopped, and Trisha smirked at the camera. *What the heck were we getting into?* My hands were suddenly clammy, and I wiped them on my shorts.

"We have a special surprise today, as well as a special reward for the winners of today's competition." Trisha held something up in her hand and pressed a button. The tablecloths lifted. Stuffed Easter bunnies and baskets of jelly beans were on the table closest to us. On the opposite side were empty quart-sized jars.

"The first part of today's challenge is The Jelly Bean Race. Each team will have three minutes to scoop as many jelly beans as they can into a spoon held between their teeth." She held up a plastic spoon and pointed it at the group. "No using your hands. The team with the most jelly beans will have an advantage in the second part of today's challenge."

Cameras were everywhere to get every possible angle.

Trisha strutted to the main camera. "The rules are simple. It's a relay; you have to wait until your partner crosses this line before you can go." She motioned to a line set up beside the empty jars. She started the contest, and I watched carefully to figure out the best strategy.

When it was Jenny and Evan's turn, I pushed my way to the front of the crowd, and Aiden followed.

I cupped my hand around my mouth. "Let's go, Jenny!"

Evan and Jenny both clenched a plastic spoon in their teeth and a buzzer sounded. Jenny raced toward the basket of beans and scooped some into her spoon. As she spun, the beans dropped. She half squealed, half growled and turned back around to scoop more. She speed-walked back toward the empty jars, dropping beans as she went. By the time she made it past the line, she only had a couple left on her spoon. Evan raced to the opposite side and scooped beans into his spoon.

"Come on, baby!" Jenny bounced on her toes and motioned for him to hurry.

By the end of three minutes, their jar still looked pretty empty. *It was gonna be tough.*

Barbie and Jake went next. It was funny to watch the ultra competitive couple.

Was that how I looked to other people?

They high-fived and chest-bumped and screamed at the top of their lungs to try to motivate their partners.

Nope.

Unsurprisingly, they did really well, filling their jar to the half-way mark.

When our turn rolled around, my lunch danced in my stomach, threatening to make a conga-line up my throat. *Please don't let me barf. Not on TV. I'd never be able to show my face anywhere again. That would be it. Dylan Kennedy, the shut-in cat lady at twenty-two.*

"You okay? You're shakin'." Aiden's hand rubbed up and down my back.

"Fine." *ish.* I bent over and unbuckled my wedge sandals. There was no way I'd get out of this without a broken ankle if I kept them on. Jenny smacked my butt as we made our way to the starting line, and I rubbed my rear. We used to do that to each other all the time. I'd forgotten how hard she could hit.

Aiden handed me a plastic spoon, and I practiced putting it in my mouth. The best position was angled, so I could clench it between my back teeth.

"You okay goin' first?" He adjusted the waistband of his shorts and nodded encouragingly.

"Yep." *Let's freaking do it.* My competitiveness had been described as "over the top," but I attributed that more to height than anything. *Okay, that was a lie. I couldn't lose. Hated it.*

The first chime sounded, and my hands trembled. I clenched them behind my back.

Buzz.

I sprinted forward, my long strides getting me to the other side in record time. I leaned down and scooped my spoon into the jelly beans. They spilled everywhere. *I'm too tall!* Dropping to my knees, I tried again. *Success.* I'd worry about the bruises on my knees later.

Aiden cheered and clapped. I shuffled across the walk, my gaze plastered to the tiny spoon. I probably looked ridiculous, cross-eyed. Mom used to say that my eyes would get stuck like that. And how could Aiden possibly find me attractive after seeing me cross-eyed? It was defamation of character.

As I crossed the line, Aiden rushed forward, and I dumped four beans into the jar.

He ran into the same problem I did. We were too tall. Beans slipped out of Aiden's spoon.

"Kneel!" I bounced on my toes as he made his way back to the line. He wasn't cross eyed. How could he look so handsome doing something so ridiculous? It wasn't fair.

As the final timer sounded, Aiden scooped me into a hug. They wouldn't let us count our jelly beans, but it would be close with Barbie and Jake.

We held hands as we watched the last few couples go. I was holding Aiden Miller's hand like it was no big deal. *It was so a big deal.* He squeezed my hand as if he knew what I was thinking. Or maybe he was just bringing my attention to the strangle-hold I had on his hand. *Oopsie.*

When the last couple finished, Trisha got in front of the camera and crew members counted jelly beans. We were staged into our original spots on the deck by the production team. *Apparently, we were infants who couldn't be trusted to remember our previous spots.*

A crew member counted us down, and nerves fluttered in my stomach.

"And now to find out who got the most jelly beans and wins an advantage in the next challenge." A man ran over and handed Trisha an envelope.

I crossed my fingers and held them behind my back. *Please, please, please. Pretty please.*

"Jake and Barbie."

Dang it. I plastered what I hoped was a gracious smile on my face and gave Barbie a thumbs up. *Shoulda been us.*

"And they tied with Aiden and Dylan!" Teresa called over the crowd.

A thrill shot up my spine, and I spun to face Aiden. He opened his arms wide for a hug. I leapt into them and he caught me, spinning me around. I placed my hands on his face and looked down into his eyes. They smoldered as he glanced at my lips and back to my eyes. *Was he gonna kiss me?* I slid down his body, and he set me on my feet.

Jenny shook my arm, pulling me away from Aiden. "Congratulations!"

Dang it. Did I want him to kiss me? I mean, he was Aiden Miller. But if we kissed, would he expect more? I tried not to take my frustration out on Jenny. She didn't know she'd broken up our almost-kiss. Or was I reading too much into it? Kissing wasn't breaking any rules. Plus, did I want him to kiss me in front of all these people?

Trisha waited for everyone to calm down and get back into their positions. "Let's head to the bow, and we'll explain your advantage."

The cameras cut, and the production crew started cleaning up the Lido deck. Trisha led the group to the bow.

Nine inflatable kiddie pools were set up on the deck, filled with some sort of colorful beads. A man came around handing out goggles. Oh, man. Whatever we were doing promised to be fun.

"Inside these pools are ten Easter eggs, hidden by these colorful beads. The men will fish the eggs out using only their mouths. Once they have one, they drop it into their hand and turn their back to their partner, then toss the egg over their shoulder. The women will catch it in one of these baskets." She held up one of the small baskets.

"Now for the advantage: the winning couples will each get one extra Easter egg, and baskets that are both wider and deeper."

Aiden put an arm around my shoulder and kissed my temple. "We got this."

As I put the goggles on, Jenny helped me with my hair so it didn't bubble out like a mushroom. The girls were given mouth guards. *Heaven forbid we lose a tooth from an errant Easter egg.* Barbie and I were handed bigger baskets, while the other girls received regular sized ones.

The men got into position in front of the kiddie pools. Aiden shucked his shirt, and everyone else followed suit. *That wasn't the best idea. I'd be distracted by his hotness and rippling muscles.*

His pecs flexed a few times, and his chuckle brought my eyes to his face. *Busted.*

He smirked. It was a little weird with the goggles, but still cute.

My cheeks heated; *I'll just attribute that to a sudden sunburn or something.*

Trisha held a whistle in the air. "You have three minutes to get as many eggs as you can. On my mark." She inhaled and blew the whistle.

Aiden braced his hands on either side of the pool and plunged his head in. I stood on tiptoe to get a better view.

Jake popped out beside him with an egg in his mouth. He stood and spun, throwing it over his shoulder. The egg went wide and dropped onto the deck. Barbie shouted, "Toss it softer, Jake!" Her words were muffled by her mouth guard.

Come on, Aiden. He popped out a second later and spun backward, glanced my way, then lobbed it softly over his shoulder. I caught it easily, and Aiden dropped to his knees to fish out the next egg.

Kourtney was on my other side and stood with her basket on one hip. "Thith ith tho thupid."

I had to muffle a laugh. She sounded like she had a lisp with the mouth guard in, and it so didn't fit with her perfect image.

Blake tossed an egg, and she didn't even attempt to catch it. The egg hit her basket. If she'd moved it even an inch forward, she would've had it. "Come on, Kourtney!" Blake's voice was edged with anger.

"Dylan." Aiden spun around and tossed another egg. It went a little high, but I managed to snag it.

Barbie and Jake had found their rhythm, and we matched them egg for egg.

The buzzer rang, and I leaned over to count Barbie's eggs. She covered her basket and raised her eyebrows at me. *Brat. Fine. I could be patient.* I pulled my goggles off and shot Aiden a thumbs up.

Trisha went around counting eggs as the producers directed her to the baskets. Evan and Jenny got eight. They were the ones to beat. We had nine. Trisha hadn't gotten to us yet. There were eggs on the ground around us, but there was no telling who they belonged to. Kourtney had only caught three.

Poor Blake.

Barbie's basket was next, and Trisha counted her eggs; she didn't announce the total, instead, coming over to me and counting my eggs.

Aiden and Jake stood behind us. I turned away from the camera and discreetly pulled out my mouth guard and shoved it in my pocket. *Gross.*

70

Trisha stood between the couples, and from off camera, producers pointed to spots on the ground.

We took our places, and Trisha beamed at the camera. "The prize our players were competing for this week was immunity!"

Kourtney gasped on my other side.

"And the winner of the challenge, and immunity this week, is..." She paused for dramatic effect, and I nearly reached over and shook her until she spit it out. "Aiden and Dylan!"

I screamed and threw a fist in the air. *Yes!* Aiden spun me and grabbed my face. He hesitated only a second to look into my eyes.

Yes.

Aiden brought his lips to mine. The kiss was chaste, but my heart did somersaults. I wrapped my arms around his neck and everyone disappeared around us. For that brief moment, it was just us. As I pulled away, one of the cameras only a couple feet away caught my eye.

My first kiss with Aiden Miller was in front of a group of strangers and being broadcast to the entire world. Not the private, intimate kiss I'd imagined, where he'd confess his undying love. *Okay, that was probably unrealistic, but I wanted the moment to be for us, not shared with an entire nation of onlookers.*

I plastered on a fake smile as bile rose up my throat. We won. We wouldn't go home this week. Emotions competed inside me for dominance. I was guaranteed another week with Aiden, but my stomach felt hollow.

Ten - Aiden

Where had Monday's Dylan gone? Tuesday, Jenny stole her, and they laid sunbathing by the pool at the back of the boat. Evan and I sat in the hot tub a few yards away, a constant stream of drinks keeping us company.

"This is exhaustin'." I finished my drink and slid an ice cube into my mouth.

The cameras were around, but no one could hear us over the noise of the hot tub.

Evan stared at the two women laying a few yards away. "Yeah, Dylan is being weird."

"She's not being herself is the problem." I glanced at her. She was on her stomach, her head turned to the side.

Evan picked up his drink and sank into the hot tub until his head was the only thing sticking out. "She's acting like Jenny. I've only hung out with Dylan a few times, but she's always been super chill. They gave her a complete makeover. Her hair used to be darker, usually curly. She never dressed like that, either." He threw back the rest of his drink and made a face as if the alcohol burned his throat.

Why would Dylan be acting like that? I'd seen glimpses of her at night and on the weekends, in our room as she lounged around in pajamas and a clean face. But in the mornings, she slipped that persona back on like a glove. *Did she think that was what I wanted? I thought I'd been pretty clear when I told her it wasn't necessary to play a role.*

"Weird." I signaled the waiter and pointed to my empty glass.

Jenny stood and pulled her towel around her. She was an attractive girl,

72

just not my type. Dylan stretched and grabbed a sheer swimming suit wrap, pulling it around her. Dylan towered over Jenny. I'd never dated a girl I didn't have to bend to kiss. It was nice. Our kids would be tall. *Whoa! Where had that thought come from?* I quashed it with the rest of my errant thoughts. *Musta been the whiskey.*

The waiter brought me another whiskey as the girls disappeared inside.

Jorge had been at the shaded bar, nursing a drink. The bartender handed him a fresh one, and he worked his way over to us, a drink in each hand.

He stumbled up the steps and burst out laughing.

Oh, good. He was a happy drunk. "Hey Jorge."

With one cup to his lips, he toasted us with the other, then sank into the bubbling water. "¡Hola, mi amigos!"

"Where's Sheena?" Evan searched the surrounding area. He hated the woman. No doubt he'd bolt if he found her.

Jorge set one of the drinks at the edge of the water and waved off the question. "Flirting with the producers? Who knows with her?"

Uh oh. "Trouble in paradise?"

He made a sour face. "Not at all. Sheena isn't my version of paradise. We know what we are to each other."

Evan laughed, his face entirely too gleeful. "Please tell me you're using her to get famous."

I cringed at the reminder that all I'd been to Sheena was a meal ticket. That would be poetic justice. I was smarter now, but apparently Sheena hadn't learned the same lesson she taught me.

"We're friends. I don't need fame. Though, it would be a nice side effect of the 'relationship.'" He made air quotes around the word with one hand and brought his drink to his lips, taking a long gulp. He shrugged. "She's hot. I'll take whatever she gives me."

The water in the hot tub was suddenly too warm. *Was that how Dylan thought of me?* "I've gotta take a break." I stood and took my drink with me, dropping it untouched at the bar.

Aromas from the different restaurants wafted through the Lido dining room. It was almost lunchtime, and Dylan was nowhere to be seen.

What was I going to say to her? *Just out of curiosity, are you just in this for the fame? Fame came with money, and if she was short on cash, this would be an easy fix.* I strode down the hall toward our room and pounded on Evan and Jenny's door.

Jenny opened it, and her face lit up when she saw me. "Hey Aiden. Looking for Dylan? She's back in your room."

I stepped closer to her. "Why did she agree to do this?"

It was almost comical, the number of emotions that crossed her face. "Um. To hang out with me and Evan, I think. She didn't know who her fake boyfriend was going to be."

"That's it?" I resisted the urge to grab her arms and shake the truth out of her.

She nodded. "And she needed the money."

I ran a hand down my face. "What about the fame? Does she want to be famous?"

Jenny laughed, and the sound grated on my last nerve.

I'd heard enough. I left her standing in the door and stalked to our bedroom. Outside the door, I paced for a few minutes as I gathered my thoughts. Why was I so bothered that Dylan was here for the money? *She didn't even know who her fake boyfriend was going to be.* So any celebrity would've been fine. The thought of her here with Jake Donahue or any of the other douche canoes made my teeth ache. I needed to know what she was thinking. What she wanted. And how I could make her stay. For me.

When I opened the door, Dylan was fresh-faced and wrapped in a *Couple's Cruise* robe, with her hair twisted up in a towel. She smiled at me and pulled her hair down before running her fingers through it.

"We need to talk." My words came out harsh, and I tried to calm my emotions. I grabbed the chair from the table, spun it around, and straddled it.

"Sure. What's up?" She sank onto the chair opposite, holding her robe closed. Her brows were drawn, and she leaned forward, placing her elbows on the table between us.

"Are you here to get famous? Insta-followers or something?" I studied her, watching for any hint of emotion.

"What? No." She crossed her arms over her chest and returned my glare.

"Why are you here?"

She shook her head, and tears welled in her eyes. She looked at a spot near the top of the wall behind me as she swiped at her cheeks. "Remember the truck I told you about? The Chevy 3800 my dad restored?"

The anger immediately drained from my body. "Yeah?"

"About fifteen months ago my dad had an accident, and my mom had to sell it to pull our house out of foreclosure." She paused and wrapped her arms around herself.

"What happened?"

"His arm got caught in a combine."

Chills raced up my body. *I'm an idiot. A complete jerk.*

"It crushed his entire arm. He had multiple surgeries and was lucky to keep it. He was getting better. They sent him home, and he tried to go back to work." Her voice broke, and I stood, rounded the table, then pulled her up and into my arms.

"It's okay. You don't need to tell me." I rubbed her back and rested my cheek against her hair.

"It got infected. He hid it from my mom. He'd go to work and lay in the toolshed, thinking if he rested, it would get better. By the time we found him, it was too late. He spent a month in the hospital in a medically induced coma. He suffered several strokes, and in the end, they couldn't save him."

I didn't know what to say. There were no words to ease the pain or sorrow.

"My mom sold the truck to some skeeze ball at a pawnshop. He said he'd sell it to me if I could get the money before his buyer got back into the country." She straightened and wiped her eyes. "So that's my plan. Get it back. It has too many memories to just let it go."

My petty insecurities seemed stupid compared to the battle she was waging. I felt stupid and selfish for coming in here to demand she stay for the right reasons, which I had deemed were me, not money. But I had it all wrong. "Let's get ya there, then."

If she needed to stay until the finals, I would stay. And perhaps my ego could take a backseat to Dylan's very noble reasons for being here.

"You're still okay staying for as long as possible?"

I nodded. "The cruise has been better for my songwritin' than I expected." *Understatement.* More lyrics had come to me in the last few days than in the last few months combined. Part of it might've been just being on a cruise, but a bigger part of it might've been the woman in my arms.

"Really?" She pulled back and looked up at me, a smile playing across her lips.

Man, I wanted to taste those lips again. To close the distance between us and lose myself in her. "Yeah." There was something between us that she felt, too. Something worth exploring.

"I have one condition." She shot me an apologetic smile and buried her face in my chest.

I tightened my arms around her. "Name it."

She glanced up at me. "No more kissing on the lips." Her cheeks turned pink, but she watched me steadily.

The words were like a sucker-punch. Had I read her wrong? I thought there was something between us, but obviously it was one sided. Or... I was right, and she was denying her feelings for some reason. Something occurred to me and I stepped back, putting much needed distance between us. "Do you have a boyfriend back home?"

She shook her head and bit her bottom lip. It was torture of the sweetest kind.

I stepped closer, but she didn't retreat. As I leaned down, her breath hitched. *She wasn't unaffected by me.* I searched her eyes. Her pupils were dilated, and her lips parted. Achingly slow, I brought my lips toward hers, our gazes locked. My hand tangled into her wet hair, and I cupped her head. Her eyes drifted closed. A mere breath away, I paused. "I promise not to kiss you unless you want me to." My lips brushed hers as I whispered the words, and a strangled whimper left her throat.

Dylan's eyes popped open, and she stepped back, brushing her hands down the robe, face a bright red. "I better get to bed."

Why didn't she want me to kiss her? I mean, she obviously wanted *me to kiss her. But why wouldn't she let me?* Maybe I was reading more into the relationship than there was. I'd done it before, and trusting my instincts wasn't something I'd learned to do. I'd just have to help her see there was more to us than she was letting us be.

Eleven - Dylan

I had an entire day and a half to stew on our conversation. My body hummed as I thought about our near kiss. It wasn't that I didn't want to kiss him. *Heaven knew I did.* It was that I wanted it to mean something. And I didn't want it to be just for the cameras. *Not that the kiss in our room would have been for the cameras! Stupid, stupid, stupid.*

Wednesday, we came into port and loaded onto the ferry. When we got to shore, they ushered us into a giant green convertible bus with a roof but no windows.

Trisha Thames stood in the front with a megaphone. "Today, we'll be testing your endurance in a zipline and rappelling challenge."

Thank the stars. I could do that. We had a climbing gym in Clearview, and I'd gone frequently as a kid. Aiden lounged with his arm behind my back, then leaned in and kissed my forehead. Jenny turned around and gave me a miserable look.

"What was that about?" Aiden whispered.

"She's afraid of heights." A sick feeling settled in my stomach. She was going to struggle today. What if she got cut? What would I do without her?

In front of us, Evan wrapped his arm around her, his lips moving. She shook her head and then let it fall back onto the bench-back.

By the time we got to the first spot, Jenny was green. *Okay, not really; she was just a very pale white.* My protective instincts kicked in, as they always did with Jenny. I'd been trying to protect her since we were in grade school and a boy teased her about her dad. The little jerk got what he deserved when I kicked him in the privates. My parents had scolded me, but privately,

Dad told me he was proud of me for sticking up for Jen.

Our guides strapped helmets with GoPros on us, then helped us with our harnesses. Jenny clung to my arm, her hands squeezing the life out of it. "I can't do this. I'm gonna hurl."

"If you hurl, will it make you feel better?" At her offended look, I said, "I'm just saying, you need to do something. And popping my arm like a pimple probably won't help."

She released my arm and smacked it. "Sorry." She stuck her tongue out, and I bumped her with my hip.

"Mind over matter, Jen. Just close your eyes and don't look down."

She pouted. "At least with the helmets on, my last moments on this earth will be immortalized on film." Jenny smiled, but it didn't quite reach her eyes.

"That's the spirit, buckaroo." I punched her shoulder lightly. "Now go get 'em slugger." *My "patronizing dad" act always seemed to cheer her up.*

She wrapped her arms around my waist and hugged me tight. "I'm really glad you're here."

"Me, too." I pulled back and looked down at her. She took a deep breath, then shook her arms out, like a boxer about to go in the ring.

Our guides led us down a dirt trail. *Goodbye, white tennis shoes.* By the time we got to the first zip line, dust was everywhere. Kourtney wasn't taking this well, which gave me hope for Jenny. *Let the cameras' focus be on that train wreck.* The head guide introduced himself as Luka and promised to take good care of us. The first ziplines went over a ravine with a dried-up riverbed in the bottom. After a quick explanation from our guides, Barbie and Jake went first, hooking in side by side on the two ziplines. They cheered and screamed as they went down the line, disappearing behind a canopy of trees at the end.

"Who's next?" Luka scanned the remaining couples. "You!" He pointed to Jenny.

She latched onto Evan's arm. *Poor guy.* He hauled her forward, and they were hooked in. I wasn't close enough to hear what he said to her, but he kissed her forehead and put his thumbs over her eyes, forcing her to close them. And off they went.

She screamed like a siren, and I laughed just the tiniest bit at her discomfort. *Bad friend, knock it off.*

"Next?" Luka raised a dark brow.

I held back. Couldn't seem too eager. Prissy girls weren't eager to go screaming over a ravine that could possibly end in death or dismemberment. *But oh, how I wanted to go next.*

Aiden glanced at me. I must not have hid my smile well enough because he raised his hand. I bounced on the balls of my feet, my heart in my throat. This was gonna be fun, but I was a teensy bit nervous.

We held hands until we couldn't reach anymore and the guides launched us over the edge of the cliff. *Holy mother-of-pearl!* The ground disappeared beneath my feet, and I sailed over the canyon, the warm wind whipping my hair. A laugh bubbled out, and I squinted over at Aiden. His smile made my stomach fizz like I'd just swallowed an entire pack of Pop Rocks. My feet touched the other side, and the guides had us jump as we unhooked from the ziplines.

Aiden and I high-fived, then hugged. Adrenaline coursed through my veins. *Amazing.* We hiked trails from one zipline to the next until we had gone through six. The last trail was steep, and my legs burned. We hiked what passed as mountains here. Jen walked beside me, and Evan and Aiden trailed behind.

She cast her voice low so only I could hear. "This hasn't been as bad as I thought. Oh my gosh! Can you believe I'm doing this?" She squeezed my arm.

"It's been really fun." We navigated the stone steps built into the trail until we reached a plateau. The top. "I'm really proud of you, Jenny." I smiled and tipped my head to the top of hers. We were dripping sweat and gross, and I was grateful that this morning I had asked Jenny to chill on the makeup. My face would have melted off. As it was, I only had on mascara, eyeshadow, and chapstick. Strands of my hair stuck to the sweat on my neck, and the humid air was thick in my lungs. The guides walked around, handing out tiny water bottles. I loved that they didn't make a fuss because half of us were celebrities, but not everyone seemed to appreciate it.

Kourtney rolled up on the back of an ATV. *Guess she had refused to walk the last leg of the journey.* She had on tennis shoes, so I wasn't sure what her deal was. She held a battery operated fan that misted water over her. *Holy diva.* Her boyfriend was already up here; he must have hiked.

Luka jumped up onto the platform in front of a cliff. Two ropes hung over the edge. *Oh my stars, we were gonna rappel.* "You made it! Good job. There are two things left, the rappel, and the Superman zipline." He gave a detailed explanation, showing us how the equipment worked. Basically, he'd hook a rope to our harness with a special pulley thing, and we just had to hold the rope down by our hip as we walked backward down the cliff. "You can do it. Who's first?"

Luka pointed right at me. "Dylan, let's go."

I grasped Aiden's hand and gave him a cheesy smile. *Prissy girl be darned.* We hooked in, and with my stomach in knots; we stepped backward over the edge. I kicked off the wall, giving myself lots of rope, kicked again and let myself just enjoy the moment.

"Race ya!" I grinned over at Aiden.

"You're on." He zipped past and I struggled to keep up.

Aiden made it to the bottom a half-second before me. He wrapped me in a hug at the bottom as the guides unhooked us. It was sweaty and hot and smelled distinctly of Aiden.

"Who is going on the Superman zipline first?" a guide asked.

I raised my hand, nerves bundling inside me. "I will."

The guides went to work unhooking my harness and putting me in a different one. *It was more like the radiation things they put on you at the dentist's office before they x-ray your teeth.* They hooked the line to my back, then had me lean forward until I was suspended above the ground, face down. "Ready?"

I glanced over at Aiden, who was being fitted with his own dentist radiation vest. "Yep!"

They launched me.

It was like being in one of those g-force machines. My cheeks vibrated, and I tried to keep my mouth closed. *Eating bugs wasn't on the bucket list.* I squinted my eyes and took in the scenery around me. The tree tops blurred by, and I giggled. It was insane. Breathing was a little hard with the wind coming at me so fast. As I approached the landing platform, two guys holding what looked like pool noodles attached to the line slid them out to slow my approach. I had perma-smile, broken up by a bubble of laughter. *It was insane.*

I jerked to a stop and more guides helped me stand and unhooked the harness and helmet, then ushered me aside. I sat on a bench and waited for Aiden.

He came flying in, his arms out in front of him like Superman. "Woohoo!" He laughed through the end of the word, making his O several syllables.

I stood, unable to keep the smile from my face. The guides unhooked Aiden's harness and helped him out of it. Our gazes locked, and he strode over and swung me into his arms, twirling us in a circle.

His eyes darkened, and he glanced at my lips, his gaze lingering. *Oh, sweet mercy.* I bit my bottom lip, and he lifted a brow.

He dropped his forehead to mine, mere inches between our lips. "I want to kiss you."

It was the adrenaline talking. "I can't." The words were a tortured whisper.

He pulled back and planted a kiss on my sticky forehead.

Son of a biscuit.

Aiden gave me a sad smile, then wrapped me in a hug, resting his chin on the top of my head.

Weird. Guys never did that to me. I was too tall, except with Aiden. "How tall are you?"

The platform started filling with the rest of the group, but Jenny had yet to show up.

"6'3. Tall enough to rest my head on top of yours." He pressed his chin into my scalp, and I swatted at his arm and ducked away.

"Ow."

He pulled me back into him. "You're the perfect height. I'm always jealous of guys who can do this to their girlfriends."

"Dork." I poked his sides, and he squirmed. *Was he ticklish? Dang it. I'd only be able to use that information for evil. He was so gonna get it later.*

The siren—or rather—Jenny went off. Her scream cut through the chatter of the contestants and crew. It didn't sound like the scream of someone who was enjoying themselves. I hurried to the platform, searching for Evan. *He must be going after her, because he was nowhere to be seen.*

As she swung onto the platform, the crew went to work unhooking her. I pushed past some cameras and wrapped her in a hug. "Shh. You did it. You made it."

Tears streamed down her face. Her eyes were wild with fright and her face was ghostly pale. I guided her off the platform, and she darted for the edge, barfing her breakfast into the bushes. I pulled her hair back and wrapped it into a bun, securing it with the ponytail holder from my own hair.

Aiden handed me a bottle of water and stepped back. I rubbed her back and offered her the water. "It's over, Jen. You did it."

She took the bottle from my hands and swished it through her mouth. She shook, and her body still heaved with her breaths, but her eyes were a little less crazed.

Evan zipped in silent as the grave. They unhooked him, and he dashed straight for Jenny and wrapped her in a hug. "You did so good, baby. I'm so proud of you." He pulled back and cupped her face in his hands. "Seriously. You're amazing." He planted a sweet kiss on her lips. Evan glanced at me over her shoulders and nodded. "Thanks for helping her, Dylan."

Shouldn't I be the one thanking him? I shrugged. "Of course."

Aiden linked our fingers together, and we loaded onto the waiting bus. Cecily Boyton, an actress, chatted excitedly on the drive home. Her boyfriend sat beside her, his eyes closed. Sleeping or just ignoring everyone? I couldn't tell.

The girl could talk. Aiden and I listened politely, and Jenny laid across Evan's lap behind us. I glanced back at them. Evan combed through her hair with his fingers. *They were so cute, it was disgusting.*

We got back to the ship and spent the night in the room. We turned on the TV, and I stole the remote. I wasn't in the mood for Forged in Fire tonight.

"This is something my parents used to do, so they didn't have to argue about what to watch. We'll turn on the tv, and each of us will press a number, and whatever comes on is what we have to watch." I held the remote out to Aiden. One side of his mouth lifted and he pressed a couple of buttons. I followed, and a few seconds later an animated movie turned on.

"Come sit by me." He patted the spot beside him on the bed.

Twelve - Aiden

Her rules of no kissing and no touching in private probably meant she didn't want me to sleep next to her, either. But that didn't mean I couldn't lay beside her and admire her sleeping form. The rise and fall of her chest as she breathed. The fan of her dark lashes over her cheeks. I grabbed my notebook and wrote some lyrics.

You play my heart strings
Just like you played my guitar
So tender and careful
I forgot to be afraid and fell hard

I propped myself on the pillow beside her, my notebook between us, and just let myself enjoy her beauty. A freckle near the corner of her eye drew my attention. She shifted onto her side, facing me. Her hand came up to brush the hair from her face, and a small smile tilted her lips.

She was beautiful.

And if I was being completely honest, I could really like her.

But once upon a time, I'd really liked Sheena, too. My fist tightened around the pen. We met at the Blue Jay, both trying to hit it big, playing gigs all over Nashville. Over the next year, our friendship had bloomed into what I mistook as love. She was my first. The first girl to make my heart race, the first girl to make lyrics flow like the Mississippi.

The day I got my recording contract, we made love for the first time. My first time. I thought we were the perfect couple and was stupidly happy, 'til I caught her in the booth with my producer.

I shook my head to banish the image, but even after six years, it was still burned into the back of my eyelids. That day marked the end of our relationship, but the beginning of her career. Less than two weeks later, I passed her in the studio, recording an album of her own.

I couldn't trust my emotions. Couldn't trust her. I wrote a few more lyrics.

Tryin' to figure out these feelings
They weren't part of the agreement

Thirteen - Dylan

Eliminations were the worst day of the week. I hated the last one more than kale chips. We had immunity, so at least I was guaranteed another week with Aiden.

But Jenny and Evan had no guarantees. The entire day, my stomach was twisted in knots. I never got to spend time with Jenny anymore, and her absence in my life left an ache that was getting harder to fill. Being around her again made me realize how important she was to me. Jenny was my rock.

She put the finishing touches on my makeup, and I slipped into a slinky red dress. It draped across my chest, going high enough that I could bend without having a wardrobe malfunction.

I adjusted the shoulder straps, and Jenny zipped me up.

"How are things going?" She walked around me, inspecting my dress and adjusting some of the folds.

"Good." Except Aiden had been really distant today. Was he regretting the decision to stay? I'd wait to analyze Aiden's actions until I talked to him.

"Yeah? Any more kissing?" She flicked an eyebrow up.

I waved her off. "Stop. No. No more kissing." *Just an almost kiss that made my cheeks heat and my heart dance.* I told him no kissing, but I would have kissed him last night. I wanted him to. *Hated that he didn't. Loved that he didn't.*

"You look beautiful, Dylan. Will you hang out for a sec and zip me into my dress?" She headed into the closet, and I followed her.

She hung her robe on the hook beside the door and grabbed a sequined green dress from a rack. It was short and strapless. I turned my back to give her privacy as she pulled it on, then helped her zip the back.

"Thanks." She gave me a sad smile.

My stomach lurched. "Jen? Are you guys getting cut tonight? Do you know something I don't?" *Please don't let them get cut.*

She shrugged her bare shoulders. "I don't know. Evan and I are fine, but we got into an argument. I think the cameras caught it. If they aired it, we might be going home."

I wrapped my arms around her and closed my eyes. They couldn't get cut. I needed her. I couldn't do this makeup by myself. This fake persona. *Malibu Dylan.*

And I'd miss her. We pulled away, and I looked into her eyes. "Wanna talk about it?"

"Nah. It's nothing." She smiled and bent, pushing her feet into some strappy heels.

"Good luck tonight, Jenny."

She nodded and pushed me toward the door. "Go, before we're late."

Aiden waited for me inside our suite. He had on a blue suit with a white shirt and no tie. His collar was unbuttoned, revealing a small patch of tanned skin. He stood and offered me his arm. "Shall we?"

"Real quick. Did I do something last night? You've been really distant today." I watched him carefully, searching for some clue as to his feelings.

His jaw ticked, and he smiled. "Nope. Everything is fine. I just had a bad night."

Something was wrong. But if he wasn't ready to tell me, there wasn't much I could do about it. I hooked my hand through his elbow and tried to ignore the unease.

We entered the auditorium. The stage was similar to last week, with one noticeable difference. There was a red couch right at the center, with eight white couches surrounding it. The pit in my stomach gaped, and I had a sinking suspicion that the red couch was for the couple with immunity. *Front. And. Center.*

Desiree appeared out of nowhere and handed us each a mic. "Hurry and mic up. We're going to do a quick interview before the elimination starts."

Aiden clipped the mic to the strap of my dress, and I clipped his to his lapel. It reminded me of prom and pinning corsages on each other. Only Aiden was taller than me. My senior prom date had been a whole head shorter.

She grabbed our elbows and half-dragged us to a small alcove backstage. A circular light was set up, and a cameraman was already there, camera aimed at the loveseat. Aiden and I sat, and he wrapped an arm around my shoulder.

All for the cameras, Dylan. I shoved my worries aside and put on my adoring-girlfriend face.

Desiree sat facing us right beside the camera. "Welcome."

I glanced at Aiden, unsure which of us should answer.

His cocky persona was back. "Thanks Desiree."

"How did you guys like this week's adventures?" Desiree gave us an encouraging nod and pointed to the camera lens.

Aiden didn't miss a beat. "We've had a lot of fun this week. The zip lines were amazing and the food." He leaned back and patted his flat stomach with one hand. "I better be careful, or I won't be ready for my next photo shoot."

I faked a laugh. *Was I the only one feeling uncomfortable?* My hands were clammy, and my throat felt tight.

"Dylan, how does it feel going into this elimination knowing that you have immunity?"

A real smile forced its way to my lips. That part did feel good. "Really good. I can almost relax."

"Almost?" Desiree raised an eyebrow.

"Well, we're worried about Jenny and Evan. They're our best friends. Jenny and I don't get as much time together, now that I've got this guy." I leaned into Aiden. "And Jenny has Evan. So I want them to stick around as long as possible."

"I see." Desiree's eyes narrowed, and her mouth twisted to the side. "So, you're worried about their relationship then?"

Where had that come from? "Um. No. I just don't want them leaving. I won't be able to breathe easy until I know they're safe. That's all."

Aiden pulled me closer to him and his fingertips brushed my shoulder, sending chills down my arms. I looked at him, and we made eye contact. He gave me a brief squeeze and turned back to the camera. And my heart seemed to lighten just a bit. *Okay, things between us weren't as bad as I thought.*

Desiree raised her hand and the camera light cut off. "That's all for now. Head on out to the red couch. Congratulations, and I'm glad we're going another week."

The red couch. The center of attention. No thanks.

Aiden rubbed my back. "You okay?" He shifted on the couch until he could see my face.

"Yeah. We get to go another week." I smiled.

He patted my side and stood. "It'll be fun." His hand wrapped around mine and he pulled me to my feet. "You look really nice, by the way."

"Thanks."

With a few minutes to spare, we made it to the dreaded red couch. Aiden twined our hands together, and Desiree shot us a thumbs up from off camera.

The set cleared. Trisha, in a skin-tight black dress, came and perched on the arm of our couch, right beside me. *Oh my gosh. I was gonna be on camera during the introduction?*

When we filmed the activities, it was easy to forget the cameras. But something about sitting here while Trisha did the introduction, being on camera, was torture.

Aiden pulled my arm down and brought my ear to his lips. "Relax, Stegosaurus. You'll do just fine."

Stegosaurus? Laughter bubbled up my throat and burst from my lips.

Trisha glared at me, and I shook my head.

The director counted down.

I clamped a hand over my mouth to hold it in.

And we were live.

"Welcome to The Results show. Live from *The Callistus*, the *Couple's Cruise* ship." Trisha gave her signature smile, and the cameras cut to play a recap of this week's events. Trisha's accusing finger pointed right at me. "Someone get this giant a tissue, and make her stop laughing."

Aiden pulled me against him, his chest shaking. "I think we found a winner."

"No." I pulled away and wiped under my eyes, shaking my head adamantly. "No. You can't call me that." But he probably had a hard time taking me seriously, since I gasped out the words between giggles.

Desiree rushed over and blotted at my face with something, then handed me a water bottle.

I took a couple of swigs and handed it back. "I think I'm under control now."

She rushed off stage, and Trisha took her place back on the armrest.

In all the commotion, I missed the clips they played of Aiden and me. I caught a sweet moment between Jenny and Evan and glanced back at her. She had her head on Evan's shoulder as they watched the screen on the far wall.

"America, this week you voted off two couples, and it's time to find out who will say goodbye."

Trisha stood and walked to an X taped onto the stage a few feet in front of us. She held an envelope in one hand. "For the first time this season, we offered immunity to the couple who won Monday's challenge. That means this week, Aiden and Dylan, you are safe."

She walked a few steps and stood beside one of the couches. "Laura and Christian, America has voted." Pause for effect. "And you are safe."

Laura threw her arms around her boyfriend, with tears streaming down her cheeks. She waved to the cameras and blew kisses. *That's why Laura has won so many awards. I was gonna be sick.*

Next up was Kourtney, hotel heiress and overall crap human being. *Okay, that was harsh.* I didn't know her well enough to judge, but I doubted the two of us would be getting together for brunch any time soon. "Kourtney and Blake, America has voted." Dramatic pause. "And you will be the first couple leaving us tonight." The light over their couch turned off.

Kourtney gripped Blake's hand, and her chin wobbled. *Ah crap. Take back*

91

what I said. She had feelings. We stood and walked over, waiting our turn to hug the departing couple.

"Good luck." The words were whispered in my ear as I released her. She squeezed my hand and moved to the next person in line to wish them well.

Hunh.

Note to self: Quit being so quick to judge people.

When we were all situated back in our seats, Trisha continued her torture tour around the couches.

She stopped between Jenny and Evan's couch and Eldon Stockman, the golfer and his new wife, Ginger.

I crossed my fingers and prayed silently. *Let them be safe. Let them be safe.*

Aiden put his hand on my knee and leaned forward, both of us seeming to hold our breaths.

"Jenny and Evan, Eldon and Ginger, there's only one spot left. The couple who will be leaving us tonight is."

If she paused for much longer, I might have throttled her.

"Eldon and Ginger." Trisha made a pouty face, and the light above their heads turned off.

I released my breath and jumped to my feet. *They were staying!* Aiden wrapped me in a hug from behind, and I spun in his arms and buried my face in his shirt, a smile on my face.

Before we went to Eldon and Ginger, I took a couple of moments to compose myself and pretend to be sad they were leaving.

As we waited in line, I wrapped Jenny in a hug, squeezing her tight. "Don't get voted off, okay? I need you."

She nodded against my chest.

Fourteen - Aiden

Monday night, after another "How well do you know your significant other game" they announced our normal Wednesday activity would be moved to Tuesday.

"You guys wanna go dancing tonight? A bunch of us are gonna go." Jenny clasped her hands in front of her. "Pretty please? I haven't had enough Dylan time."

Dylan's face was so hopeful that I couldn't refuse. I shrugged. "I'm game."

Jenny squealed, then grabbed Dylan's hand and hauled her off the stage and toward the elevator. Evan bumped my shoulder. "How's it going?"

"Good."

"I'm glad you came, man. It's been too long since we've hung out."

The elevator dinged, and we squeezed in with a group of contestants.

I faced Dylan and put my hands on her waist, letting my fingers graze the bare skin between her jeans and blue crop-top. Technically, I wasn't breaking any rules, because this wasn't in private. Hopefully, she didn't add "no unnecessary touching" to the rules list. Because unnecessary touching was my favorite kind of touching. Her breath hitched, and I couldn't help my answering grin.

"You're awful," she whispered.

"Guilty." I winked at her.

We came to a stop, and the bass from the speakers vibrated me to my core. The group migrated out of the elevator, through a corridor, and into a dimly lit bar. A DJ spun records near the dance floor surrounded by pink neon lights, and a bartender and servers greeted us.

Jenny and Dylan cut to the dance floor and started dancing. The two spun in circles and doubled over with laughter.

Evan and I hit the bar, getting the draft on tap. We wandered to a table and sat. My eyes were drawn to Dylan's dancing form.

A slow song came on, and Evan took a long swig of his beer and stood. "Gotta go dance with Jen. She'll kill me if I don't."

Guess that meant I should dance with Dylan. I stood and approached, my hands a little sweaty. It was odd. During our times in our room together, I wasn't nervous. But here I was, my heart picking up speed as I closed the distance between us.

"May I have this dance?" My voice was oddly quiet.

She held her hands out, and I took them in mine. I pulled one up to my shoulder and brought the other to my heart, cradling it between us. Wrapping my arm around her waist, I inhaled the floral scent of her shampoo. Blue and green neon lights alternated pulses with the beat of the song as we swayed to the music.

"What's your favorite ice cream flavor?" Her words were breathy next to my ear.

"Rocky Road. You?" I could go for some right now.

"Mmm. Mine is Grasshopper."

"Come again?" I pulled back and wrinkled my nose.

"Grasshopper. It's mint Oreo. It's so good." She leaned her head on my shoulder. "This is nice."

The song ended too soon, and the next song started. It was fast-paced. A few more couples joined us on the dance floor. There was something freeing about raising your hands in the air and just letting the music move you. As we danced, the crowd separated us.

When Jenny's song, *Stars Align*, came on, Dylan found me and wrapped her arms around my shoulders. She whispered through the first verse and on the chorus she sang quietly, "When the stars align and we're feeling fine, I'll take your hand and make you my man. Give you my heart. They'll never tear us apart. Yeah, when the stars align. When the stars align."

I pulled her tighter against me. Her voice was an addiction. Every time I heard it, I wanted more.

"I waited up for you to call again, to beg me back into your arms again—"

"Your voice is beautiful." I placed a kiss on her temple.

"Thanks."

She picked up the chorus one more time, and my eyes drifted closed. I could listen to her sing all night.

We danced a few more songs before I escorted Dylan to the table and left her there to go grab her a drink.

"Can I get an ice water?" I patted the bar top and sat on one of the stools. Sheena sauntered up. "Hey, Ace."

"Sheena." I forced a smile. *Wasn't in the mood for her.*

She walked two fingers up my sleeve, and I grabbed them before she got to my chest. Sheena pouted.

"Stop." I glanced over her shoulder to where Dylan sat, watching Jenny and Evan on the dance floor.

"Aiden, don't you miss us?" Her voice was a purr, and she pressed up against me.

I stood, putting much needed distance between us. "I have a girlfriend. You need to knock it off."

Sheena stepped closer, wedging herself between me and the bar. She looked up at me with wide, vulnerable eyes. "I don't like having regrets, Aiden."

"Stop," I repeated, backing away.

"You're my regret." The corner of her mouth tilted up into a smile. "Call me when you two break up."

She was delusional. *What was her game?* Because with Sheena, there was always a game.

Her hips swayed as she walked away. The bartender slid the water to me. "Good job, buddy. I wouldn't have been able to resist."

Great. He'd probably interpret that interaction in the worst possible way, then leak it to the tabloids. I slapped a fifty on the counter. "For your discretion."

He pocketed the money and nodded.

I grasped the glass and headed to the table, the light condensation wetting my hand. The bass of the music was suddenly too much. I set the glass down and leaned in to speak into Dylan's ear. "I'm not feeling great. I'm gonna head to bed."

"I'll go with you." She sipped the water, then caught Jenny's eye and jerked her hand in the general direction of our room.

Jenny waved, and Dylan grabbed my hand. "Do you need me to get you anything? Broth or pain killers or anything?"

I shook my head. "I'll be okay. Seriously, stay."

She placed a hand on my forehead. "You're not hot." She blushed. "I mean, you don't feel like you have a fever. Are you sure you don't want me to come?"

She sure knew how to boost my ego. I forced my face to stay neutral. "I just need to sleep. Stay. Have fun."

I made it back to the room, stripped to my boxers, and set up camp on the chaise lounge, then picked up my writing notebook.

Fifteen - Dylan

I didn't get it. *Why did Aiden want to leave? Had I done something wrong?* I wished I'd heard his conversation with Sheena. *Why was I not good enough?* When he came back, he probably realized how much more sophisticated Sheena was, then faked an illness so he could go back to the room and sleep.

Fresh air. That was what I needed. I wandered up the stairs to the deck near the front of the ship. The only sounds were the waves crashing over the bow and the wind whipping my hair. I gathered it as best as I could.

To the west, the clouds were pink and orange, and the sun was moments from disappearing behind the horizon. I inhaled the ocean air, salty and humid.

I weaved through the beach loungers on the deck and leaned against the rail, staring out at the water under the sunset. If Aiden liked girls like Sheena, I didn't stand a chance. *I was only here for the money, anyway. Yeah...*

~

Tuesday morning, I woke early and snuck to Jenny's room. "Help."

"What's up?" She opened the door, and her silk robe gaped open, revealing slinky silk lingerie.

I shrugged my shoulders, and my chin trembled. "I don't know." *I'm not good enough for him.*

"Come on in." She ushered me into the bathroom and kicked the door closed. She came up behind me and held my shoulders as we stared at my reflection in the mirror. "You guys are cute together. We just need to doll you up a little bit. Image is everything in this business." Jenny angled me toward a chair and then perched on the counter in front of me. "Now tell

Grandma Jen all about it." She grabbed some pasty stuff and squirted it onto a spongie thing. "Open your mouth."

I obeyed. "I'm not sophisticated enough." My words were muffled by the lack of lip movement.

"Pshaw. Says who?" She smeared the cream under my eyes and along the bridge of my nose.

You. Everyone. His interest in other women. I shrugged. "Just observing."

"Stop being so insecure. Don't take this the wrong way, but insecurity is super unattractive." Using a pinky, she wiped a spot on my nose. "Just fake it til you make it."

"Fake what?" *I was faking everything. How much more could I fake?*

She unscrewed another cream and began spreading it over my forehead. "Confidence."

Easier said than done.

"Dyl, you're a great catch." She paused and grabbed my shoulder with her clean hand, staring into my eyes. "Any guy would be lucky to have you, and if he can't see that, then who needs him?"

Ugh! Did she hear herself? She'd just told me to change everything about my outward appearance, and she'd been telling me to be fake from the get-go. I clenched my teeth to bite back the words that would alter our friendship. I nodded my head, and she finished in silence. Jenny couldn't see her own hypocrisy.

"There. You're so pretty. I love you, and I hate you." She air kissed my cheeks.

What the heck was that? "Um. Thanks."

She escorted me to the door. "Are you sure anything isn't wrong?"

I squeezed my eyes shut. Should I tell her? "This is just hard. I can't read him at all. One minute he's all touchy feely and the next, he's completely hands-off."

"Aww, Dylan." She rubbed a hand up and down my arm. "How does he act when the cameras aren't on?"

"Like we're buddies but nothing more."

"He might not be interested, and that's okay. That's on him, not you. Just stay on the ship as long as you can, and if you're lucky, you'll make enough to get your dad's truck back. Then you never have to see him again." She pulled me in for a quick hug. "Now get dressed before he sees you in these jammies. It wouldn't hurt for you to wear something more sexy and less 'forty-year-old virgin'." She pushed me out the door and closed it.

What was wrong with my jammies? They didn't even have any holes in them. A T-shirt and boxer shorts were perfectly acceptable attire for sleeping. *Weren't they?*

When I walked in, a towel was slung low around Aiden's waist. *Leaping Lizards. I was going to faint.* I beelined for the closet and shut myself in. I flipped through the clothes and settled for a pair of white linen shorts, a teal T-shirt with what Fabian called "peek-a-boo shoulders" and tan wedge sandals.

There. That was more prissy.

Aiden knocked on the door. "Dylan? I kinda need my clothes."

I kicked my pajamas into the corner and made a mental note to wear something more appropriate to bed that night. *Alright Dylan, confidence.* I pushed out my breasts and attempted to saunter to the door. My ankle twisted, and I caught myself before I really injured myself. "Son of a..."

"Dylan?" Concern laced Aiden's voice.

Great. Wedges would never work. I unlaced them and kicked them off before slipping my feet into my jeweled flip-flops. *Here we go, grace. Don't trip this time.* I pulled open the door and brushed past him. "Sorry. Beauty takes time." Wow, I sounded just like Jenny. And my voice was way too bubbly.

Aiden's muscles flexed before he disappeared behind the closet door. *Ahh, it was working.*

I folded the blankets from the lounger thing and laid across it. Draping myself was the goal, but I was more like a thanksgiving turkey in a display window. *Nope.* I sat up and glanced around the room. It was useless. I couldn't pull off "kitten." Heck, I couldn't even pull off "giraffe." *Well, maybe giraffe.*

Aiden came out of the closet bare chested with his arms threaded through his T-shirt.

99

My mouth dropped open, and I physically reached up to snap it closed.

He smiled, and that dimple flashed. He pulled the shirt over his head and smoothed it down his chest. *Dang, if my eyes didn't track every move he made. Gah, I thought he was hot five years ago when his first album came out. But like a fine wine, he'd aged well.*

He held a hand out to me. "Shall we?"

I stood and giraffe-walked over to him. *Okay, I tried to saunter, but let's be honest, it was awkward. Fake it til ya make it, right?*

We linked hands and headed down to the Lido deck.

Everyone was gathered around Trisha, and she was shouting orders. *Were we late?*

"Let's get to the ferry." Trisha waved an arm and led the way.

My stomach growled, and I pouted miserably. I pulled a tube of gloss from my pocket and spread it over my lips; it smelled like strawberries, so it had to taste like them. I sampled a small bit. *Nope.* It wasn't gross, but it definitely had no flavor. *Arg. What's a girl gotta do to get some food around here?*

Aiden pulled me down the gang-plank, and I bit back a joke about walking the plank. *Probably for the best.* He helped me into the ferry, and we settled in next to Jenny and Evan.

"Where have you guys been?" Jenny smirked.

I opened my mouth to answer, but Aiden beat me to it. "That's none of your business." He slung an arm around my shoulders and pulled me into him, planting a kiss on my temple.

My cheeks flamed, and I gave Jenny a tight smile. *That was us, the couple who were late because we lost track of time during our passionate love making.* I curled my hands into fists, digging my fingernails into my palms. *I really had to figure him out.*

We made it to the shore and a crewman who spoke broken English helped us out. We were escorted to Limousines. *Now that was cool.* Cameramen already waited inside. *While this was my first time in a freaking Limo, I had to play it cool. No opening the sunroof to wave to my adoring fans. Not that I had any.* I squeezed Aiden's hand and grinned like a psycho.

Aiden gestured for me to get in first. *Good thing I wore shorts and not one of those mini skirts. I'd flash the whole group.* I climbed in and grinned. Tiny lights along the ceiling illuminated the interior. The seats were laid out in a square. I picked the far bench and sat. The leather was soft and smooth. Aiden climbed in and sat beside me.

He put his arm behind my back and snuggled close. Jenny and Evan got in, and Jenny didn't even react to the Limo. *Gah, who was she?* She looked at me, and I gave her a cheesy thumbs up. She returned it, then turned to Evan.

"First time in a Limo?" Aiden's lips tickled my ear. I tilted my head just the tiniest bit to encourage him. *Here Aiden, Aiden, Aiden.*

I tried to make my voice breathy. "Yes." But it was more of a croak. *Good job, kermit.*

"You okay?"

I cleared my throat. "Yeah, sorry."

His fingers skimmed the back of my neck.

I let my head fall forward, inviting the touch. He chuckled.

"You really are a like a kitten. I can practically hear you purring." He squeezed my neck, then continued his caress.

What did I care? It felt good, and if a hot guy was going to tickle my neck while whispering sweet nothings in my ear, who was I to stop him? "Don't call me kitten." I'd already tried being a kitten this morning. I wasn't good at it. *Baby giraffe is more up my alley.*

"What should I call you then?" His fingers made their way over to the peek-a-boo part of the shirt. Chills spread across my skin.

"I don't know, but not that." Though I wouldn't mind rubbing my body all over him like a scratch post. *Dylan, stop it.*

The Limo set off, and I watched the city pass by. Most of the buildings were older, with chunks of cement missing, or roofs patched with plastic.

We pulled up to wherever it was we were going. A hotel? It looked fancy. Men in valet uniforms opened the Limo door for us. Aiden and I were the last ones out.

Aiden brought his lips to my ear. "Did you catch what we were doing?"

I twisted my lips; we had gotten there too late. No one had really been talking about it, but Jenny seemed in a good mood. "No clue."

The air outside was muggy. The aroma of spices and cooked meats drifted in the breeze. I held Aiden's hand but kept some distance between us.

A man wearing a brightly colored button-down shirt came out to greet us. He held his hands wide. "Welcome to Rio! Follow me."

Rio? As in Rio De Janeiro? I missed that part. *Oh, my gosh.*

Aiden pulled on my arm. "Quit bouncing, you look like a kangaroo."

I was bouncing? Whoops. "Sorry."

"Do you think kangaroos purr when you pet them?" His eyes sparkled, and he winked.

"Aiden Theodore Miller, don't you even *think* about nicknaming me kangaroo." I channelled my best school teacher's voice. Or, more accurately, the voice Mom used when Colby or I had done something particularly bad. And I also revealed that I knew his middle name... *Well, we can chalk that one up to stupidity.*

Sixteen - Aiden

I planted a kiss on Dylan's temple. We'd have to talk about how much she actually knew about me later, cause I hadn't told her my middle name.

We followed the guide to a lobby, where women and men in white greeted us with bright smiles.

"Welcome to Spa-Day!" Teresa held her arms up like a younger version of Vanna White.

Kill me now. I'd rather watch paint dry. I glanced at Dylan. She was smiling, but it didn't reach her eyes.

A woman and man came up to us and gestured to a door. "This way."

Inside the room were two massage tables covered in white sheets. This was the only part of spa-day I could get behind.

"Disrobe and slip between the sheets. We'll be right back to start your massages." They closed the door.

Dylan's panicked gaze met mine. "Were they serious? Get naked?" Her mouth opened and closed a few times. "I mean, yeah. But I mean, you're here."

Oh, it was about to get interesting. "And we're supposed to be datin'." I unbuckled my belt, then unsnapped my button, holding back my grin.

Her cheeks flamed a bright red, and she spun, giving me her back.

I unzipped my fly and pushed my pants down my legs. Luckily, I'd worn flip-flops today, so I kicked them, along with my pants, all off into one big pile. "You're cute when you blush."

"Just hurry and get under the sheets, please." She put her hands over her eyes and peeked through two fingers over her shoulder.

My shirt was next. I flexed my muscles and peeled the shirt over my head. She turned back away. I finished undressing and slid between the cool sheets, putting my face in the headrest. "Go ahead. I can't see you."

Clothing rustled, and I deserved a medal for not looking over to watch her slide between those sheets.

A minute ticked by and our massage therapists still hadn't returned. "So, you didn't wanna see Aiden Miller naked?" I didn't know why it bothered me so much. I didn't consider myself an especially egotistical guy, but she hadn't even tried to make a move.

She gasped and tried to cover it with a cough. "Don't talk about yourself in the third person. It's creepy."

Skillful dodge. Let's see her dodge my next one. "Why not? Millions of girls would kill for a glimpse." It was eating at me.

Silence thickened the air between us. How would she get out of that?

"I… It's just that… I want it to mean something." Her voice was slightly muffled by the headrest.

Interesting. I lifted my head and looked over at her. She had pulled the sheets so high that her feet were poking out the bottom, kinda like mine, but I had her by five inches. "It wouldn't mean something?"

There was a tap on the door, and I cursed the timing of our masseurs.

"Ready!" I dropped my face back down onto the table. It'd been a while since my last massage.

The masseuses entered, and the man spoke softly in my ear, asking if I had any problem areas.

"Nope. Relaxation is the goal." *Especially after realizing Dylan didn't think making love to me would mean something.*

Music started, a soft piano number.

His warm hands started on my shoulders, and I forced myself to drift off. I didn't want to think about how much Dylan's words stung.

I woke up to Dylan giggling. "Ahh. Stop. You have to stop. It tickles."

My eyes cracked open, and I lifted my head. Her masseuse was massaging her feet. Mine were being rubbed, too. Dylan kept jerking them back as she clung to the top of the sheet. *Darn.*

"I'm so ticklish on my feet." She straightened her legs and did some weird shiver.

"It's no problem." The woman squirted more oil on her hand and rubbed it onto Dylan's calf; she shifted the sheet to expose her entire thigh. I dropped my head back and squeezed my eyes shut. *If I watched much more, there'd be trouble.*

When our hour was over, they left, leaving Dylan bright red and buck naked. I wrapped the sheet around my waist and stood. "You gonna lay there all day?"

She clutched the top of the sheet and stood, sweeping it behind her like a wrap. "Just put your robe on."

"Gladly." If she wouldn't pass out, I'd just drop the sheet. I waited until she'd turned around to pull my clothes on. "Your turn, kangaroo."

She clung to the sheet and bent over to wrestle with her clothes.

Should I feel bad for watching? Yeah, probably. "I'll turn around and give you privacy. I won't peek. Scout's honor." I held up my fingers in the boyscout sign and faced the wall.

A thump and some creative cursing later, she tapped on my shoulder.

"Finally ready?" I chanced a glance over my shoulder. She was adorable in her short shorts and teal shirt. Dylan must've gotten a scalp massage, because her hair was messy. I *really* liked the laid back version of her. *Darn it. How was I supposed to keep doing this? I was like a puppy, begging for affection.* I set my jaw and took a deep breath.

We exited and were met by our original guide and a cameraman. "How were your massages?"

"So good, thank you." Dylan leaned into me.

"We have shops in the main area, little boutiques, tourist places. You will like it very much." He nodded and pointed out the door we had come through. "We also have mud bath, or facial, or we can treat you to manicure and pedicure." *Was it me, or did he sound a little too delighted at the thought of putting me through that?*

Dylan glanced at me over her shoulder, her bottom lip between her teeth. "What do you think?"

It all sounded like torture. "Whatever you want, cupcake."

She quirked a brow. "Let's browse the shops."

I wrapped my arm around her waist and rested my hand on her hip. "Shall we?"

We wandered the shops for over an hour, and knowing my other exes, it was like speed shopping. She picked out a few trinkets. Nothing too expensive, and she paid for them with her own card.

"Okay. I'm going to buy you something." I took her hand and led her to a clothing shop.

The female shopkeeper met us at the door. "Welcome. What can I help you with today?"

"My girlfriend has her eye on a bikini." I gave Dylan a wicked grin.

She smacked my arm. "I have enough swimwear. What about a sweatshirt?" She let go of my hand and pushed into the shop.

Hideous, even by my standards. Sweaters lined one wall. *Tourist bait.*

She laughed out loud and held a sweatshirt out to me. "Rio is calling, and I need a vacation."

I raised an eyebrow.

"Aren't you going to get anything for your family? What would Brin like?" She walked over to a carousel of brightly colored necklaces and spun it around. "What about this?" She held up a cheap stainless steel necklace with a seashell dangling from the end. The word Rio was painted on it with red, green, and yellow letters.

Dylan gasped. The counter was a glass case with the more expensive merchandise inside. "Look at that." She pointed to a string of alternating pink and black pearls. *Okay, Dylan would look beautiful in that.*

She pointed to the necklace and made eye contact with the clerk. "Can we see that, please?"

The clerk unlocked the glass case and slid it open. She pulled the necklace out and set it on a velvet cloth before laying it on the counter.

Dylan lifted the small tag and looked at the price. "Eight hundred dollars?" Her voice was barely loud enough to hear.

"What about that?" I pointed to another pearl necklace, this one made entirely of black pearls.

The woman smiled and laid it atop another piece of velvet. "This is a fine choice. It would look lovely on this young lady."

But I had Mom in mind. She'd love it. She'd probably only wear it to church on Sundays, but she'd love it. I bought two necklaces; a pink pearl necklace for Brin, and the black one for my mom. A tie clip for Dad and the hideous Rio sweatshirt for Dylan. And I secretly threw in the black and pink pearl necklace for Dylan.

I turned to the cameraman. "You have a name?"

He glanced over the eyepiece. "Carlos."

"You want some ice cream, Carlos? I saw a shop a few doors down." I grabbed the bags from the counter and thanked our clerk.

"Sure." He grinned.

I pocketed my wallet, then slipped my hand into Dylan's. "Shall we?"

We weren't the only ones with the idea to get ice cream. Brock Edgerton, the actor, and his fiancé, Stacy Phillips, an aspiring actress, were already there. They had somehow escaped without a cameraman.

Stacy's lips were pinched, and she glared at Brock as he tried to coax a bite into her mouth. "You know I can't. I'm getting ready for a role."

I held back my laugh. *Her role. Ha. I'd heard her bragging about a toothpaste commercial.*

"But they won't see your body, just your beautiful smile. You're still allowed to enjoy life, Stace." He held out the bite again.

She stood and slapped the spoon from his hand. "Don't be ignorant, Brock. This business is so much different for women." Stacy turned on her heels and froze when she saw the camera. Her anger melted, and she smiled before spinning back to Brock. "Thanks for practicing that fight scene with me, babe." She lowered to the chair stiffly.

"I can't do this. Good luck with your career." He took his ice cream and left her sitting there.

Dude.

Dylan unfroze before I did, pulling me to the counter to order our ice cream. I was embarrassed for both of them. That was not how I wanted our time on *Couple's Cruise* to end. I never wanted Dylan and I to have a similar scene.

I draped an arm around her shoulder. "Thanks for not creating a scene like that."

"It's not too late." She winked at me, and the employee came over to take our orders.

I glanced back at Carlos, whose camera was focused on Stacy. She pounded her fists onto the table and stormed from the restaurant.

"Carlos, what'll you have, man?"

He put the camera on one of the tables and came over to join us. After we each had our ice cream, Rocky Road for me and Carlos, and Mint Oreo for Dylan, the three of us sat at one of the tables. About fifteen minutes into the conversation, I realized the camera was pointed at our table, and the red light was on. He recorded our whole conversation? We hadn't said anything wrong, had we?

Seventeen - Dylan

That night we sat on the bed together, both propped up by pillows. We'd fallen into a familiarity, but his proximity still gave me heart palpitations. The edited recap of today's events played on the TV. Stacy's "scene" and following break-up made the cut. Guess they'd be out of here tomorrow. I hadn't had a chance to get to know them, but she seemed like high drama.

Our conversation with Carlos also made the cut. We sat side by side across from Carlos, and by the angle of the camera, you could see Aiden's hand on my knee. We talked and laughed, probing Carlos about his family and if he liked traveling with *Couple's Cruise*.

We looked like a real couple. *Like, a* real *couple.* I glanced at him. His expression was unreadable. Why couldn't he wear his emotions on his sleeve? I'd give just about anything to know what he was thinking.

After our portion was over, he turned off the TV, and I shifted so I was lying on the bed.

Aiden grabbed his notebook and started furiously scribbling.

I watched and waited as the minutes ticked by until the pencil slowed and he looked up from the page.

"How're the songs coming along?"

He glanced at me, and a small smile curled his lips. "Really good, pumpkin."

"Ugh." I shook my head and readjusted my pillow to hide my grin. "Not pumpkin." I liked nicknames, but my parents had always called me "Bean Pole" which had evolved over the years to "Dylie Bean." The nickname and memories of my parents made me smile.

I loved hearing Aiden come up with his own nicknames. *Stegosaurus was my favorite so far. Not that I'd admit that to Aiden.* Not so much the actual nickname, but the timing of it. I'd been on the verge of a panic attack. Well, maybe not a real one, but I'd been nervous, and he'd cured me with a few words. It was like he knew me, knew what I needed, like we were on the same wave-length. *Like he cared.*

Aiden adjusted his position and hunkered down beside me. He kept his notebook angled away and put the pen to paper once more. The look on his face was familiar, the unfocused eyes, the parted lips. It was the same look I got when I wrote lyrics. There was nothing like the feeling of creating something others would hear, opening your heart to the lyrics and putting them on paper. *It was cathartic. Therapeutic.* When I wrote with Jenny, and we'd get on a roll, it was amazing.

We always listened to music while we were writing, though. "Do you mind if I play your guitar?"

His pen froze, and he glanced at me. He hesitated for a second, his gaze never leaving my face. Aiden closed his notebook, and his eyes narrowed momentarily, like they had the first time I played for him. His expression finally smoothed and he nodded, a quick up and down of his head. "You know where it is?"

"Yep." I stood and forced myself not to rush to the closet. Something about playing for him both soothed and terrified me. He was an artist. He understood the feeling of baring your soul to another person, the raw emotion that played into writing your own songs. But I knew what song I was going to play, and that part sent my pulse into overdrive. *Like, double overdrive.*

His case was on the top shelf, and I snagged the handle with shaking hands and pulled it down, then placed it on the ground and opened it. The redwood guitar gleamed, and I ran a hand over the body. It was almost too pretty to touch. *Almost.*

I scooped it out of the case and cradled it with the gentle respect it deserved. *Holding the guitar made me feel lighter, almost as if I was floating.* I entered the room with a bounce in my step and Aiden watched me, a crooked grin on his face that made my insides wobbly.

The leather shoulder strap was a little long, and I adjusted it before perching on the edge of the bed. I strummed a chord, the movement familiar. It had been about three weeks since the last time I played, longer than I usually went without touching an instrument. The guitar's vibration soothed me, and for a minute I got lost in the movements, in placing my fingers on the chords, in the back-and-forth strum on the strings.

Aiden scooted closer, close enough to touch. Close enough to make my breaths pick up their pace and my hands to sweat.

Jenny and I had worked on a song together, but it didn't quite fit with her image, so she buried it, never to see the light of day. *Until now.*

Be brave. Jenny's words echoed in my head. If I wanted this, I had to go for it. I'd never know unless I took the chance. And if I wanted a relationship, then Aiden needed to know why I was waiting.

I took a deep breath and played the chords of the song; the music filling the room. Then my voice joined in, singing the melody. When I closed my eyes, I was able to lose myself in the song *Saving My Love for the Right Man,* the lyrics I had written and connected with.

"Her heart broken,

She took the walk.

His promises were all just talk.

He took all she had to give,

For one night they loved and lived."

I continued through the verses, losing myself in the emotion. As I finished the last note, I let my eyes drift open.

Aiden had a soft smile on his lips. His eyes scanned my face. "Wow." His voice was barely a whisper.

My heart stuttered. The way he was looking at me was the way I wanted to be looked at by a man. For the rest of my life. The way I imagined a man would look at me as we joined hands and said our vows. *Snap out of it Dylan. He's Aiden Miller. His life is parties and world tours, not monogamy and vows.*

"You wrote that?" He ran a hand through his hair and shook his head.

"Co-wrote it. It didn't make it on Jenny's album." I fidgeted with the guitar strap, unable to make eye contact. Couldn't let myself look at him again.

111

Couldn't see that look on his face and not be affected by it.

I'd lose my heart.

"Why don't you have your own album? You've got the chops."

So many reasons. "The timing was never right." It was a partial truth. I didn't need to scare him off by telling him I hated being in front of a crowd.

"Tell me about the lyrics." His tone was warm, like my favorite blanket or a cup of cocoa on a cold morning.

Our gazes locked. I had to see if he was genuine.

He nodded his head, as if encouraging me to open up.

I went back to watching my fingers as I placed them on the strings.

The more time I spent with him, the harder it was going to be when this was all over. But we didn't have a chance if I couldn't be open. *Didn't have a chance? A chance at what?* I stole another glance at him and found him staring at me, his gaze intense, helping my confidence soar. This was what I'd wanted, what I waited my entire life to find. *Why, of all people, did I have to find it with Aiden Freaking Miller?* There was no way there could be a chance. We were all wrong for each other. His fame, the constant cameras. It would never change, and I couldn't live that life.

But this feeling, the feeling of floating. How could I give it up? Maybe there was some middle ground, some way to compromise. He offered a small smile of encouragement, and my heart halted before resuming its galloping pace. I had to try. But trying meant being honest about everything. *Well, almost everything.*

I pulled the guitar strap off and stood, placing it on the lounger. If we were having this conversation, I couldn't look at his face while we did it. I laid beside him on the bed and stared up at the ceiling.

"The idea came from our friend in high school. She and her boyfriend had sex. After he broke up with her. She was crushed." My cheeks burned, and I didn't dare look over to see his reaction. I plowed on before he could stop me, or tease me. *Complete honesty.* "Jenny and I made a pact: to wait until marriage." I didn't think she'd kept her end, but I kept mine. "This song was inspired by our friend's experience and our decision to wait for love, real love."

The bed shifted beside me, and I could feel his gaze on my face. I chanced a glance over at him. His expression was open, and he reached over and grabbed my hand. I snapped my gaze back to the ceiling.

"So you've never...?" He let the unspoken word hang between us.

Kill me now. "Nope."

"I respect that. A lot. Dylan, I—" He cut himself off. "Yeah. I respect that."

What was he going to say?

After a minute, I turned on my side to face him. "How's writing going?"

He rolled on his back, grabbed his notebook, and dropped it between us. "Good." He stared into my face. "Really good."

I placed a finger on top of the notebook and raised an eyebrow, sliding the notebook toward me. "May I?"

He put a palm on top of it, stopping its movement. "Let me find the right one." He flipped through the pages, then turned one to me.

My eyes scanned the words, and a couple of lines jumped out at me.

I don't know how,

But baby you've found a way

Over my walls

With every smile of your unpainted face

It was a love song. *Holy moley! It was a love song?* I brought my gaze to Aiden's. His lips were slightly parted, and eyes were wide and vulnerable.

"It's not done yet." He sounded hesitant, unsure. He watched me as he pulled the notebook back to him.

I met his eyes. "It's beautiful."

He reached up and tucked a strand of hair behind my ear.

Holy mother.

His knuckles grazed my cheek, and my breath caught in my throat.

His thumb brushed back and forth along my jaw. "I wrote it for you."

Eighteen - Aiden

My gaze focused on Dylan's lips; pink and slightly parted. Her breaths rushed through them in short puffs. She stared at me and wet her lips, begging me to kiss them. I wanted to pull her into my arms and show her I was different. Prove to her I could be the man she wanted me to be, the man who put her before anything else. Being with her turned my world on end. She made me dream of things I didn't think I'd ever want again. Looking at her gave me hope for a future I never thought I'd have.

Our ragged breaths filled the space between us, and I stared down at her in wonder. I hadn't even touched her, and we were already out of breath. Being with Sheena had never been like this. It was all touch and no feeling. *But this? This was feeling.* Feeling like I'd never imagined possible. If laying next to her, almost kissing her, could feel like this, kissing her was going to destroy me. In the best possible way. I'd never be able to kiss another girl again.

I desperately wanted to break her no kissing rule.

Dylan watched me beneath lowered lashes. They fanned out over her cheeks, highlighting the freckles splashed across the bridge of her nose. She caught her bottom lip between her teeth and gently bit down. She wanted a man willing to wait until marriage, and as bad as I wanted her, she was worth waiting for. We had chemistry and not just physically. We understood each other, connected in ways I didn't know were possible. *What was I waiting for? The rule. The darned rule. No kissing.* What if I kissed her and she got upset? Thought I wasn't respecting her beliefs? But it could be earth shattering. Change everything.

Chemistry sparked between us, and when she leaned into me, and her hand cupped my cheek, warmth filled my chest.

It was all the invitation I needed. Consequences be darned.

I cradled the back of her head and drew her into me, her pulse beating a frantic rhythm at her throat. I brought my lips agonizingly slow toward hers, giving her every opportunity to pull away. Her mouth molded to mine, soft as silk, still tasting of the chocolate mousse she'd eaten for dessert.

Dylan's hands dove through my hair, tugging me closer, urging me on.

I pressed her onto her back, covering her body with mine and deepening the kiss. I explored her mouth, getting lost in her sweet sighs and panted breaths. Our bodies fit perfectly, like the long-lost, missing piece to a puzzle. My heart galloped in my chest, thundering out a frenzied beat.

Kissing her was everything.

She curled her fingers into my shirt, pulling it upward as she did. It felt good, too good, but this wasn't what she wanted. As much as it killed me, I broke the kiss and gripped her wrists, stopping her. I stared down at her, our lips still close, close enough I could feel them despite the air separating us. "Dylan. Stop."

Her cheeks flamed a cherry red, and she turned her head to the side. "Sorry."

The quiet apology was a kick to the gut. Did she think she'd done something wrong? I took her chin in my fingers and gently turned her back toward me. After only a moment of hesitation, I brought my lips back down to hers, reassuring her. The second kiss was no less intoxicating than the first, but it was shorter. I'd already taken more than she'd intended to offer.

She pulled back, gasping for air, her hands pushing at my chest. Dylan turned her head to the side. "Aiden." My name was panted between breaths, barely above a whisper, and it sounded so good on her lips.

I pressed my nose to the side of her neck, sucking in breaths. Regaining my control. "We have to stop."

A little whimper escaped her, and the temptation to kiss her again almost overwhelmed me.

I rolled onto my back and stared up at the ceiling. *Destroyed.* The memory of that kiss would haunt me for the rest of my life.

"Is everything okay? Did I do something wrong?" Dylan's voice was small and her words a knife to my heart, cutting me open and leaving me raw.

Nothing. She'd done everything right. I laughed and shook my head, still trying to get control of my emotions. "No, Dylan. You didn't do anything wrong."

She shifted beside me, and I turned my head to face her. Her hand pillowed her cheek, and she stared at me, wide eyed, pupils dilated. "Then why'd you stop?" Her voice was quiet. Breathy. Her insecurity was clear in her eyes.

I groaned. "Because if I didn't stop now, I might not be able to."

Her eyes widened, and her mouth shaped an adorable "O."

Her mouth. It'd felt so right against mine. I closed my eyes to shut out the temptation, but her rapid breathing next to me was still a painful reminder.

"We have something special, Dylan, and I don't want to ruin that." I would have said anything to take that hurt from her eyes, but I owed her the truth.

Dylan rolled onto her back. Her chest rose and fell dramatically with each breath.

We sat in silence until my heart slowed and beat in time to the ballad ambling through my head. Every lyric seemed to start and end with her, every thought.

Every. Thing.

Every Breath
Since we met
I have spent
Tryin' to figure out these feelings
They weren't part of the agreement

I sat up and grabbed her hand, bringing it to my lap. I picked up my pen from the nightstand and put the tip against the inside of her wrist. "The truth is, you're my muse." I drew the lines of a bar and traced the melody from the first line of the song I'd started to think of as hers.

As I drew, she tried to sit up to get a better view, but I covered it with my hand, giving her a teasing grin. "Patience."

116

She flopped back down onto the bed, a smile tilting her lips.

"I don't care about the show, about the publicity." I filled in each note, nice and dark. "I don't care about anythin' on this boat." I closed off the bar with two short lines. "But you."

A gasp brought my eyes up. Hers were red-rimmed, and she shook her head.

"Oh, kitten. Don't cry, what's the matter?"

Her sad smile turned into a frown. "It's not real. I'm not real."

My stomach clenched. How could she say it wasn't real? What we had was the most real thing in my life.

She shook her head and dashed away a tear from her cheek. "I'm not some trophy girlfriend, Aiden. I hate the camera. I hate makeup, I hate fashion. The girl you like doesn't exist."

I put the finishing touch on the drawing on her arm and laid down beside her. She stared up at the ceiling, tears dripping down her temples. "Dylan, I don't like that girl. I like the girl who walks around without makeup and PJs when I'm the only one around. The girl who fishes, and zip lines and rappels. The girl who eats an entire plate of Sweet and Sour chicken and polishes it off with chocolate mousse." I brushed the hair from her face.

Her lashes were thick with tears as she turned her eyes to me, her gaze searching mine.

"I don't want a fake version of you, Dylan. I want the real thing."

Nineteen - Dylan

I slept curled in Aiden's arms. Deliriously happy, my heart soaring. He wanted me, the real me. After our talk, he turned out the lights, forcing me to wait until morning to see the drawing on my wrist. As soon as the sun hinted at giving me a sliver of light, I got out of bed and went out onto the balcony to stare at his drawing. The bottom line was slightly longer, protruding out past the bar lines. I sat on the beach chair and softly caressed the image.

It was about two inches long and an inch tall, and I recognized the melody. He'd played it for me before. Fresh tears stung my eyes. I didn't deserve him. He was so sweet and hearing his words last night sent butterflies fluttering in my stomach. *I was his muse.*

I leaned into the balcony door and stared at his sleeping form. It was the most romantic thing anyone had ever done for me, and I wanted to remember it for the rest of my life.

Eliminations weren't until later that night, so I had time to add, then cross off something from my bucket list. Leaving Aiden asleep in bed, I threw on jean cut-offs and a flowy white shirt, then slipped my feet into my flip-flops. I snuck down the hall to Jenny's room.

She was dressed and just finishing her makeup. "We'll do you next. Have a seat."

I shook my head. "Nope. I'm not wearing makeup today." My smile overtook my face, and I let out a little squee.

Jenny paused and gave me an assessing look. "Oh my gosh, did you lose it last night?"

"What? No-"

"You lost it to Aiden Miller after you were so adamant about waiting?" She laughed, a humorless sound, and went back to her makeup.

"I didn't lose anything to Aiden Miller last night." *Except my heart.* "I'm just happy, and I want to commemorate my time here by doing something crazy."

She put the lid on her lipstick and rubbed her lips together, staring at me in the mirror, eyebrows raised. "What?"

"A tattoo." I held up my hand to show her my wrist.

She grinned, one side of her mouth tipping up. "Yes. I love this wild Dylan. Let's do it." She stood and put on her high heels. "This has been good for you, Dyl. Opening up, experiencing new things. I'm proud of you." Jenny wrapped an arm around my waist and stuck her hand in my back pocket.

The producers wouldn't let us leave without a cameraman, so Carlos volunteered to accompany us and Desiree came to produce and translate. A boat ferried us to shore, and a couple of security guys escorted us. We crowded into a twelve passenger-van, *which seemed a little extreme for what coulda been a two person outing,* and headed to a tattoo parlor Jenny and I scoured the internet for. All the reviews said it was clean, and we loved their style. One of the artists had multiple pictures of music notes and lyrics that I fell in love with. And she squeezed me in once she heard there would be TV exposure involved. *Who knew there'd be a good side to fame?*

"So, is this your first tattoo?" Desiree sat in the passenger seat, and Carlos rested the camera on the headrest, pointed directly at me.

I nodded. "Yeah, I always thought if I got a tattoo, it would be something special. Something I wanted to remember forever."

"What are you getting?" Desiree's voice was low, conspiratorial.

The story was mine, but the tattoo would be for everyone to see. I held up my wrist, showing off the line of notes. "Just a couple measures of music."

"Does it have any sort of significance?" She raised her eyebrow as if daring me to open up.

"I just want to get it to remember my time on *Couple's Cruise.*" *And my time as Aiden's girlfriend.*

119

"Hey, can we make a quick stop at the pharmacy? My lady's days are here, and I need supplies." Jenny pointed to what looked to be a pharmacy on the corner. The driver pulled off, and Jenny and one of the security guys made a quick run inside.

Desiree made a twirling motion with her finger and rolled her eyes. Carlos shut off the camera.

When Jenny got back, she grabbed my hand, giving it a squeeze. "I'm so excited, I can't believe you're actually going through with this." She clutched it with a death grip and didn't release me until we were through the tattoo parlor doors.

Guess she thought I'd chicken out. But no, my mind was made up.

The tattoo parlor wasn't what I would describe as upscale, and after living in the lap of luxury for the past three weeks, it was a definite step down. The walls were covered in drawings and posters of celebrities' tattoos. The counter was a display box with jewelry for every type of piercing imaginable.

A woman met us at the counter. Her ears were gauged with big black hoops, and tattoos covered nearly every visible surface. When she saw the cameras, her smile turned genuine and her posture straightened. "You must be Dylan. I'm Maira." She spoke in heavily accented English and grabbed a couple of papers from the shelf beside the register, then put them on the counter in front of me. "I create sketches after our conversation."

I lifted my wrist and compared it to the drawings on the page. They were more perfect, more symmetrical, and less like Aiden had drawn them. I showed her the drawing on my wrist. "I want this. Exactly this."

She grabbed my hand and turned my wrist from side to side, studying the drawing. "You want imperfections on there? This line is longer than others." She pointed at the bottom bar.

I looked at Desiree for help. "Yes. Exactly like it is, please."

Desiree spoke in Spanish for a moment, then turned back to me and nodded.

Maira's gaze met mine, holding it for a beat. "Who drew?"

Heat suffused my cheeks. It was stupid to be embarrassed about it, but I was. I saw the red blinking light of the camera out of the corner of my eye.

"My boyfriend." The lie felt more like the truth than it was.

She nodded her head once. "Alright." She released my arm and slid a clipboard to me. "Fill this out. We'll get you right back."

Jenny grabbed my arm and shook my shoulder, her excitement transferring to me. "You're actually getting a tattoo!"

I walked to the small waiting room, crowded with our entourage, and sat on one of the padded chairs. One by one, I filled out the questions. With each answer, something in my stomach coiled tighter. I was going through with it. Getting a tattoo. When I was finished, I took the clipboard to Maira.

She looked it over and turned her latest sketch around so I could see it, then motioned for me to hand my wrist over to her again. Her eyes went back and forth between her work and my wrist, and went so far as to lay the sketch over my wrist for a comparison. Once she was satisfied, she met my gaze. "Yes?"

It was perfect, down to the last flaw. Warmth filled my chest at the thought of putting it permanently on my skin. "I love it."

She pulled out a new paper and began drawing it again, getting every detail. When she was done, she showed me. "Still okay?"

"Yes." *Leaping Lizards, what would Aiden say?* Would he think it was cute or creepy? I had a brief moment of panic. What if he hated it? *But it wasn't for Aiden. It was for me.*

Maira jerked her head toward the back room. "Good. Follow me."

My heartbeat kicked up a notch. *What was I doing? Getting a tattoo?* I glanced at Jenny, who followed me with a bright smile. She was like a proud parent, sending her child off to kindergarten for the first time. Jenny gave me a thumbs-up, and just like that, my nerves settled.

Maira brought me into a room. The walls were plastered with hand-drawn pictures of everything from flowers to sugar skulls. The pictures were broken intermittently with a full-color photo of a tattoo or the occasional poster, but it was the drawings that caught my eye. Each one gave me more confidence that I'd chosen the right artist. Even the darker images had a soft edge to them, and it was that edge I needed to capture Aiden's strokes so perfectly.

Along one wall was a table similar to what you'd see at a doctor's office, and in the middle was a piece of furniture that looked like a massage table with a hole for your face until Maira repositioned it and it transformed into a chair. She motioned for me to sit as she pulled a table over and draped a sterile blue cloth over it. "You want all black?"

I nodded.

She pulled down tiny cups from a cupboard that resembled thimbles and squirted black ink into several of them, then she squirted some silver into one, a deep green into another, and a navy blue into a third. If she was planning to use all black, why on earth would she need those other colors?

At my silence, she looked up. She said something in Spanish, and Desiree translated. "It creates depth. It will look black, I promise. You want it all black, right?"

I nodded, dropped onto the chair, and placed my arm on the table she gestured to.

This was a big step, a bucket list item, and I couldn't help the surge of pride that traveled up my spine. I was doing it. Actually doing it.

Finally, Maira straddled a stool and rolled it toward me. She squirted a foul smelling soap over my wrist and followed by shaving the area with a disposable razor.

"Ready?" She held the tip of the tattoo gun in one of the thimbles of black and used the foot pedal to bring the gun to life. She dipped it in a few times, examining it in between, and once satisfied, she held it, poised to begin the torture process.

I nodded again, not trusting my voice to stay steady if I spoke.

Maira spoke again, and Desiree relayed her words. "It's gonna burn a bit. Try not to move your arm. The tattoo is only as good as the artist and the client."

Burn was an understatement. I glanced at the clock on the wall, noting the time: Eight minutes past nine. The first few strokes weren't bad, but it quickly built to a stinging that caused my toes to curl. On one particular pass, I gasped and fought the urge to pull my arm away. *Son of a biscuit. Why had I agreed to this? I hated needles. Hated. Them.* A shudder worked through

122

me. Needles reminded me too much of hospitals. Closing my eyes against the memories, I fought to keep myself in the present.

The camera alternated between my face and the tattoo forming on my wrist. And my gaze alternated between the clock on the wall and the torture on my arm.

Maira held a wet paper towel in one hand, and every few seconds, she wiped the extra ink away.

Blood bubbled on my skin, mixing with the ink and smearing across my arm. *What if it didn't turn out?* The green, silver, blue, and black streaked my wrist, making the tattoo look less like a bar of music and more like a psychedelic, gothic rainbow.

"I hear getting a tattoo on the wrist is really painful. How does it feel, Dylan?" Desiree's face was entirely too amused to ask me such a garbage question. The urge to smack that smirk was almost overwhelming.

"Hurts." I forced a smile and began a silent mantra inside my head, repeating it like a broken record. *I can do this. I'm brave.* Twelve minutes down.

It felt like a rubberband snapping on my wrist, again and again. *And again.* But the pain would all be worth it. To have a memory of this time, the perfect moment with Aiden. *The way it felt, the melting butterflies when he told me I was his muse.*

The constant buzzing of the tattoo needle was the only sound as the minutes ticked on. Maira stopped part-way through, opening a sterile package. She switched the needle then continued. This time the sensation was more of having someone touch a sunburn, tender but not unbearable.

She kept alternating between the colors, adding depth to the black. I couldn't watch. I turned my head away. This would either be the best thing ever, or I'd be on one of those bad tattoo shows getting it fixed or removed or covered up or whatever they did.

Twenty-two minutes later, the buzzing stopped. She wiped more of the rancid soap over my skin and patted it dry with a paper towel. Maira cut a small piece of clear tegaderm, the self-adhesive plastic that hospitals use to secure IVs, then smoothed it over my arm.

I turned my wrist over and stared at the perfectly imperfect bar of music. Tears welled in my eyes, and I cradled my arm to my chest.

She pulled off her gloves and threw them on the table beside the rest of the mess. "Follow me up front, and we finish."

Carlos walked backward in front of me with his camera going, while one of the security guards watched his back so he didn't trip. Desiree, Jenny, and the other guard were behind me, following quietly.

Maira went behind the counter and set a gift bag on top of it. She put a couple pieces of paper on the table and began circling care instructions.

I glanced at the one she was working on and let out a relieved breath when I saw it was in English. She was reading the Spanish version as she circled things on the English one.

Desiree translated, "Okay, just keep the wrap on it for twenty-four hours. Keep it out of the sun for at least a week. Sunscreen like crazy. Try not to scratch it. If it itches, and it will, slap it, don't scratch." Maira flipped the page and circled more things.

How much could there possibly be?

Desiree continued, "Ibuprofen will be your best friend. Take it. If you have any questions, feel free to call." Maira circled the phone number for the tattoo shop, then started pressing buttons on a register.

I handed her my card and signed for the total, then looked down at my new tattoo. *My. New. Tattoo.* A smile spread across my face. *I did it. I was brave.*

Twenty - Aiden

Evan and I sat in the hot tub at the back of the boat. Dylan was gone when I woke up, which was perfect. I needed to talk to Evan.

"So what was so important that you dragged me out of bed before noon?" Evan stretched and adjusted his sunglasses.

He was gonna think I was a pansy. "You and Jenny have been dating for what? A year? When did you know she was it for you?"

Laughter burst from him, and he splashed water at me. "She's got you! I knew it. She's perfect for you."

I launched an armful of water back at him, hitting him square in the chest. "Shut your face. She doesn't have me. I'm just…" *Whipped? Smitten?* "Considering my options."

"Like what? What gifts you should put on your wedding registry?" He smirked and whipped his hair back, slinging water at me.

"Don't be a dick. I'm serious. I like her. She's the first girl who's made me think that maybe a relationship wouldn't be all give and no take." The best way to describe how I felt when I was with Dylan was to compare it to being on stage. The rush of adrenaline, fans screaming, palms sweating, exhilaration. Mix that up with the connection I felt with my music, and you had Dylan.

We were connected.

He leaned back and sank down into the water until his shoulders were covered. "So you like her."

"I really do."

"That's huge, dude. Did you tell her about Sheena?"

"Why would I tell her about Sheena? That's the stupidest thing I could do."

He turned his head to the side til he was looking at me. "Dude. Chicks like honesty. If you're really giving this thing a go, you gotta tell her about Sheena. That wench screwed you up. If you're going to have a relationship, it has to be based on honesty."

"When did you become a relationship expert?" He was wrong, though. I couldn't tell her about Sheena. Not yet, anyway. Maybe when the cruise was over. Dylan didn't need to deal with Sheena and all her deceit.

"Never claimed to be. So you like her." He laughed again, a mocking sound.

"I like her."

"I'm glad. It's about time you got past what that chick did to you." He submerged for a moment, then came up, wiping the water from his face. "I'm thinking of asking Jenny to marry me."

Wasn't expecting that one. "What?"

A goofy smile overtook his face. "Yeah. You said it, we've been dating for a while. She'd make being married easy."

That was it? That was his reasoning? It'd never been more apparent to me than now; he didn't write his own songs because he couldn't. He wasn't a romantic. Practicality wasn't a good reason to marry a woman. *Love. What about love?* A song lyric came to mind, and I made a mental note to write it down as soon as I got back to the room.

We sat in the hot tub for another hour before a group of people exited the dining room door. Dylan and Jenny among them. I nudged Evan, and he sat up to get a better look.

"What's going on?" Evan stood, water dripping from him and hitting me.

My gaze met Dylan's, and she gave me one of her sweet smiles. My insides heated as she walked toward us.

Evan got out, and I followed, grabbing my towel and rubbing it through my hair before wrapping it around my waist.

"Hey." I gave her a quick peck on the lips, the simple action sending a zing through me.

The camera crew surrounded us. What were they up to and why were they in our faces?

"I did something." Her voice was small, and she had a slight crease in her brow.

Was she nervous? I held my hand out, and she put hers in mine. Her wrist was wrapped in plastic. *Holy crap, she got a tattoo.* I brought her arm up and turned it over. It was the measure of music I'd drawn. She got it inked onto her skin, permanently. Her words from one of our first conversations came back to me; if she got a tattoo, it would only be if it meant something to her. I pulled her against my chest, wrapping my arms around her and holding her tight.

She laughed into my bare chest, her body shaking against me. Dylan's arms came up around me, her arms like a blanket, comfy and right. The world disappeared around us, and it was just the two of us.

Dylan and me.

I was losing my heart to this woman, and it didn't scare me like I thought it would.

"You got a tattoo." I pulled back and brought her arm back up so I could stare at it. They were more than just notes. They were her song, and they were the first notes that came to me in over a year. A lump formed in my throat.

Who was I kidding? I was gone. My heart was hers.

Twenty-One - Dylan

Can you die of happiness?

I let Jenny put the barest amount of makeup on so I wouldn't look like a drowned cat. Her words, not mine.

The white dress I picked for tonight went to mid-thigh and had a lace overlay. The dress itself didn't have sleeves, but the lace added short sleeves and gave it an extra couple of inches on my legs.

Jenny pulled my hair up into a chignon, curling a couple of loose tendrils near the back. Not that the camera would see them. They were for Aiden. He liked to play with my hair, and I wanted him to have easy access. The thought flooded my chest with warmth. If these butterflies flapped any harder, they'd probably need medical attention.

"You okay?" I looked over at Jenny. Her face was drawn, and bags formed under her eyes. "What's going on? I say this with love, Jen. You look like crap."

She smiled and waved my concern away. "I'm fine. Just tired. I haven't been sleeping well lately. I think being on the ship this long is messing with my body."

"Do you get motion sickness?" I put my hand on her forehead. Was there even such a thing as delayed motion sickness? I had no idea. She didn't feel hot.

"I've gotta get ready. Go find your *boyfriend*." She winked at me and shoved me out the door.

I had a boyfriend, a real boyfriend. A grin overtook my face, and I forced myself to not skip down the hall toward our room.

Aiden stepped out of the door in a tux, and my breath caught. He looked up at me, and his face transformed. His eyes roved my body, sending a flash of heat through me. If I was older, I'd swear it was menopause.

"You look incredible." He came toward me, his long strides eating up the distance in seconds. When he was close enough to touch, he stopped. His hand came up, and he brushed my cheek with the back of his knuckle. His eyes darted to my lips, and he leaned in.

I was gonna need a defibrillator.

Our lips met, and my eyes drifted closed. My arms had a mind of their own, coming up to clutch at his lapel and drag him closer. The kiss deepened of its own accord and had nothing to do with my need for this man in front of me. I could taste the mouthwash he used and smell the aftershave on his skin.

We broke apart, and he pressed his forehead to mine. "You. Are. Amazing, Dylan." His chest heaved with each breath. He pulled me close once more, tucking my head under his chin and wrapping his arms around me.

Definitely the defibrillator. My heart beat so fast it probably sounded like a cat purring.

When he finally released me, I reached up and wiped the lipgloss from his lips. I'd seen Jenny do it with Evan a lot, but I'd never had the opportunity. It felt like a milestone, a rite of passage, and I just stepped into a new age.

He laced our fingers together, and we walked to the auditorium. There was no immunity this week, so there was no red couch, only seven white ones.

Desiree escorted us to the back row, which was either really good or really bad. A pit formed in my stomach. What if we went home this week? Would Aiden want to continue our relationship, or would that be it? Lights out, curtains closed. *Holy crap. Holy. Freaking. Crap.*

My heart picked up its rhythm as we sat on our couch. I leaned into Aiden, and he draped an arm behind my back and brought his lips to my temple, brushing them lightly over the tender skin there.

"You okay? You look like you're about to puke." His tone was soft, but the words just made the pit bigger.

I tried taking a deep breath, but something in my chest ached, preventing the entire breath from filling my lungs. "I'm freaking out a little bit. What if we go home tonight? What will happen to us?" I couldn't believe I'd been so bold as to voice the words.

Aiden pulled away, scooting to the edge of the couch and turning to face me. He took my face in his hands and held it until my eyes focused on him. "We're not going home, Dylan. And if by some chance we do, it won't be the end for us." He searched my face, his thumbs brushing my cheeks. "I promise."

Darn these butterflies. If they didn't stop twitching, I *was* going to puke. But they replaced the pit in my stomach. *It wouldn't be the end for us.* We'd still see each other. Still be together.

Trisha's high heels clacked along the stage as she took her place at the front of the set.

Aiden planted a chaste kiss on my lips and scooted back, pulling me into his side.

Cameramen took up their positions around the stage, covering every possible angle.

Someone counted down, and Trisha began her perfectly rehearsed spiel. *We could do this. We were going to make it through this round.* Aiden's hand came up and brushed the bare flesh at the back of my neck, his fingers dragging along the small chain of the necklace I wore. Chills made their way up my body, and I fought to keep my eyes open. His breath tickled my neck, and he whispered a few words.

"I'd been looking for a muse
From the Rockies to the Gulf Coast
Then you got under my skin like a tattoo
Now your touch is the one I crave the most."

The light above Felicity Black and her fiancé, Peter, went out. *What the heck? Had I zoned out so much that I hadn't noticed the elimination?* Her dad was a famous singer in the nineties and she said some nasty things to me a couple of weeks back.

I stood to go say goodbye and Aiden grabbed my arm.

130

"You don't owe her anything. She was rude to you." He shook his head.

"That's not who I am." I pulled out of his grip and made my way over to the departing couple. She might not have been my biggest fan, but I'd be the bigger person. I hugged them both and wished them well, Aiden following behind to do the same.

He gave me a half smile. "That was really nice of you."

One of my shoulders went up in a shrug. "We all say stupid things sometimes."

Trisha took her spot back at center stage.

We weren't going home. I repeated the mantra over and over.

Finally, Trisha made it to our couch. She stood between us and Brock and Stacy's couch.

My insides sagged in relief, but I kept my posture perfect. Brock and Stacy had the blowout fight at the ice cream shop. There was no way they were staying.

"The final couple leaving us tonight is…" The seconds ticked by as Trisha waited for the off-camera cue. "Brock and Stacy."

The light above them went out.

I turned to Aiden and flung my arms around his neck. He enveloped me in a hug, and it just felt right. *We were safe, and we were together.* I plastered a gracious smile on my face and hugged Brock and Stacy goodbye.

When the cameras cut, Jenny ran over and squeezed the life out of me. *Well, she tried.* "I'm so glad you guys didn't get cut. This cruise wouldn't be the same without you."

"Right back atcha, kid." I nudged her under the chin with my fist. *Sometimes my inner nanna came out and I just let the old bird do whatever the heck she wanted.*

"So? Dancing?" Jenny did one of her signature dance moves, and I shook my head.

"Not tonight. I think all the stress wore me out. I need to sleep." I gave her one last hug. "You guys have fun, though."

Jenny loved dancing. There was a place in town growing up that did country-western swing dances, and we'd found ourselves there every weekend without fail.

Aiden grabbed my hand and towed me to the elevator. He pressed the call button, and while we waited, he stared at me, his eyes a little smoldery.

Was that a word? I'd have to add it to the dictionary.

"What?" I patted my hair to make sure it wasn't sticking up at a weird angle.

He took a second to answer. "You never cease to amaze me."

Heat crept up my neck and bloomed on my cheeks. "Thanks?" *What prompted that comment?*

"It's like you read my mind. I like going back to our room and just hanging out with you. I don't need to go dancing. Every now and then is fine, but I don't care for those places. Dark. People grinding all over each other." His dimple flashed and one brow raised. "On second thought, let's go next week."

My cheeks had probably reached lobster-red. *Air. Where was the air?* I took a step back and fanned my face dramatically.

He chuckled. "You're so easy to make blush. It's one of my favorite things about you. Your innocence." The last words were a husky whisper, the back of his hand came up and brushed my burning cheek.

The elevator arrived, and we stepped inside. It seemed the moment was lost, and I took a deep breath. *Definitely a good thing. I'd spontaneously combust if he kept that up.*

Back in our room, I searched my bag for my ugliest jammies. The flannels I found felt like the armor I so desperately needed. I pulled them on, then exited the closet, pulling the pins from my hair.

Aiden watched me with hooded eyes. He had his jacket off and slung over the chair and his fingers worked the tie at his neck.

Holy Georgia.

Twenty-Two - Aiden

Waking up with Dylan in my arms was darn near the best thing since sliced bread. Taking a cold shower afterward was probably the worst.

We spent the weekend in our room, Jenny and Evan, our constant companions. Ordering-in, playing games, watching TV or movies. We learned the staff didn't like bringing us drinks all day, as if we were hanging out on the Lido deck. We made it worth their while with tips, though.

Monday afternoon we gathered for filming. Five double producer chairs and one single were set up under an awning. Wow, the final five couples. It occurred to me that the show didn't matter to me anymore. I had my inspiration. Now I just wanted to stay for Dylan, to see her every day, and to wake up beside her every morning. And to help her get the money she needed for the truck, that meant so much to her.

I grabbed her hand, and she laced our fingers together, leaning into me and planting a kiss on my jaw. My heart did a little flip. She was getting more comfortable, kissing me just because she wanted to and not because there was a camera on us.

Desiree came over, handed us mics, and pointed us to our director's chair. "Three questions today. No points. It's purely for entertainment. You'll do great."

There were chairs set up facing the stage where a bunch of the wait staff were currently seated. *An audience? Guess they wouldn't have to use the laugh track.*

Trisha Thames teetered onto the stage in four inch high heels. She perched on the single director's chair at the end of the row. An assistant ran a glittery mic to her, and she smiled, inspecting it.

The director counted down and called action.

"Welcome to our Game Show Edition of *Couple's Cruise.*" She paused as the intro ran. "We have our final five couples here, and we'll be asking them questions to see how well they know each other."

The camera panned over the five couples and returned to Trisha. "Let's begin. Write your answer on your whiteboards. Who said I love you first?"

I glanced at Dylan. She grinned as she wrote. Warmth flooded my chest, and I wrote my answer on the whiteboard.

Trisha went down the row, revealing everyone's answers. The audience clapped for each one and laughed when the couple disagreed.

"Aiden and Dylan. On the count of three, show us: Who said I love you first? One, two, three."

I held up my sign and stared over at Dylan's. We both said, "I did."

She leaned into me, and I kissed her temple.

The audience "awed," and she laid her head on my shoulder.

"You guys are sweet." Trisha winked at the camera and continued down the row.

"Next question: What animated movie character is your partner most like?"

It was a no-brainer. Her long, blonde hair, the joy she took from nature, and her endearing naïvety.

Trisha went down the row.

I was curious what Dylan came up with. How would she describe me?

"Aiden and Dylan, on the count of three. One, two, three."

I flipped my sign and looked over at Dylan's. Flynn Rider. Of all of the animated characters, she picked Rapunzel's love.

She looked at my sign and smiled. "Aww, Rapunzel."

"Dylan, why Flynn Rider?" Trisha perked up as if waiting for the juicy details.

She shrugged one shoulder. "Look at him. He's perfect and pretty." Her cheeks flushed red. "And he's a thief. He stole my heart."

I put an arm around her and pulled her against me. *She was perfect.*

Trisha looked at the last card in her hand and gave an evil smile. "What are you most likely to argue about?"

Dylan covered her board and wrote her answer.

My pen moved over the whiteboard. Trisha already started down the row. "Aiden, Dylan. What are you most likely to argue about? One, two, three."

When I saw the look on Dylan's face, regret wasn't a strong enough word.

Why was I such an idiot?

Trisha read Dylan's. "What board games to play."

Dylan's face was a bright red, and her smile looked forced. "He always wants to play Scrabble, but I prefer Boggle."

"That's because she whips me every time." How was I gonna dig myself out of this hole?

"And Aiden, you said, 'intimacy.' Care to elaborate?"

Was there any saving it? "No. I don't."

Trisha tried prodding me more, but I just shook my head.

Dylan's eyes were glued to her lap. She folded her arms over her chest.

I had to fix it.

"I couldn't think of anythin'." I turned toward her, begging her to believe me.

Her eyes came up and searched my face.

"I'm so sorry." I said it just loud enough for her to hear.

Her lips twitched into what might pass as a smile if you didn't know her as well as I did.

I screwed up.

Trisha moved on to the next couple, and I leaned into Dylan.

"I don't know where that came from."

She sat stiff, not giving at all.

The crowd gasped, and Jenny shot out of her chair. "Why would you bring that up right now?!" Jenny stood beside us and glared at Evan. "That's something between couples. You don't air dirty laundry on national television."

Evan stood, folding his arms across his chest. I knew that determined look in his eye. "It wasn't a big deal until you made it one."

135

Jenny threw her arms up in the air. "I can't. I just can't." She marched off, leaving a ticked off Evan in her wake.

"That's it for this episode of *Couple's Cruise—Celebrity Edition*. We'll see you next time for this week's adventure." Trisha gave her signature sign off and smiled her plastic smile at the camera.

Dylan stood and darted the direction Jenny had gone. My heart lurched as she disappeared into the elevator. I rubbed a hand down my face and sat back in the director's chair. *Moron.* I'd been suffering silently, and it was the first thing that came to my mind. I even knew *why* she was waiting, and I still opened my big mouth.

Evan groaned and wandered over to me, pushing a hand through his hair. "Dude. Chicks are crazy."

Tell me about it. "But we're crazy about them."

He nodded. "Let's grab a drink. It'll give them time to cool off."

We wandered toward the bar and the bartender served us some drinks. We were predictable; we didn't have to order. He just gave us our usual.

Evan slumped onto the stool. "What am I going to do? I was just talking about asking her to marry me. I don't understand her."

I had nothing. No advice. Evan was my go-to for advice, and if he was at a loss, I was even more so. "What did your whiteboard say, anyway?"

"Some bull about kids." He threw back his drink and slammed the cup down on the bar. The bartender refilled it, and he tossed back a second and a third in quick succession. "Can I stay in your room tonight?"

"Um. Sure." Dylan would probably stay with Jenny, anyway.

He shot back another glass. "Thanks, man."

I left him sitting there and headed for my room. As I passed Jenny and Evan's room, I heard the distinct sound of shouting. *Should I? Yeah.* I paused and listened at the door.

"...so sick of the same argument!"

It was Jenny's voice. I already felt guilty enough for listening to that much. I continued down the hall to my own room.

The bed looked warm and inviting, and I flopped down on it face-first. *What a day.*

Twenty-Three - Dylan

Jenny said she didn't want to see Evan, and that she didn't want to be alone. I didn't know if she'd completely missed my moment with Aiden, or if she was just so absorbed in her own problems that she forgot to ask about mine. My stomach was in knots, but I listened to Jenny rant until she'd worn herself out and fallen asleep.

Aiden had tried to backtrack, but there was always some truth in jokes. He knew why I was waiting. Knew it was important to me. I was an idiot to ever think a relationship with Aiden Miller would work. How had I gotten so deep?

My stomach growled, and I sat at the edge of Jenny's bed, then shook her awake. "I'm going to go get some dinner. Are you hungry?"

She cracked an eye open. "I'm fine."

Down on the Lido deck, I wandered the restaurants that lined the perimeter of the dining room, settling for Mongolian BBQ. I filled my plate with veggies, noodles, and shrimp.

Sheena and Jorge hopped into line behind me. *Ugh. The ex.*

She gave me a sugar sweet smile. "Where's Ace?"

My gut twisted. It really bothered me she had a nickname for him, that their relationship had been to the point where they'd given nicknames. Granted, Aiden had given me several, but they were like being in the dressing room with Fabian and Jenny; they were cute but didn't quite fit.

"He and Evan are having a guy's night." I grabbed my tray and retreated to a table alone in the dining room.

A few minutes later, Sheena sauntered over and slid into the booth across from me. "Thought I'd keep you company. You shouldn't be alone on a couple's cruise." The words themselves were sweet, but the look on her face, the slight upturn of her lips, the glint in her eye, she was up to no good. I scanned the dining room for Jorge, and found him sitting at the bar on the far end.

"I don't mind." I kept my tone light and my smile plastered to my face.

She tsked. "Girl, I know how Aiden is. A guy's night could last all night. You'll want some company. One time he went out for a guy's night and came home the next morning smelling of perfume and hungover." She tried to make her face look hurt, but the amount of botox, or whatever, made her attempts almost comical.

But her words weren't. "Do you think he cheated on you?"

She hesitated. "I don't think so. We were so in love, he wouldn't have cheated."

And my appetite was gone. After the remark about intimacy, hearing he may have cheated on Sheena was the last thing I needed. *If I wasn't giving it to him, would he go to someone who would?*

"He's a good guy, though. I'm sure you have nothing to worry about." She took a bite of her food and Jorge came to join us.

"I better go check on Jenny." I stood and left her and Jorge to their dinner.

When I got back to the room, Jenny was still asleep.

A few minutes later, I called room service and had them bring me an extra blanket and pillows, then made myself comfortable on the lounge thing.

~

Jenny and I hung out all day Tuesday, watching TV and eating junk food. Pointedly not talking about the men in our lives. Which meant I spent the whole day with my eyes on the TV, but my mind on Aiden.

I understood what prompted the comment. It was easy for me to wait; I didn't know what I was missing. But he knew, and he had *seemed* to be okay with it. He even said he admired me for it. *Apparently, not.* Because on national television, he said we disagreed about intimacy.

Was I overthinking it? Over analyzing it? Probably. But I couldn't help the hurt that one word had brought. And what was worse? He wouldn't elaborate. Like, we disagreed about how intimate we should be, but did that mean he had to tell the world about it?

Sheena's words about Aiden smelling of perfume flooded my mind, and I pictured him at one of the dance clubs, enjoying the company of someone else.

Wednesday morning, we waited until the guys had passed our door on their way down to breakfast, and I went to my room to shower and get ready.

When I caught the first glimpse of Aiden's face, my heart ached. *How was it possible to miss someone and be mad at them at the same time?*

"Get that look off your face, Dylan. You need the money," Jenny murmured.

I forced myself to smile as I approached him. "Hey." I did a finger-wave and avoided really looking at him. Scanning the set, I noticed several cameras on us. *Crap on a cracker!*

"I missed you." Aiden put an arm around my waist and planted a kiss in my hair. "I'm really sorry about what I said."

"It's fine." My smile felt forced, and when he held my hand, I didn't pull away.

Jenny and Evan hugged and spoke in low tones, then linked their arms together.

Trisha's amused look should have been the first indication that this week's challenge wasn't going to be easy. "Welcome! We'll meet out on the beach for the intro today. You'll want to wear tennis shoes. So if you don't have them on, you've got ten minutes to get them before the ferry leaves."

She wound her hand in a circle, dismissing us. Of course, I had on my tennis shoes. They were my go-to these days. The four of us headed down to the ferry. We were the first ones on, with Barbie and Jake right behind us. A few minutes before the ferry left, Sheena and Jorge, and Laura Gilchrest and her fiancé, Christian, got on. We were all given mics, and the boat took us to the beach.

"Welcome back to this episode of *Couple's Cruise—Celebrity Edition*. We've tested our couples, but we've never challenged them with something like this." Trisha grinned and paused while the opening montage ran.

"We have the obstacle course to beat all obstacle courses today. Whose relationships will survive? We'll find out. Stay tuned."

Trisha's perky, singsong voice was grating on my nerves.

Why did she always have to sound so gleeful when she was announcing something she knew people wouldn't like?

The group was ushered to a waiting bus where we were all shoved on and taken inland to a lake.

There were huge foam pillars sticking out of the water in the shape of a circle. A giant pillar in the middle held what I could only assume was a huge freaking *sweeper arm!* I bounced in my seat, my hand squeezing the crap out of Aiden's. There were other colorful foam obstacles sticking out of the water, and I might have made a high-pitched squeaking noise. *Okay, I definitely did. Oh my gosh, I was so excited.* I caught myself and released Aiden's hand, shooting him a quick glance. I wasn't one to hold a grudge, but every time I tried to forgive and forget, I thought about that word written on the whiteboard.

I released a breath and scanned the bus. Jenny was pale and had her eyes closed. Her chest rose and fell with her exaggerated breaths. *Uh oh.* She was gonna puke.

Aiden leaned into me and whispered, "It's been too long since I've seen you this excited."

I forced a smile. I had a feeling I'd be really good at forcing smiles by the end of this.

We got off the bus, and Trisha explained the first obstacle. It was a race with multiple rounds. Each round would have one winner, and the first couple to get both of their players to the final platform and press the buzzer won an advantage.

Trisha took entirely too much joy in announcing the obstacle, which was a legitimate obstacle course.

They helped us into helmets and lifejackets, then put us on an adult-sized merry-go-round.

The sadistic look on Trisha's face would have sent me screaming if I hadn't been so excited. She counted down, then pressed a giant red button.

We spun in circles until I couldn't think straight. The spinning stopped abruptly, and I lurched sideways.

The group stumbled like a group of drunken monkeys to a teetering platform where we had to leap a three-foot gap and land on a log roll. My vision was starting to focus, and Aiden and I leapt at the same time, landing face down and teetering on the top of the platform. *Holy Moses.* I slid on my stomach to the center, then stood up, ready to launch myself to the next obstacle.

As the platform leaned forward, I jumped, stomach-first, onto the log-roll. *Oof. I didn't really need to breathe, anyway.* The log rolled, and I reached up to grab the handle, hefting myself up. Aiden was right behind me.

From there, I frog-hopped across some forty-five-degree platforms that were spaced in a zig-zag and placed about six feet apart, and onto a giant foam triangle. Two ropes went up and over the top. I grabbed a rope and hauled myself up and over the triangle. The last obstacle was a rope swing over the water to a bubble-covered platform with a four-foot pole in the center. The final buzzer was on top of it.

I panted, and glanced over my shoulder at the other contestants. Aiden was in the water, swimming back to the starting line. As soon as I hit the buzzer, this round would be over, and they'd start again.

I shook out my hands and grabbed the rope, then swung myself over the gap and landed on the platform. My legs slipped out from under me and I landed hard on my back as my body skidded across the platform. Reaching out a hand, I managed to grab the pole with the final buzzer, and hauled myself up to my knees. With a victorious grin, I slammed my hand on the buzzer. A bell rang, alerting the rest of the contestants that someone had finished.

Aiden cheered from one of the platforms. "Cannonball!" He launched himself into the air and curled into a ball, making a huge splash. He came up, shaking his hair from his face like a dog.

Jenny sat on the grass, her head between her knees. Her lifejacket was stripped, and her helmet sat beside her. I jumped off the final platform and swam to her.

Evan and Aiden were already on the giant merry-go-round, ready for the second round.

"What's going on, Jen?" I plopped down beside her on the ground.

Desiree brought me a towel and disappeared back into the group of spectators.

"I'm not feeling well, is all. I can't do this stupid challenge with my stomach. I'll hurl everywhere." She lay back and stared up at the sky.

"Where are we, anyway?" I laid beside her.

The buzzer rang, signalling the next round, and I popped up to watch Aiden.

"Heck, if I know. We're over half-way through the cruise now." Her words came out slow between breaths.

"Why is Evan even trying to win? Both people in the couple need to cross the finish line." I cringed as Jorge leapt to the log roll and slid off before he could get his hand up.

She huffed. "He can't deal with me when I'm 'like this'." Jenny made her voice low, imitating Evan's baritone.

I jerked my gaze to her. "Like what? Sick?" *What kind of garbage boyfriend didn't want to deal with his significant other because she was sick?*

"Emotional. Crazy." She looked out at the obstacle course. Her eyes were red-rimmed and tears trailed down her cheeks.

"Oh, Jenny." My heart ached for Jenny. I wrapped my arms around her, and her shoulders shook as she whimpered into my chest. "What are you going to do?"

Her voice cracked. "Break up with him." A sob accompanied the decision, and her arms wrapped around me. "It hurts so much."

They really were such a good match. I couldn't believe she'd just throw it away. I opened my mouth to say something, then snapped it closed. I rubbed circles on her back and shushed her. "We'll get through it, together."

She nodded against me. "Love you, Dyl."

"Love you too, Jen."

Twenty-Four - Aiden

I lost the second round. Freaking Jake Donahue and his darned Trojan's training. *Just have to beat Barbie now. How hard could it be?*

By the third round, I felt like I was failing a sobriety test. I couldn't have said the alphabet forward, let alone backward. This didn't seem like such a good idea, having celebrities do this, especially the athletes. The Trojans would probably freak out if their star quarterback was injured in a stupid reality TV show. *One of us could fall and knock ourselves out. Drowned in the lake, injure ourselves.*

Barbie and Jorge were both on my heels throughout the entire race. As I scaled the final obstacle and grabbed the rope to swing to the last platform, Jorge was beside me and Barbie right behind.

I swung onto the platform a split second before Jorge, and I skated ungracefully toward the final buzzer.

Jorge shot onto the platform like a bullet. He held his arms wide and managed to take my legs out from under me before he slammed into the pole with the final buzzer.

I scrambled to grab something to keep me on the platform, but I slid into the water just as Barbie pushed the buzzer.

When I surfaced, Barbie called, "Medic!"

An hour later, Jorge had been taken to the hospital; they suspected a broken rib.

The sweeper obstacle had been prepared. Basically, there were eight twenty-four-inch platforms set up in the shape of a giant clock. The sweeper arm, a huge foam pole positioned horizontally, acted as the second hand

and swept in a circle around knee-height while the contestants leapt over it. Contestants were tied together like we were doing a three-legged race and stood on our platforms. Since Barbie and Jake won, they were given a thirty-six-inch platform instead. I looped an arm around Dylan's waist.

Trisha used a megaphone to announce the next torture device. "The sweeper arm will spin in a circle, going a little faster and a little higher each pass. When the sweeper arm knocks you off your platform, you're out."

Barbie and Jake cheered, both amped up and bouncing on their toes. "Let's go!" Jake screamed.

A buzzer sounded, and the sweeper arm started its rotation.

With Jenny and Evan sitting out, and Jorge injured, there were only three couples left.

As the sweeper arm made its way to us, we jumped, not quite in sync, but we remained on our platform.

"Next round, put your free foot up first, then we'll jump with the tied foot at the same time." I glanced at Dylan, and she nodded.

The sweeper arm made its next loop, and we jumped, clearing it easily. From our vantage on the platform we could see the other couples, and they both cleared it without issue.

Dylan grinned, her eyes never leaving the sweeper arm. "This is fun."

Once again the arm came around, and we cleared it. Laura and Christian had no such luck. Their timing was off, and as the name indicated, the sweeper arm swept them off their platform and dumped them into the drink.

"We got this, kangaroo." *Still not quite right.* I had to find a nickname that really worked for her, and as of yet, I had nothing.

Her laughter distracted me as the sweeper arm came to us again. We jumped, our back legs catching, but we were able to stay up.

"Don't fall!" Jake shouted, cupping his hands over his mouth.

Arrogant bastard. I hope he choked, but not so much that he injured himself. I liked the Trojans.

"My heart feels like it's going to pound out of my chest." Dylan grinned and tightened her hold around my waist.

"Mine, too."

The sweeper arm came around, slightly higher than my knee. How was Barbie clearing it? Darn dancer's agility.

The next jump, I literally picked Dylan up and put her over the arm, but my back leg got caught, and we were ripped from the platform.

We dunked into the water, and I un-velcroed the straps around our legs, then pushed to the surface. Dylan was treading water, and I ached to reach out and hold her. She'd avoided me yesterday, and had been really distant today. The pole for the platform we'd been on was in arm's-reach, so I grabbed it, then turned to her.

"Dylan. I messed up."

She looked at me, *really* looked at me for the first time all day. Her lips were drawn into a frown, and she raised her eyebrows.

"I couldn't think of anythin' we really disagree on. Things with you have felt so right. I just panicked." *It was the truth.* I reached toward her, and she clenched her jaw, but grabbed my hand.

I pulled her to me and held her up.

"When you were with Sheena..." Her voice trailed off.

I looked at her. "What? When I was with Sheena, what?" What had she heard? What was she going to accuse me of? Had Sheena said something?

"Nevermind. I don't want to know." She shook her head and swam toward shore, leaving me to stare after her.

I cursed Sheena. It wasn't enough that she crushed my heart, she had to continue to torment me by sabotaging my relationship? I clenched my teeth so hard my jaw ached.

Back on shore, we gathered for Trisha's final remarks. She spoke to the camera, while we stood in a crowd behind her like fans trying to get their fifteen minutes of fame. Dylan stood by me, but avoided my touch.

It didn't sit right. A lot of things weren't sitting right, suddenly.

Dylan sat by Jenny on the bus, and Evan slumped beside me. "Shouldn't you be sittin' by your girlfriend?" I asked.

He glared at me.

Alright, never mind. I held up my hands in surrender.

145

It felt odd that song lyrics started scrolling through my head. Like they shouldn't be, cause I was pissed. It wasn't a song I'd been working on thus far. I turned to our producer. "Desiree? You have a pen and paper?"

She shuffled around for a minute and handed me what I'd requested. I should've brought my notebook, but didn't want to risk losing it, or getting it wet.

I jotted down the lyrics. An angry song. It was perfect.

That night, Evan slept in our room again, and Dylan disappeared to Jenny's. How the heck had this become our norm? It had been three nights in a row, and I was darn near sick and tired of it. I just needed her back in our room. Needed to talk to her somewhere out of the camera's line of sight. Every time I'd started trying to apologize, she'd left me staring after her. In our room, she'd have to listen. Have to forgive me for being an idiot. *If Jenny and Evan went home tomorrow, I wouldn't miss them.*

Twenty-Five - Dylan

My stomach was tied in knots. Double looped, criss-crossed, and an all over colossal mess. Eliminations were an hour away.

This morning, I'd finally convinced Jenny to go to the doctor, and she'd come back with a diagnosis of food poisoning. They'd given her IV fluids and told her to get plenty of rest.

When she got back, we'd spent the afternoon watching chick flicks, then put minimal effort into getting ready. I just needed to sneak back to my room for a dress and probably take Evan some clothes in the process.

"Hey Jen? I'm gonna run to my room real quick, okay?"

She whined from the bathroom, and I snuck into their closet.

So much black. His closet looked like it belonged to the Addams Family.

I grabbed a pair of black slacks, a black button-up, a black belt, and black socks. I completed the ensemble with a black tie and boxer briefs. *Land sakes.* Black seemed appropriate though; mourning the death of their relationship.

"Be back in a jiff." I snuck out the door and down the hall.

When I entered our room, Aiden sat on the bed, wearing a tailored blue suit with a purple dress shirt. He bent over, tying his brown dress shoes. Seeing him caused a physical ache in my chest. I hated how things were between us. Hated that I couldn't get over my hurt.

Evan was on the lounger, looking as if he hadn't showered in a week. Though I had seen him yesterday, so I knew that wasn't true.

"You doing okay, Evan?" I asked.

He ran a hand through the train-wreck he called hair. "Peachy."

I held up the clothes in my hand. "I brought your clothes. Maybe you want to take a shower or something? Get ready? Eliminations are in like thirty minutes."

His gaze wandered to me, took in the bathrobe, then went back to the TV. "This Forged in Fire show is cool."

"C'mon man. Get ready. You have to go or the show'll sue you for breach of contract or somethin'." Aiden toed him with his dress shoe.

Evan swatted at him, and it occurred to me, he was drunk. *This wasn't going to end well.*

I had an idea. Mom had done this to my uncle once. I just hoped like heck that Evan didn't react like my uncle had. I marched into the bathroom and grabbed the ice bucket, filled it with cold water, then dumped it over Evan's head.

He spluttered, waving his hands in the air as if he could slap the water away.

"Shower, get dressed, then march your butt down there and do it graciously. Don't let your fans see you like this. It'd be terrible for your image." I dropped the bucket onto his lap and spun on my heel, making a beeline for the closet.

A slow clap started, and I turned around. Aiden had a grin on his face as he applauded. "Bravo, I haven't seen someone talk to him like that since his mother."

I glanced at Aiden, then away. It was too painful. "I channelled my inner mom."

Evan said a few choice words as he made his way to the bathroom, but he was moving, and I called that a win.

In the closet, I found the purple satin gown that would go perfectly with Aiden's shirt. I slid it over my head and adjusted it until it draped over my body like it was supposed to, stared at myself in the mirror for a few minutes. If we made it through this week, I'd have fifteen-thousand dollars.

Everything felt so out of control. The sale of Dad's truck, my relationship with Aiden, Jenny and Evan, the entire cruise. I pressed a hand to my stomach and took a deep breath, stopping when the ache in my heart became too intense.

There was a knock on the closet door.

"Come in."

Aiden cracked it open and froze. "Wow. You look beautiful."

Our gazes met, and those darned butterflies started flapping; they hadn't gotten the memo about him yet. "Thanks."

He came in and stopped a foot away. "Is it bad that I hope Evan goes home tonight so I can have you in our room to myself?"

The butterflies flitted faster, and my cheeks heated at his implication. I studied the buttons on his suit, avoiding eye contact.

"Dylan." His hand came up, and his fingertips brushed my cheek. "I can't keep doin' this."

My stomach lurched, and I nodded. I could kiss Dad's truck goodbye. Aiden was breaking up with me. A tear trailed down my cheek, and I dashed it away. I'd never see him again. Never get to play with the hair on the back of his neck. Never get to kiss those lips. As the list continued, I had a revelation. I was more sad about losing Aiden than I was about losing the truck. *Don't get me wrong, I'd be torn up about the truck.* But I was falling for Aiden.

"My mom says that when you're going into a relationship, keep your eyes wide open." I chanced a glance up at him, and he froze.

His posture stiffened, and his brow wrinkled in confusion.

"But when you're in a relationship, she says keep them half shut."

Aiden squinted at me. "So, I guess the question is, are we goin' into a relationship? Or are we already in one?"

I stepped closer, closing the distance between us. My hand reached up, and I traced my thumb along his jaw. I inhaled the scent that was distinctly him. It invaded my senses, reminding me of the good times we'd shared. His hands lightly rested on my hips and he pulled me closer.

Aiden's head tilted toward me, and our lips met. My eyes fluttered closed, and I draped my arms over his shoulders.

He broke the kiss and pressed our foreheads together. "Dylan. I respect you. I will never force or pressure you into doing more than you are comfortable with. I will wait for you as long as it takes." He brushed another stray tear from my cheek, and kissed my forehead.

My breath hitched. He softly cupped the back of my head and brought our lips together again, washing away the hurt I'd been holding onto.

As I broke the kiss, I said, "Promise not to tell? I've been hoping they go home, too. I miss our nightly talks, and laying beside you as we watch TV and fall asleep."

"I added another bucket-list item." He pulled me flush against him and leaned down, his chest rose as he inhaled. "Mmm. I love the smell of your shampoo."

"Are you going to tell me the bucket-list item? Or let me sit in suspense all night?" I pulled back to look into his eyes. They were dark and hungry and just the sight of them set my heart into overdrive.

He leaned down and whispered against my lips. "Tonight."

A crash in the bedroom tore us apart. "I better go check on Jenny. Meet ya on stage?"

Aiden squeezed my hands. "See ya there."

Jenny was also dressed all in black. She even had a black veil that I made her take off.

"This isn't a funeral. Quit being so dramatic." I pulled the veil from her hands and held it out of reach.

She gave me "the look," brows drawn, lips pursed, laser-beam eyes. *Yikes.*

"I'm not giving it back. You can stop trying to explode my head with your mind." I raised an eyebrow.

"Sorry. I'm having a hard week."

I draped my other arm around her shoulder. "I can tell."

She checked the clock. "We better get down there."

We were gonna be late. *Desiree was probably freaking out.* I rushed into Jenny's closet and set the veil on the top shelf, then grabbed her by the arm and hauled her to the elevator.

Less than two minutes later, we emerged into the auditorium. Five white couches were set up, and everyone was sitting except us. Desiree ran over, handing Jenny and I both mics, which we quickly attached and climbed the stairs to the stage. Aiden was already sitting in one of the couches, and I joined him.

Trisha Thames was all cued up and ready to go in a dress that made her look like a peacock, royal green, blue, and yellow eyes. *And feathers. Lots and lots of feathers.*

Aiden followed my gaze to Trisha and leaned toward me. "If you're hungry later, we can kill Trisha's dress, and I'll cook it for dinner." His voice was low, and his breath tickled my neck.

My gaze locked with his, and I burst into laughter.

Trisha pointed a manicured fingernail at me. "Not again! Someone make her stop. I can't work like this."

I sat up straight and zipped my mouth with an imaginary zipper, locked it, then tossed the key over my shoulder. My eyes watered with the effort, but I had learned the trick of waterproof mascara after week one, so I blotted my tears with my fingers and tried to make myself look innocent.

Trisha marched to the front of the stage and took her position on the X. "Welcome aboard *The Callistus* and the Live Eliminations on *Couple's Cruise—Celebrity Edition.* I'm your host Trisha Thames."

The camera broke away and replayed the events of the week. Jorge had indeed broken two ribs, but wanted to stay. They gave him pain medicine, and, judging by the vacant look in his eyes, he was loving every minute of it.

"America, you have decided. Your votes have been cast, and tonight, we find out which couple leaves us, and which four couples will continue on to next week." Trisha walked as she talked and perched on the edge of our couch.

She was coming to us first. That was a good sign. They never eliminated the first couple.

Trisha continued, "Aiden and Dylan, America has spoken, and you… "—pause for effect—"are safe."

She turned her attention to Jake and Barbie beside us. "Safe."

Laura and Christian. "Safe."

Even though I knew it was coming, as she stood between Jenny and Evan; and Sheena and Jorge, I couldn't help but hope Sheena left. I crossed my fingers and leaned on the edge of my seat. *Let them stay.*

"Evan and Jenny, America has spoken." The seconds ticked by as Trisha gave the camera a compassionate look.

I squinted at Trisha, telepathically sending her Sheena and Jorge's names.

"And you'll be leaving us tonight. Which means, Sheena and Jorge, you're safe."

The light turned off above Jenny and Evan's couch.

I let my eyes drop closed and took a deep breath. The nerves bundling in my stomach had nowhere to go. My heart ached. I stood and headed straight for Jenny, tears falling unabashedly down my cheeks as I wrapped her in a hug. "Love you Jen."

"Love you too, Dyl." Her voice was rough, as if she was choking on emotion.

I held her for a few more seconds before the other contestants butted in for their turns. Waving goodbye as she left the stage felt like saying goodbye forever. It was so final.

Aiden pulled me in for a hug, his hands stroking up and down my back.

That was how it would feel when Aiden and I got booted. *Final. The end. Finished.* Jenny told me the show was notorious for destroying relationships, and here I was, opening my heart to a man I barely even knew. The show would destroy our relationship, and the man would destroy my heart.

Twenty-Six - Aiden

The floral scent of her shampoo wrapped around me the next morning. I pulled her tighter against me, keeping my eyes closed. *Didn't want to wake up yet.*

We pushed the limits last night, and I paid the price. Our activities after dinner included her accidentally kneeing me in the Rocky Mountain Oysters. Needless to say, we ended up just cuddling.

Dylan wiggled, and I released her. She rolled onto her back and stretched. "Morning." She turned to me, a soft smile on her face.

"Morning." I reached a hand and brushed my fingertips down her cheek.

She put a hand over her mouth. "I'm gonna go brush my teeth."

I rolled onto my back and chuckled as she retreated into the bathroom. I looked at the clock: 9:46. It'd been months since I'd been able to fall asleep at a normal time. Or had woken up before noon.

We spent the entire weekend in our room. I didn't want to pop our little bubble. *I'd found happiness, and I'd do anything to maintain it.*

Monday's immunity challenge came too soon.

Trisha stood in front of the group with a microphone. "Welcome to Shaw's Island. The private island boasts over a mile of white sand beaches and untamed jungle, and it's ours for our final immunity challenge."

Desiree came over and handed us two backpacks, and a piece of parchment with a list of ten items written on it. Some had pictures beside them, others were just words. Five pink seashells, a piece of sea glass, a palm frond, a hibiscus flower, and more.

"Each couple will have their own camera and will be filming their own scavenger hunt." Trisha glanced at her watch. "You'll want to wear tennis shoes, so if you're not prepared, we'll give you twenty minutes to change and meet down at the gangplank."

Dylan and I rushed back to our room. She was already wearing tennis shoes, so while I changed, she dumped the contents of the backpacks on the bed. "Water, granola bars, sandwiches, rope, snorkeling masks, chips, a knife, waterproof flashlight, an umbrella, an empty plastic jar, and a poncho." She started repacking the bags. "The second bag is empty, probably for us to put all of our scavenger hunt items in."

"Divide the food and water, in case we get separated." *Not that I planned to let that happen.*

Dylan glanced up at me and searched my face for a second. "Alright." She shuffled things around and a few minutes later, handed me a backpack.

I slung it over my shoulder and took her hand in mine. "We need to stay together, if possible. Work quick and hopefully, we'll be done first."

"Yes, captain." She saluted me, and a smile tugged at the corners of my mouth. *I was falling. Hard.*

We boarded the ferry right behind Sheena and Jorge.

Carlos gave me a hand-held camera. "This button records. You can flip this screen around like this." He flipped open the screen and spun it around, then clipped it back into the device. "Just make sure you're getting good footage. When you find something, back up, turn on the camera, and pretend you're finding it for the first time. You don't need to let it run the entire time if you don't want to. Try to alternate between the cameraman, so we can see you each finding items."

"You got it." I stuck a hand out and shook his.

He gave me a wide grin. "I hope you two win."

Laura and Christian came a minute later. Then Barbie and Jake shuffled on last. As we were taken to the island, they were each given cameras and similar instructions.

We hit the beach, and there was a small podium set up.

Trisha took her position in front of the camera. "Contestants, you have two hours. If you aren't back in the allotted time, you won't be eligible for the reward. The couple with the most items on their list will be awarded immunity." She held up a stopwatch. "Ready?" Her eyes searched the crowd. "Go!"

People rushed in every direction.

We pulled out our list again and went down it, trying to figure out what to get first.

Five pink seashells

A piece of sea glass

A palm frond

A hibiscus flower

A lava rock

A minnow

A piece of driftwood

A coconut

A piece of litter

A sand dollar

I'd been to the beach hundreds of times and never found a sand dollar. It was gonna be interesting.

Dylan grabbed my hand. "Let's get as much on the beach as we can before we go deeper on the island."

Smart. "Okay."

We scanned the beach, and I manned the camera.

"Over here! I found a piece of driftwood." Dylan ran toward a small piece of wood, and I captured it with the camera. She held it up to me, a bright smile on her face, then pulled her backpack forward, hanging it on one shoulder and putting the wood in it.

My chest was light watching her, like nothing bad could happen when I was with her.

"What's next?" She pulled the parchment from her back pocket and read it. "Pink seashells?" Her face scrunched in a cute little scowl. "Or a sand dollar, a piece of sea glass, or a minnow." Dylan dropped onto her butt in the sand and pulled her shoes off, stuffed the socks inside and set them aside, then put the parchment in the pocket of the backpack and pulled out the plastic jar.

I laughed and stepped farther from the surf. "What are you doing?"

"We need seashells and sand dollars and a minnow." She grinned at me and dipped a toe in the water. The surf washed over her feet, and she squealed and ran back. "I didn't expect it to come up that high." Her words came out between a laugh.

"Go catch me a minnow." I kept the camera aimed at her as she splashed around in the water.

She launched an armful of water at me. And just like that, the game was on.

I stripped my backpack and set the camera on top of it; all the while she screamed for mercy. She waded in up to her waist, probably hoping I wouldn't want to get that wet. *She was wrong.* The water was warmer than I expected, and I dove in and swam to her.

"Stop!" She held up her hands, palms out.

"You wrote a check you can't cash." I scooped her up into my arms and dunked us both under the water.

Dylan came up sputtering and wrapped her arms around my neck, her legs around my waist. "No more." She laughed, and I dunked us again.

She released me and pushed away, swimming out of my reach.

I came up for air, and she disappeared under the clear water, her body gliding beneath the surface right toward me. Dylan grabbed my legs and yanked. I lost my balance and toppled into the water. I grabbed her by the waist and pulled us both to the surface.

Our bodies pressed together, and our breaths mingled between us. Her arms wrapped around my neck. She was suddenly serious, and my body reacted immediately.

I wrapped my arms around her, savoring the feel of her body against mine. "We should be doing the scavenger hunt, little otter." My lips brushed her jaw as I spoke.

"What's keeping you?" She tangled her fingers in the back of my hair. Her jaw was close, and I leaned forward and nipped it.

"You're keeping me." I growled and untangled her arms from around my neck.

We waded in the shallows, collecting the seashells and the sea glass. Dylan even managed to find a partial sand dollar, but we weren't sure if it would count.

We'd tried to catch a minnow in the little plastic jar they'd provided, but the little fish never got close enough.

As we emerged, our feet were covered in sand. "How are we gonna get our socks and shoes on now?" I tried unsuccessfully to brush the sand from my wet feet.

She picked up her shoes and stuffed them in the backpack. "We'll just have to let them dry, then brush the sand off."

An hour later, our feet were dry, and we'd also found a hibiscus flower, a coconut, a piece of litter, and a palm frond. We put our shoes on and hiked a trail that led inland.

After twenty minutes, we came out the other side on top of an outcropping of rocks overlooking the sea.

"Look!" Dylan gasped, picked up a lava rock, and spun, showing me and the camera the small piece. She placed it in the backpack, and I held the camera on her as she took in the scenery from this side of the island. Her wide-eyed wonder never ceased to get my heart going.

We picked our way through the rocks to the edge of a cliff overlooking the sea.

"Help!" a raspy voice called from below.

Twenty-Seven - Dylan

Aiden edged toward the drop of the cliff and cupped his hands around his mouth. "Sheena?"

Ugh, why couldn't it be someone less gorgeous and less connected to Aiden.

"Ace?" Her voice was barely audible over the roar of the ocean. "I'm down at the beach!"

He turned back toward the jungle. "We're coming!"

My heart started pounding, and I said a silent prayer that she wasn't hurt. "Where's Jorge? Why is she alone?" My voice edged on irritation. "Why would he leave her?"

"We'll figure it out later. Right now, we need to focus on finding her and getting her to safety."

I knew he was right, but his concern for her had me second-guessing everything. Did he still have feelings for her?

Speed made us sloppy, and we picked our way down the rocks to the sand below. By the time we hit the bottom, my legs and arms were covered in scratches and mud.

We rounded the outcropping and finally laid eyes on our damsel in distress.

"Ace?" Sheena's voice was laced with pain. She was just out of the water's reach, wearing a tiny white bikini and nothing else. *Where the heck were her clothes?*

Aiden rushed to her and dropped by her side. Her foot was the size of a football. *Okay, that was an exaggeration, but it was pretty swollen.*

"My foot was stung by a jellyfish." She clutched her calf like she could keep the pain from spreading if she applied enough pressure. "Jorge saw something about peeing on it, but that just made it worse."

Bile worked its way up my throat, and I exchanged a horrified look with Aiden. *What moron peed on a jellyfish sting?* I pulled my backpack off and poured the rest of my water bottle on her foot to clean it.

On the top of Sheena's foot were three wavy lines with welts that reminded me of leopard print. I glanced around the area. She didn't have food or drink or her bag. *Or clothes.* "Where's Jorge?"

She shrugged. "He went for help. With his broken ribs, he's really slow and can't carry me. And I can't put any weight on it."

"How long ago was that?" *And why hadn't the moron left her food and water?* Another shrug. "A half hour? Maybe longer."

I peeled my tank top off and gave it to Sheena. I had my swimming suit on.

She pulled it over her head and put her arms through the sleeves. It looked like a minidress on her.

"Alright Sheena, I'm going to carry you, and we'll get you back to the ship for medical attention." Aiden scooped her up like a baby and she clung to his chest, her arms slithering around his neck.

A little green monster perched on my shoulder. *Did she have to plaster herself to him like that?*

Sheena met my gaze, a grimace on her face. "Sorry, Dylan. It's probably weird to see your boyfriend carrying a beautiful woman." Her words were a slap in the face.

And a little too close to what I was already thinking.

I glanced at Aiden. His jaw worked, but he didn't deny her words.

He wouldn't even look at me. "Let's just get you back to the ship, Sheena."

I snatched his backpack from the ground where he'd dropped it and shoved its contents into my own bag, then jerked the zipper closed. A lump formed in my throat and the back of my eyes stung. I took the lead, so I didn't have to see the two of them.

"You know why I call him Ace?" Sheena called over the rush of the waves.

"I don't care." *Liar.* I cared, and I really wanted to know, but I'd rather hear it from him.

Sheena made a whimpering sound, and I glanced over my shoulder in time to see Aiden jerk his gaze to her, his eyes scanning her body for additional injury.

My stomach twisted. He wasn't over her, and here I was like an idiot, permanently branding myself with a reminder of this man. *I was going to be on one of those terrible tattoo shows.*

She shot me a smirk, then began humming as if she didn't have a care in the world. After a minute, the tune registered. It was his very first hit. The song that started it all. *Love, Always.*

Each note was like a dagger to my heart.

What kind of idiot was I? I knew, *knew* from the get-go not to trust him, not to get too close. *Why didn't I listen? Why didn't I just get kicked off the first week, collect my ten grand and hit the road?* He was still in love with her.

"Stop, Sheena." Aiden's words were hissed, likely just for her, and carried to me by the breeze.

I stopped walking. "Go ahead. I need to pee." *Brilliant, brain. Give Sheena more ammunition.*

As they passed, Sheena locked gazes with me over Aiden's shoulder and batted her eyes. "It's our song. You wrote it for me."

How many girls had Aiden written songs for? *The dumb tattoo on my wrist. Was I just a number? Just one in a crowd.* A traitorous tear dripped down my cheek, and I wiped it away and glared at Sheena.

"Where's Jorge?" I didn't mean for the words to sound so clipped and petty. But I wanted to remind her that she had a boyfriend of her own. *And to get her hands off of mine.*

Off in the distance, a horn sounded, marking the end of the challenge.

Twenty-Eight - Aiden

I stopped for a second to rest, setting Sheena on a rock.

Dylan marched past. "I'll go see if they can make an exception, since we had to rescue Sheena."

"Wait. We'll just go in toge—"

"It's fine." She kept going until she disappeared around some trees.

Sheena scooted closer and put a hand on my shoulder. "Let her go. She needs to cool off."

"You were needlin' her. What's wrong with you? Can't you leave well enough alone?" I pulled her hand off my shoulder and dropped it on her lap.

"She wanted immunity." Sheena pointed in the direction Dylan went, her voice defensive. "This had nothing to do with me and everything to do with your girlfriend. What does she stand to gain if you guys are here another week? More exposure?"

I debated throwing her over my shoulder like a sack of potatoes. "Dylan isn't like you, Sheena. She's different." I was proud of myself for keeping my tone so neutral.

Sheena gave me a pretty pout, one that used to get her anything she wanted when we were dating. "Dylan's tall." She fingered the hem of Dylan's shirt. "I thought you liked your girls pocket-sized?"

"Stop comparing yourself to her, Sheena. I already told you, she's nothing like you." I resisted the urge to shake her.

Her laugh made my hair stand on end. "Wake up, Aiden. That girl is exactly like me. You think she's different? She's just a better actress. You don't have a voice like that and *not* want to be recognized for it."

We sat in silence for a few minutes, and I pondered her words. I'd asked Dylan about singing, and she said the timing wasn't right. Was the timing right now?

"I miss you." Her fingers scorched a trail down back. She threaded her arm in mine and put her chin on my shoulder. "I wasn't lying before, Aiden. I regret what I did to you. Fame is fun and all. But it's hollow without you by my side."

I pulled my arm free and closed my eyes. "Sheena, maybe five years ago, I would've wanted to hear those words. But it's too late, now."

I felt her shift beside me, then her body was on mine. She put her hands on my shoulders and pushed me until my back hit the tree. Her mouth was on mine before I'd even had a chance to process. Her hands sank into my hair, tugging and pulling me closer.

But it was wrong. I broke the kiss and turned my head to the side. "Sheena. Don't do this. You're better than this." *We both were.*

She perched on my lap, and guilt overwhelmed me. I stood, pushing her onto her butt in the dirt. I paced back and forth while running my fingers through my hair.

She whimpered and held her foot, but I ignored her. She'd brought the pain on herself.

What happened? How was I going to tell Dylan? Would she believe that it was just an innocent kiss?

Sheena's laugh broke me out of my thoughts. She shook her head. "You're so gullible."

I froze.

"You thought that was real?"

I could tell by the hurt in her eyes that her pride was wounded, but I didn't press it.

"I was acting. Just like your precious Dylan." A stray tear broke free, and she dashed it away. A second later, she seemed to compose herself, and whispered, "You know why I call you Ace?"

I shrugged. "Because we were each other's first."

She shook her head. "Because you were the ace up my sleeve. My ticket

162

to fame. You're hers, too."

The words echoed in my mind. *The ace up her sleeve. Her ticket. Was she right? Was Dylan using me?*

Sheena was poison, trying to seep into my veins. "Ever heard the phrase, too good to be true?"

I left her sitting on the dirt and jogged down the trail. But hadn't I thought those same words about Dylan? She was too good to be true. She herself had admitted that she wasn't real. She'd tried to tell me, and I'd ignored it.

A medical crew met me part-way, and I pointed down the path toward Sheena. "She's about five minutes back."

I searched the crowd, but Dylan was nowhere to be seen. As I exited the treeline onto the beach, I saw Jorge on a stretcher under an awning with a drink in his hand.

Producers rushed about, setting up chairs and getting everyone into their places. Trisha stood, perfectly done up, waiting for the mess to start. The cast filed in, and after I sat in the director's chair, Dylan came to sit beside me.

Guilt over the kiss twisted my gut, and I reached out a hand and grabbed Dylan's. We needed to have a serious talk.

Trisha took her position in front of the camera. "The time has expired, and we've had a very eventful day here on *Couple's Cruise.*" She paused and waited until they signaled for her to start again. "And now, it's time to reveal who won this week's immunity challenge."

Both of our teams were disqualified. It didn't matter that we were rescuing a lost cast member. We missed the time limit.

Laura and Christian, and Jake and Barbie sat in the producer's chairs closest to Trisha, and she walked over and stood between them.

"These two teams made it back on time. Now let's see who got the most from the list."

She led them to a table where their backpacks were set up. One by one she had them pull items out until Barbie reached her hand in and it came back out empty, while Laura produced a smashed flower.

Laura and Christian hugged each other and cheered, while Jake and Barbie

163

high-fived.

We all applauded politely, and I studied Dylan from the corner of my eye. She smiled, but it looked forced.

"Join us next time on *Couple's Cruise*, where our couples will face the ultimate test in patience and endurance. Until next time, America." Trisha gave her signature smile, and the director called cut.

Dylan stood and stalked to the ferry. She didn't sit by me, instead she stayed curled against the wall of the boat, her tall frame looking small and vulnerable.

What had I gotten myself into? Was she really like Sheena, using me for fame? Was it all just an act? Telling Dylan about the kiss would only make things worse.

Scenes from the past replayed in my mind. Sheena curled up next to me, seeming for all the world as if I was the only person in her life. I replaced Sheena with Dylan, and my gut twisted. *I was an idiot. A complete and total moron. I'd ignored the obvious.*

Carlos told us on the boat trip to the island to alternate between which of us found items, but Dylan had been content to let me man the camera the entire time. Hadn't even offered to take it from me. It didn't matter that I wouldn't have given it to her, being too content to watch her through the screen. She was hogging, *no*, basking in the spotlight.

When had it happened? When had I tipped over the precipice from like to infatuation? Because that's what it was, infatuation. Not love. I wasn't falling; I was being fooled. She hooked me with her innocent act, then reeled me in. All the while, me, a willing participant. I'd be nothing more than a trophy on her wall, a shell of my former self.

I wouldn't let that happen.

Back in our room, she jumped in the shower and came out ten minutes later. She slipped into the closet and came out wearing a pair of shorts and a cute blouse.

My chest ached.

"I'm gonna go eat in the dining room. I need some time to think." Dylan slipped her feet into her flip-flops.

"Fine." *Because I needed the same.*

After two hours, I debated going to look for her. *How dare she just leave me in here by myself. We were supposed to be a couple. It was a breach of our contract. She was supposed to pretend to be my girlfriend, and that didn't include running off in the middle of the night and not coming back.*

I had a moment of complete clarity, and my heart stuttered. *What if she was out there with one of the producers right now? What if it really was a repeat of Sheena?*

Pulling on a T-shirt, I stalked to the elevator and punched the button. She wouldn't get away with it. I'd give her a piece of my mind.

She wasn't on the Lido deck; it was virtually empty, and the dining room was a ghost town. I stopped at the Chinese restaurant. "Have you guys seen Dylan today?"

The cook nodded. "She came for dinner. I haven't seen her since."

I stormed to the back of the boat, searching the pool and hot tub. The chairs along the back were all empty, too. Where was she?

The bartender made eye contact and raised a brow.

"Have you seen Dylan?" I set my hands on the bar, palms down to keep from balling them into fists.

"Earlier. She left, though."

"Was she alone?" The words almost wouldn't come out.

He nodded. "Yeah."

Thank heavens. I followed the rail, walking along the perimeter of the boat. The sun was low in the sky, and the water on this side of the boat churned dark and ominous, like my mood.

As I neared the bow of the boat, Dylan's laughter floated to me. I narrowed my eyes and stalked the last steps to the bow, ready to unleash my fury. Rounding the corner of one of the upper decks, Dylan came into view.

She stood at the bow of the boat, alone. Her arms stretched wide and her head thrown back as the wind whipped her hair. "I'm the queen of the world!"

I stopped and just watched her, momentarily taken aback.

Dylan spun in circles, then stopped, clutching the edge of the rail.

What was she doing? Celebrating my idiocy, or was this genuinely Dylan?

The carefree girl who made me forget my worries and helped unlock the songs stuck inside of me. I couldn't be sure.

If she was just using me for my fame, she was a heckuva actress.

I slunk back into the shadows and walked back to the room. *What was I doing? She wasn't Sheena.* She'd proven it time and time again, and I let Sheena's words today get in my head. *Aiden, quit being a douche.*

As I walked back to our room, I repeated the words over and over. Dylan wasn't Sheena; she was completely different. I hadn't handed my heart to another snake in the grass.

Twenty-Nine - Dylan

I needed Jenny. She wasn't supposed to go home and leave me here to muddle through my emotions alone. *I thought I was falling for Aiden. Like, for realsies.*

But seeing Sheena in his arms, her tentacles wrapped around his neck as she hummed "their song"... *Yeah, I was having second thoughts.*

The movie scene I played out at the front of the boat helped clear my mind, but the storm didn't stay away long. A physical ache started in my chest the night Jenny left, and the feeling was still there. We'd been apart for longer than this in the past, but never when I needed her strength and advice so much.

Ace. *What the heck kind of nickname was that, anyway? It was stupid. I could come up with a better nickname for him than that. Arvin, Alvin, Alpha? Bahaha. Alpha. Why was I stuck on A? Guitaro? Oh my gosh, I sucked at this. PMS-Panty Melting Singer? Eww, did I really just come up with that? Yeah, I had nothing.*

I lounged on a deck chair until well past my usual bedtime. *Still didn't have a nickname for Aiden, and still didn't know what to do with this ugly, green monster on my shoulder.*

"This spot taken?" Aiden snuck between the loungers and pointed to the one beside me.

"Nope, have a seat." I took a deep breath to steady myself. It was going to eat me from the inside if I didn't address it.

"Talk to me." He sank down onto the seat and kicked his feet up onto the lounge, crossing his ankles.

I shook my head and rubbed my eyes. "Did you love her?" *Whoa. Yeah, guess we were starting there.*

He laughed without humor and looked up at the black sky. "You know, there was a time I thought I did."

A time? What does that mean? "And now?"

"Now." He ran a hand through his hair and turned to me. The light from the cabins behind us illuminated his face and our gazes locked. "Now, I know it wasn't real."

My voice didn't want to work, but I had to know. "The song she was humming?"

His mouth turned down, and his eyes softened. "Was written for her."

A lump formed in my throat. Some of the lyrics played in my mind. He wrote those words for Sheena.

"Sorry, I'm trying to be mature about this." A traitorous tear trailed down my cheek, and I brushed it away. "We're just two strangers, who became friends through this. I don't know why I'm making such a big deal out of it." I put my feet down on the ground between us and looked up at the sky, willing the breeze to dry my tears.

Aiden mirrored me, caging my knees with his and taking my cold hands between his warm ones. "I'm hoping it's because we're more than just strangers. More than friends. More than Sheena and I ever were." His gaze never left our hands as his thumb stroked over my knuckles.

Hope fluttered in my chest like a caged bird.

"Something real." He reached his hand up and wiped a tear from my cheek.

Our gazes collided, and I leaned forward. Our lips brushed, tentative at first. His were like a balm, soothing me, smoothing over the rough patches and washing away my fears.

He pulled me to my feet without breaking the kiss and wrapped his arms around me.

I threaded my fingers into his hair. I loved his hair, with just the slightest curl. The silky feel of it between my fingers.

Aiden broke the kiss and pulled back. He reached between us and grabbed a lock of my hair, rubbing it between his thumb and forefinger. "Sorry I didn't stand up to Sheena for you today, Dylan. I let her words get under my skin, and I began questioning everything we have."

It was news to me. "What did she say?" I didn't want to know, but I couldn't help myself.

"She told me why she calls me Ace." He searched my eyes, his thumb stroking my jaw. "I thought it was because we were each other's firsts." He shook his head, his eyes vacant.

My eyes fell closed and the pain in my chest flared. I was going to regret asking this. "Why?"

His eyes focused again. "Because I was the ace up her sleeve. Her secret weapon. She rode my coattails all the way to the top." He opened his mouth as if to say more, but snapped it closed.

"Hey." I grabbed the wrist of his hand cupping my face. "You can tell me."

"That you were using me, too. For my fame." The words were barely more than a breath.

I scoffed. *That was ridiculous.*

His lips thinned into a line, and he pulled me in for a fierce hug. "I have to tell you something else."

The tone of his voice gave me pause, and I pulled back and looked at him.

His eyes went distant, and he shook his head. "When I was out there with Sheena, after you left. She kissed me."

"Wha–"

"I didn't kiss her back. I stopped her right away. Then I left her sitting in the dirt while I went for help. But I needed you to know. I want to be one-hundred percent honest with you, Dylan."

Dread dug a pit in my stomach, and Sheena's words from our conversation in the dining room came back to me. She'd thought Aiden had cheated on her. Tears welled in my eyes and I turned away from Aiden so he couldn't see them. Was it his fault? She obviously wasn't over him. I couldn't compete with Sheena Renfro.

"Are you sure you're over her?" As much as I dreaded the answer, I had to know. I studied him, watching for any sign he wasn't being honest.

His clear gaze met mine. "I don't have feelings for her, Dylan. I got out of there as soon as I could."

She had kissed him. Not the other way around. How could I blame him for that? I inhaled to clear my mind, then said, "Let's go to bed."

We held hands on the way back to the room. I felt lighter. We had opened the lines for communication and had come out the other side stronger than before.

~

On Wednesday morning, there was a note on our door. I brought it into the room and broke the seal. "We're supposed to wear closed-toe shoes."

"Sounds like fun." Aiden ran the towel through his damp hair, and my eyes were drawn to the muscles working on his arms.

Mmm.

I was already dressed for the day, hair in a ponytail. *Cause that's what I could do without Jenny. That was a lie. I could straighten it, too, but none of the pretty waves and curls that Jenny could pull off.* I had on a blue T-shirt with a vintage rainbow, paired with denim bermuda shorts and my no-longer-white tennies.

Aiden threw on his tennis shoes, and we walked down to breakfast, ready for a day of adventure in our closed-toe shoes.

Looking around the dining room at the few of us left was weird. Four couples of the original twelve remained. *Good gravy, what a weird thought.* America liked us better than eight other couples. We were in the final four. I got an omelet and Aiden got waffles and we shared. I always wanted savory for breakfast until I saw his sweet, then suddenly, I had to have sweet too. And vice versa. He was always stealing bites of my breakfast.

The speaker crackled to life, calling everyone to the Lido deck. Three of the four couples gathered and Trisha stood on the podium, which had become a semi-permanent part of our daily lives.

"Welcome, contestants. Today we were supposed to have an activity, but due to some recent events, the plans have changed." She paused looking at each of us. "Instead, we'll be running a short recap, along with interviews from each of you. After lunch, please meet in the auditorium."

Aiden and I exchanged a look. They were breaking the schedule. Something wasn't right. The ache in my chest intensified momentarily.

It had to be Sheena and Jorge. Between them, they were completely out of commission.

"You may have noticed that Sheena and Jorge aren't here. After their injuries the past two weeks, they'll be leaving us this week. They'll both attend the elimination ceremony on Thursday to make it official. Since we have no need for a competition, we're cutting the activity. We'll see you in the auditorium at one." Trisha stepped down from the podium and walked to the three couples, all standing in a group.

She never mingled with us.

"We're saving this week's activities for next week." Her smile was sadistic.

Yup, that was why she came over. She couldn't wait to tell us that our torture was being postponed, not cancelled.

"Thanks, Trisha." Jake smirked and grabbed Barbie's hand. "We'll see you after lunch."

Aiden and I followed suit, disappearing into our room.

"So Boggle?" I raised an eyebrow.

He grinned. "Scrabble?"

"Can't stand to lose, huh?" I pulled my bottom lip into my mouth, testing my feminine wiles.

Aiden grabbed the Boggle box from our board game stack. "Fine. One game."

I leaned in and planted a feather soft kiss on his lips. "Two."

He slid his hand into my hair, cupped the back of my head, and pulled my mouth to his. "I just can't say no to you." The kiss was sweetened by the syrup from his waffles.

Game momentarily forgotten, I slid onto his lap and wrapped my arms around his neck. We had an almost moment a few nights ago, and my fumbling had been so... *ugh.* Embarrassingly bad. I nearly took out his manhood. The moment was shattered, and as embarrassing as it was, I was grateful it happened.

Truth be told, I'd already given my heart to Aiden, and if I gave him more than that, it would be real. Scary, real.

Too, real.

Thirty - Aiden

After lunch, we were split into different rooms in the auditorium. Dylan and I met Carlos and Desiree in one of the rooms with a familiar white couch.

Carlos extended his hand. "Hey, man"

"Hey, buddy." I shook his hand, and he wrapped Dylan in a hug.

"Hey, beautiful."

She laughed as he released her. "Hi, Carlos."

We sat side by side, and Desiree took a few minutes to fix Dylan's flyaways. She looked beautiful with or without the stragglers. I tried not to be bothered by the fact that Dylan wouldn't have typically cared about flyaways, but she didn't complain once as Desiree worked.

"Before we get started, I wanted to say thank you. You guys have done a really great job being a couple. We're going to be asking you questions and the two of you have been pretty well dubbed the sweethearts. Your interactions have been heartwarming and adorable, and the audience loves it." She smiled, but it didn't reach her eyes. "The questions I'm asking are designed to paint you in a bad light. I shouldn't tell you that, but Carlos and I both agree, we'd love to see you win. Also, the further you get, the more money I make." This time, the smile did reach her eyes.

Dylan grinned at her. "So, you do well when we do well?"

Desiree glanced around the room as if looking for a hidden camera. "Or if you break up in an epic fashion, I get paid for that, too."

Dylan gasped and put a hand over her mouth as she laughed. "That's terrible."

"The audience loves drama." Desiree shrugged. "So as we go, keep in mind that anything you say, any reactions you make, if the producers think it's worth airing, will see the light of day."

Dylan sat up straight and jammed her hands between her knees, one of her tells.

I put an arm around her and leaned close to her ear. "Don't be nervous."

She smiled at me and bumped me with her shoulder. "How'd you know I was nervous?"

"I just know." Warmth filled my chest. *I was toast. This girl owned me.*

Carlos sat behind the camera and turned it on, the red light flashing. Desiree sat by the lens and picked up a notebook from the floor.

"So, Dylan. Was it weird to watch Aiden rescuing his ex-girlfriend last week?"

Ouch. I squeezed Dylan's shoulder to let her know I was here. My gut was sick with guilt at the mention of Sheena's name.

"It was a little weird, but I'm pretty secure in our relationship, so it didn't really bother me." Dylan pressed her thigh against mine.

Desiree nodded and gave us a silent thumbs up. "How was it for you, Aiden? Bring back any memories?"

I scrunched my face, thinking. "Not really. I was just worried that Sheena's cattiness would hurt Dylan. So I thought about Dylan the whole time, and how I'd make sure that *she* knew that she was the only woman I wanted to hold that way."

Desiree twisted her mouth and tilted her head from side to side as if she was deciding if she liked my answer or not.

"Aiden, you were there when Jorge was injured. Anything go through your mind as he broke his ribs?"

"Cracked." I held up a finger. "Cracked. And not really. He took my legs out from under me, and I just slid right off the platform."

"Dylan, the first week, you choked and began coughing. There was a heated exchange with Felicity Black afterward. Can you tell me what was said?"

I knew words had been exchanged, but I hadn't been close enough to hear

173

what they were.

Dylan looked down at her lap for a moment then back up at the camera. "She called me an attention whore and told me my fifteen minutes of fame were almost up."

My stomach felt like I'd just eaten a whole cow, heavy and sick.

"What was said back?" Desiree sat wide-eyed, nodding her head almost imperceptibly.

Please don't let Dylan have gone all mean-girl on that chick.

"Jenny told her not to say anything like that again, or Jenny would fix her nose-job with her fist. Something like that."

I breathed in carefully through my nose, trying not to crack up.

Desiree looked like she was doing the same thing. She put a hand over her mouth, stifling her laughter. After a few seconds, she turned to me. "Aiden, we hear Dylan sang back-up on Jenny's latest album, *Stars Align*. Will we be hearing her on your next album?"

Dylan's cheeks turned bright red, and she stared at her lap, while I did my best to control my reaction, which was to snap at Desiree.

"Time will tell." *Vague. Neither a yes or a no.*

"Dylan, would you sing back-up if he asked you to?" Desiree softly closed her notebook.

She shrugged. "I love singing. If I could get away with it without going on tour, I'd be all about it."

If she could sing without going on tour? Why was that so confusing? Maybe she just got stage fright. That might be the only thing holding her back.

Carlos signaled, then turned off the camera.

"Thank you both." Desiree ushered us out of the room. "There isn't any more filming scheduled for the day, but remember, the cameras are always rolling."

I took Dylan's hand and pulled her back toward the room. "That was ominous. Big brother is always watching."

"No kidding. Remember, we're watching you." Dylan held up her free hand and wiggled her fingers spookily.

We made it to our room and flopped onto the bed side by side.

"Wanna go to the pool?" I turned my head to look at Dylan.

She met my eyes. "Can we go on the water slides?"

I laughed. This woman just made everything better. "Of course."

The rest of the day was spent poolside, either playing Scrabble, Boggle, or going down the water slides. If every day could be like this, it'd be heaven. Between games, I flipped over the scoresheet and wrote a few lyrics.

Thirty-One - Dylan

It was weird getting ready without Jenny.

I straightened my hair, put some mascara on, and a tiny bit of lip gloss. The dress I chose was gold and white, reminiscent of ancient Greece. It had a square neck lined in gold and a gold belt. The skirt itself was white and flowy. I just needed dark eye makeup and a black wig, and I'd be all set for Halloween. *Oh, and one of those gold tiara things that looked like a snake ready to strike.*

Aiden was handsome in a gray suit. He didn't wear a tie, instead opting to leave his top two buttons open.

I rubbed my chest right above my neckline. "I know we aren't going home tonight, so why am I wound so tight? My chest feels like it's being squeezed by a giant fist." There wasn't a good reason to be nervous. Sheena and Jorge were going home, so we didn't have to worry, but I was jittery anyway. The idea of seeing Sheena again had my stomach in knots. My conversation with Aiden helped, but knowing their history made me really dislike her.

"I feel the same way." Aiden finished tying his shoe and stood, offering me his elbow.

"Oh, so debonair." I looped my arm through his. "Shall we?"

When we arrived on-set, Sheena and Jorge were already sitting on one of the white couches, while Laura and Christian sat on the red one.

The quick staccato of Trisha's heels across the stage announced her arrival. She had on a tight red dress and her hair swept to one side and held in place by a jeweled clip.

Barbie and Jake came and sat a second later.

Aiden helped me up the steps, and we sank onto our loveseat together.

Trisha took her place at the front of the stage, and the director counted down. "Hello America, and welcome to the elimination show. I'm your host, Trisha Thames, and this is *Couple's Cruise—Celerity Edition*, live from *The Callistus*."

Eliminations went exactly as I thought they would. Sheena and Jorge went home for medical reasons. They were given a nice tribute with lots of airtime before they were sent on their way.

"Join us next week for the semi-finals, where our final three couples will have the adventure of a lifetime." Trisha gave her salute, and the camera lights turned off.

My feet didn't want to walk to the couch where the two of them lounged. Jorge had been nice to me, though. Well, not overtly hostile. *Which I counted.* And I felt a little bad that he cracked his ribs.

Really, it was peer pressure. The other two couples were going over to say goodbye and wish them a speedy recovery. *What kind of monster would I be if I didn't join them?*

Aiden grabbed my hand and tugged me forward. "Just a quick goodbye, and they're out of our lives forever." He spoke through the corner of his mouth as he dragged me along.

Neither of them stood, and to the side, there were medics with wheelchairs ready to help them.

Barbie and Jake already wished them well and were on their way out of the theater. Laura knelt in front of them, gushing about how much she'd miss them. *Man I wished my acting skills were that good. She deserved an Oscar. Oh, wait. She'd already won one.*

Aiden stuck a hand out to Jorge, who slowly brought his up to shake Aiden's. Jorge winced, but his smile never faltered. *Maybe he was the one who deserved the Oscar.*

"Hey, Ace." Sheena's foot was propped on Jorge's lap and wrapped in a bandage.

How dare she call Aiden that? To think I'd envied that nickname.

"Take care, Sheena." I leaned down and gave her a stiff hug, then moved on to Jorge.

Sheena's foot didn't look swollen anymore. It must have been a short time deal. I briefly considered kicking it, or at the very least bumping into it "accidentally."

Aiden gave her a tight smile, then grabbed my elbow as if he knew my intentions to harm her.

Was I that obvious? He towed me toward the exit.

"Why don't you say something to her?" I glanced back over my shoulder. Sheena watched us walk away; her eyes narrowed and her mouth pinched.

"Like what? She doesn't deserve any more of my time or energy." He slid his hand down my arm and threaded our fingers, then brought my wrist to his mouth and planted a kiss on my tattoo.

Yeah, I melted. My heart was a puddle of goo on the floor.

"You have a really good point, but the petty side of me wants to kick that stupid foot of hers." I leaned into him as we walked, my head resting on his shoulder.

"And I'm glad you want to defend me, but I think Sheena's pettiness is a little more advanced than yours. She'd probably sue you for damages and emotional distress." He dropped a kiss on the top of my head.

He was right. I could totally see that.

"Chinese? I'll order dumplin's." His tone was light and teasing, and a smile played across my lips.

"Abso-freaking-lutely," I whispered, and Aiden laughed, a deep throaty sound.

Back in our room, we changed out of our "be on TV clothes" and into our "lounge in front of the TV clothes." *Translation: jammies.*

Aiden ordered while I found Forged in Fire and cued up the next episode.

The cleaning staff quit moving our table back to the corner of the room it belonged in, and instead left it where we dragged it every day to watch TV and eat: right in front of the lounger thingy Aiden said I should call a chaise, but I refused. It was funnier to call it a lounger thingy. Chaise sounded so snobbish. So upper crust. And it was really funny when he said it with his southern drawl.

He plopped down beside me, one leg tucked under him.

I could feel his eyes on the side of my face, and I spun to look at him. "What?"

"I'm just happy. That's all. You make me happy." Aiden's hand came up and brushed a strand of hair from my face.

My heart fluttered, and my cheeks heated. "You make me happy, too."

He leaned in and planted a kiss at the corner of my smile. I loved when he did that. *Loved when he kissed me just to kiss me. Loved when he didn't push me for more than I wanted to give, even when I was an idiot and tried to give it to him, anyway.*

The next morning, I wasn't feeling right. I had a headache and a mild fever. I wasn't sure if it was homesickness, or maybe I'd gotten some food poisoning like Jenny. But we spent the weekend in the room.

Aiden was the ideal nurse, making sure I had something to contain my fever, or ordering me juice and toast. The medicine actually made me almost-normal for a few hours. He had a nurse come and check in on me. She thought it was a bug of some sort. She said give it a few days, and if I wasn't feeling better, they'd get me in to see the doc.

By Monday, I felt a little better, and they told us to get ready for a getting to know you game with a twist. We were supposed to wear bathing suits. I popped a couple of ibuprofen and slipped into my royal blue swimming suit. Jenny would probably sigh when she saw this episode and noticed I didn't put on makeup, but what was the point if I was getting wet? It'd just wash off. I pulled my hair into a high ponytail; it wouldn't help with my headache, but it would keep my hair out of my eyes.

Aiden knocked on the bathroom door. "Almost ready?"

"Yeah." I looked in the mirror one last time. Small, dark circles were forming under my eyes. *Yeah, Jenny would definitely scold me for not figuring out makeup when she was here to teach me.*

I opened the door and stepped into Aiden's arms. He'd gone down to the dining room and grabbed muffins, toast, and orange juice. They were the things we'd discovered upset my stomach the least over the weekend.

"You doin' alright this morning?" He pulled back and looked into my eyes, lightly rubbing a thumb over the dark circle under one.

"Fine." I smiled at him.

He grabbed my hand and pulled me to the elevator.

We met the other two couples on the Lido deck. Barbie wore a maroon and gold bikini with the Trojan's logo across the butt.

Laura and Christian wore matching swimming suits, white with teal patterns. There was entirely too much coordination put into their outfits. And I had a feeling they'd be a meme after all this was over with the hashtag *#relationshipgoals.*

"Good Morning everyone. Welcome to *Couple's Cruise*—The ultimate test." Her eyes sparked, *legitimately sparkled,* with what I could only guess was anticipation.

Why did Trisha always seem so gleeful when she was about to torture us?

"Let's head to the ferry, and I'll explain more on location."

Thirty-Two - Aiden

I was going to cross another item off my bucket list, and my hands were sweaty just thinking about it.

A shark cage hung from a pulley at the side of the boat as cameras were secured to every side, facing both inward and outward.

"You'll go down in the cage as a couple. You'll be able to hear me and have to answer the questions I ask at the same time." Trisha held up a facemask that would enable us to speak and hear her. "You'll stand back to back, being circled by the ocean's top predator as we ask you questions. For example, 'Who made the first move'?" She switched out the facemask for two paddles, one blue, one pink. "If the answer is her, you raise the pink paddle. If the answer is him, you raise the blue one."

She continued, "No points will be rewarded. This is just for fun. You'll be able to hear each other, but you must be back to back when each question is asked."

Someone held an upside-down hat for Trisha, and she reached in and pulled out a piece of paper. "Laura and Christian, you'll be going first."

Laura shrieked and plastered herself to Christian's side. Crew members circled them, and I turned my attention to the ocean.

The waters had been chummed with fish guts to get the sharks over. And every now and then, a dark shape emerged. One of the crewmen had a giant fish head attached to a rope with a small buoy to keep it afloat. He tossed it into the water and dragged it across the surface. Within a couple of seconds, a shark was stalking it, and a second after that, the huge creature had taken a bite out of it.

My heart beat erratically in my chest. Sharks both fascinated and terrified me. The apex predators circled the boat and could easily kill a person in seconds. Another crew member chummed the other side of the boat. The cage was positioned on a platform at the back of the boat and lowered into the water so only the top six-inches stuck out. The crew attached the cage directly to the platform and opened the top. Laura and Christian climbed in.

I wished we were first. I wanted to go in with no expectations. No preconceived notions. Just raw terror with no one to tell me about it.

Dylan came over and leaned against me, resting her head on my shoulder.

"Come with me to the bow." I grabbed her hand and pulled her away.

She wrinkled her brow. "Don't you want to watch?"

"Nope." I glanced down at our joined hands and caught sight of her tattoo. Warmth filled my chest. At the bow, I stopped and brought our hands to my mouth, planting a kiss on the inside of her wrist, right over top of the tattoo. *My tattoo.* "Does it hurt anymore?"

She shook her head, her cheeks stained pink.

I loved her blush, loved that I could so easily read her. Loved that innocence.

We stared down at the water side by side, our pinkies linked on the rail.

"How're ya feelin'?" I was worried about her. She slept a lot last weekend, barely ate, which wasn't like her at all. That was another thing I loved about her. No more kale chips. I banned her from them. *That sounds dick-ish. I really just banned her from pretending.*

"Kinda excited, mostly scared. Colby is gonna freak out when he sees this episode. I'm really going to swim with sharks!" She sounded normal. Maybe she was on the mend.

"I meant, physically. Are you feeling sick?"

"Nah."

"Aiden and Dylan, you're next." One of the crewmen flagged us over and helped us into wetsuits. My hands shook as I pulled up the zipper. Adrenaline coursed through my body, making me edgy.

They strapped oxygen tanks to our backs and taught us how to use our masks. Then a crew member handed us our pink and blue paddles. *This was it. We were going down.* I bounced on my toes and looked over at Jake. He nodded and shot me a hang-loose sign.

Laura and Christian climbed out of the cage. The crew unhooked them and they laughed, wrapping their arms around each other.

Carlos gave us a thumbs up from behind his camera, and I climbed out onto the cage. The tempo of my heart sped. There was a rail about hip-height around the cage, and I gripped it to catch my balance.

Dylan grabbed my arm and came out onto the cage beside me. "Ready?"

"You want to go first?" *I had to offer.*

"No, this is your bucket-list item. Go ahead." She grabbed the rail and released me.

That's why I was falling for her. She knew me. I crouched down and let my legs hang into the cage, pushed myself off, so my tank wouldn't catch, and dropped into the ocean.

Bubbles surrounded me, blinding me momentarily. It was so quiet. The only sound was the steady inhale and exhale of my respirator. I gripped the edge of the cage and pushed myself down, giving Dylan room to come in. A muted splash sounded outside the cage and a flash of red caught my eye near the surface. A fish head skimmed across the water, and seconds later, a tiger shark came into view. Its striped body powered through the water with effortless ease. The large mouth opened. Rows of sharp teeth sent my pulse into hyper-drive, and the jaws clamped shut on the fish. Its head shook violently back and forth as it tore a chunk of flesh from its victim.

It was magnificent.

Another splash preceded bubbles exploding beside me. Dylan grabbed the cage and pulled herself down.

Her muffled shriek sounded through the earpiece. "Oh, my gosh! This is amazing."

Dark shapes below us grew closer and more clear until we were surrounded by the apex predators.

"It's beautiful." I grabbed her hand and squeezed it, glad to be sharing this moment with her. *There was no one I'd rather be with.*

"When you're ready, get back to back. Pink paddle in your left hand, blue in your right." Trisha's voice was tinny and not at all the silky smooth sound she was known for. "Let me know when you're in position, and we'll start."

Pink left, blue right. I positioned myself in the center of the cage and a second later, Dylan's oxygen tank clinked against mine. I glanced over my shoulder at her, and she waved.

"We're ready." I spun back, watching as another shark swam toward the cage.

"Who's more romantic?"

I lifted my right hand. *I was way more romantic.*

"Me." Dylan laughed, and I looked over my shoulder. Her pink paddle was up.

"No, I am."

"Ready for the next question?"

We faced forward.

"At restaurants, who's the better tipper?"

Oh, she better pick me for this one. I held up my blue paddle and looked over my shoulder.

"He is."

"No arguments here," I added.

Dylan shrieked, and I spun to see a shark powering through the water straight for her. Instinctively, I pulled her behind me and the shark wedged between the gaps of the cage, its mouth gaping open. I pushed its nose with my hand, feeling the rough skin with my fingers and redirecting it away. I rubbed my fingers together and took a deep breath. *I can't believe I just touched a shark's face.* I'd seen it done in videos, but never thought I'd have the chance.

"You guys okay down there?" Trisha asked.

I laughed, and adrenaline coursed through my veins. "We're fine."

Dylan grasped my hand and hugged it against her chest. We'd both dropped our paddles in the commotion, and I pushed off the bottom of the tank and grabbed them from the surface of the water. I handed Dylan her paddles, and we went back to back again.

"Ready," I called.

"Who's most likely to talk themselves out of a speeding ticket?"

I raised the blue paddle, then thought better of it. She was sweet and innocent. I raised my pink paddle. "She is."

"He is."

Trisha laughed. "Any story behind that?"

We both spun to face each other, our gazes locked.

"Well, she's hot, and she can be incredibly persuasive." If we hadn't been masked, I would've kissed her right then.

Our legs brushed, and my blood pulsed in my veins.

"Ready for the next one?"

The cage shook and Dylan gasped. Her eyes widened at something over my shoulder.

I spun and a massive shark had its teeth sunken into one of the plastic buoys at the top of the cage. A smile split my lips, and my stomach flipped. *Incredible.* Dylan's fingers dug into my forearm, her paddle forgotten.

The shark released the buoy and disappeared into the depths.

"I lost my paddle, again." Dylan's voice wasn't what I expected. It was laced with excitement. She enjoyed our close encounters as much as I had.

I swam up and grabbed her paddle, then pulled myself back down.

"Ready."

"Who's the better shower singer?" Trisha's voice sounded flat, annoyed at the question. Maybe to her, it was obvious. But she'd be wrong to assume I was the better shower singer.

I'd enjoyed many a shower concert from Dylan. I raised my pink paddle. "She is."

Dylan laughed, and I glanced over my shoulder expecting to see the blue paddle, but her pink one was up, too. I reached my foot back and nudged her with my toe. *Arrogant woman.*

"Interesting. Next question. Who snores louder?"

Dylan doesn't snore. I held up my blue paddle. "I do."

"He does." Dylan's voice was off. Not quite the playful tone I'd expected. More painful.

I spun and dropped my paddles, grasping her arms. "Are you okay?"

She nodded. "My heart just hasn't recovered from the shark attack."

"That was the last question. You guys can come on up."

I pushed Dylan to the hatch and helped boost her onto the ledge of the cage. She disappeared a second later, and I took one last look around, then swam to the surface. One more item crossed off my bucket list.

Two, if you count falling in love.

Thirty-Three - Dylan

Kill me now. Don't get me wrong, glad the sharks didn't get me. But my chest was still hurting the next morning, and I was pretty sure I'd sweated through the sheets.

Aiden ran to grab breakfast, and I made the embarrassing call to housekeeping for new sheets. I collapsed onto the lounge while I waited for them to come, shivering uncontrollably, praying for the painkiller to kick in. My head throbbed, and my entire body ached.

When someone knocked at the door, I just shouted, "Come in" and didn't even bother to open my eyes. *It could've been an ax murderer, and I wouldn't care.* As long as they changed the sheets after they killed me so it didn't look like I'd peed the bed.

"Did you want me to change them, or just leave the sheets with you?" Her perky voice was like nails on a chalkboard.

I raised my head and cracked open an eye. The tiny woman holding the sheets probably came up to my waist. I dropped my head with a groan.

"I'll go ahead and take care of it. Did you need anything else?" Her voice was less perky this time. *Way to read the room, chicka.*

My response was a whine.

She worked quickly. I knew because every now and then I felt a breeze as she walked by. It sent chills over my body, and my shivers became more violent. *Come on ibuprofen, work.*

"Want me to send a doctor?"

Another whine.

There was another knock on the door a second later, and I moaned. The

187

door opened. A man and a woman came in. The woman pushed a wheelchair. *Holy crap, the housekeeping lady was a ninja, or I fell asleep again. One of those was probably right.*

"Dylan? We're here to take you to the clinic." The woman laid a hand on my forehead. "She's burning up."

They lifted, with almost zero help from me. I kept my arms down so I didn't slip from their grasp. *Which I thought was super duper helpful.*

Once they had me positioned in the wheelchair, they rolled me out. My head pounded, and I closed my eyes. The intermittent bursts of light behind my eyelids told me we moved down the hallway. We took a different elevator down a few floors, and they wheeled me into a clinic looking room.

A man in khakis and a blue golf shirt assessed me, taking my temperature, blood pressure and listening to my heart and lungs. "Dylan, I'm Doctor Whittaker. Can you tell me what's going on?"

My teeth chattered. "I'm cold."

"You have a temperature of a hundred and three, young lady." He put his hands under my chin and probed my tonsils. "How long have your symptoms been going on?"

My eyes closed, and I struggled to reopen them. "Fever has been for a couple days."

"What else is going on?" He moved onto checking my reflexes, tapping my knee with his knuckle. "I heard you got a tattoo that might be infected. May I see it?"

I held out my wrist, and he touched the spot. It wasn't even tender.

I thought back. When had the symptoms started? "I've had an ache in my chest for about two and a half weeks." *Oh, my gosh. I'm an idiot. A complete and total moron.* My hand jerked to my chest and prodded the tender area under my left breast. *No.* I whimpered and shook my head. I was supposed to be better, supposed to be healed. "I had non-Hodgkin's lymphoma when I was seventeen. I've been in remission." *Had been. Past tense.*

The doctor's brow creased, and he turned to the two people who'd wheeled me in. "I need bloodwork on her ASAP."

Needles. Always needles. It was the worst-case scenario. My throat was tight, and I let out a shaky breath. I laid back, and dropped my head against the padded table, with my eyes squeezed shut. *It was a dream. I'd wake up and be back in my bed at home in Montana.*

It had to be.

The nurse walked in with a few tubes, a kit to place an IV, and a bag of fluids. *Not a dream.*

Calm. I needed to breathe. There was no use jumping to conclusions until I was sure. I had to wait until the test results were back. "How long until we get results?"

"We should get them back tomorrow morning. We'll try to get you the results before your excursion." Doctor Whittaker patted my hand. "I'll contact your oncologist."

My eyes lost their focus, and I stared blindly at a spot on the wall while the nurse inserted my IV and drew my blood. My stomach was an empty pit, and I exhaled a shuddering breath. The nurse hung the fluids and pocketed the vials of blood. She twisted the tube to the IV, hooking me to the fluids.

At some point during the visit, my pain killer kicked in, and my head cleared. What would Aiden say? I didn't want his pity. What if he felt obligated to stay with me because I was going through chemo? What if he couldn't handle it and broke things off? I couldn't let him see me like that. *Couldn't put him through cancer.*

Twenty minutes later, I checked the bag of fluids hanging beside me. It was almost gone. I'd have to pull the bandaid off before I got back to the room. Until I had absolute confirmation, I wouldn't breathe a word of it. I'd pretend everything was hunky dory. "Am I done?"

When the bag was empty, the nurse pulled the tape off my arm and wrapped it with that purple stretchy stuff.

"You're free to go. Let's have you follow up tomorrow morning, say nine? I believe you're going on the activity at ten. That should give you plenty of time. Did you have someone that could come with you for emotional support?" Doctor Wittaker had a laptop open and typed something on it.

"Desiree?" She was the closest thing I had to a friend on the ship, besides Aiden.

"I'll have her meet you here at nine."

"See you then." I laid there for another few minutes. My shivering subsided, and my head swam, but I was able to stand without assistance. My body still ached, but I could walk.

After exiting the office, I found an elevator and took it to the deck. When I was inside the ship, it was too easy to get lost. I had to go to the deck to get my bearings. Figure out which way to go. I wandered the deck, trying to look normal for the cameras.

I walked toward our room, and made it to the second elevator the same time Aiden did. He had a tray in his arms, with those stupid plastic covers over the top. It was too reminiscent of the hospital stays. Bile rose in my throat, but I forced a smile. "Hey, you."

Aiden planted a kiss on my forehead. "You slept late."

"Mmm. I was tired." I reached out and snagged the bottle of orange juice from his tray. I fought with the cap for a minute and finally took a sip.

Back in the room, the bed was freshly made, towels cleaned up. *Dang it*. She cleaned the entire room. How was I going to pass it off like I'd just gotten out of bed?

"Housekeeping came while I was in bed, and I helped clean." *Liar, liar, pants on fire. It was just until I found out for sure.* Maybe I was just sick. Maybe I had an infection or something. It was the flu. I was having a weird reaction to shellfish. *Something. Anything.*

It was another day of vegging out. We watched The Office. Both of us had seen episodes but never the whole series. It was my new favorite show. *And it kept my mind off of the Big Maybe.* We binge watched the whole first season and ordered in lunch. I took more meds to keep my fever away. Then eight hours later, as we were finishing season two, we ordered a late dinner and dessert. Chemo diet was crazy strict, and I was going to eat as normally as I could until they told me to stop.

That night, Aiden fell asleep before me, which never happened. I couldn't get my thoughts to settle. Between that, and being worried I'd wake up, and we'd both be in a pool of my sweat, I didn't sleep. The night dragged, and I found myself out on our private patio, lounging on a pool chair, staring at the moon and listening to the waves as they broke against the side of the ship.

I took more medicine for the fever and finally fell asleep shortly after three.

The next morning, Aiden woke me. He knelt on the deck beside my chair and gently brushed the hair off my forehead.

I cracked open my eyes and stared into his blue ones; they seemed darker, deeper. He smiled, crinkling the skin at the corners, and I smiled back.

"Morning, sleepyhead." His fingers teased the skin along my brow. "You don't have a fever."

A yawn escaped, and I put a hand up to block my morning breath. "What time is it?"

"Just after eight. You've got plenty of time. You feeling up for it?" He grabbed my hand and brought my wrist to his mouth, planting a kiss on my tattoo. *Our tattoo.* He'd been doing that more and more. Each time made me more gooey. *I'd have to be careful, or I'd be putty in his hands.*

"I have a quick errand to run right before nine. Can I meet you in the dining room for breakfast?" *A quick errand? Way to go brain. That sounded normal. Just had to run to the grocery store, or the dry cleaners. Don't mind me.*

"Okay. Why'd you sleep out here?" He stood and held his hand out.

I took it, and he pulled me to my feet. I pressed a quick closed-mouth kiss on his lips. *Had to contain the morning breath.* "I had a rough night, couldn't sleep. See ya in a bit?" I rushed to the bathroom before he could ask any follow-up questions.

Desiree met me outside our door, a sad smile on her face.

At nine, we stood outside the doctor's door side by side. *It would be nothing.*

Three after nine. *The flu?*

Five after nine. *Food poisoning?*

Eight after nine. *Tattoo infection?*

I had to know.

My hands trembled as I twisted the handle and pushed the door open. The doctor was sitting at his computer as we walked in.

He turned to us. *It wasn't good.* The doctor's expression told me everything

I needed to know. I'd seen that look before, five years ago when I'd been diagnosed the first time.

My legs gave out, and I dropped to the floor, my hand drifting to my mouth to cover the squeaking sounds trying to escape.

The doctor and Desiree took my arms and helped me onto the padded exam table.

I shook my head, and my eyes wouldn't focus. *No. It couldn't be happening again.*

Dr. Whittaker sat on his rolly stool and positioned it in front of me. "Your test results are back, Dylan. Your white blood cell count is high, with an extraordinary number of immature cells. Your lymphocytes count is high too, indicating a relapse."

Black spots dotted my vision.

There was a six-foot, human-sized pit in my chest.

My grave.

Tears sprang to my eyes as I struggled to fill my lungs with air. The sharp pain indicating the cancer's return stopped me from getting enough. I dropped my head and curled my legs to my chest, hugging them. *What was I going to tell Aiden?*

Desiree put a hand on my shoulder, rubbing soothing circles. "What can I do? I feel totally helpless."

What could anyone do? "Pray?"

She pulled me into a hug and rubbed my back. "Oh, sweetie. I'm so sorry."

My shoulders shook, and a sob worked its way up my throat. Tears streamed freely down my cheeks.

"We'll get you out of here as soon as possible, Dylan." Her voice choked with emotion and when she pulled back, tears shimmered in her eyes.

"How?" I whispered. There was so much to think about. Too much to consider.

"We'll have a courtesy vote, fudge the results. We've done it before. You'll be out of here by tomorrow. Does that work?"

A conversation we had a couple weeks back niggled at the back of my mind. I couldn't put Aiden through cancer treatments. Couldn't let him see me like that. "How much of a bonus do you get if we break up on camera?"

She shook her head. "You don't have to do that, Dylan. That's sweet, but don't do that for me. You two are so perfect together." Desiree grabbed my hands. "Watching you two fall in love has been so rewarding."

Love. Hearing it confirmed only made it hurt more. I was desperately, hopelessly, in love with Aiden. *Which is why I had to spare him from this.* If I broke it off now, he'd be able to move on, be able to get over it. It would be fast and easy. Drawing it out, going through cancer, watching me die. That was something nearly impossible to come back from.

It would crush him.

I couldn't do that to him.

Wouldn't.

"You said if you captured an epic break up on camera you got a huge bonus. I want to know how much?" My voice was flat, emotionless. Disconnected.

A small sob broke from Desiree's lips. "Thirty grand." She shook her head, her blonde hair a mess of curls. "I can't ask you to do that."

She was right. If she'd asked, I wouldn't have done it. "You didn't. I'm volunteering." My voice broke, and I cradled my head in my hands.

Aiden couldn't know the truth. He'd insist on staying. Insist we could be together. He'd have to watch as I shriveled up and died.

A vice tightened around my heart. It would crush him. But it was for his own good.

Tears dripped from my chin and ran down my legs. I held up my left wrist and stared down at the tattoo. He didn't deserve the pain, the worry. He deserved happiness. He deserved a normal life free of chemo appointments, nausea, weight gain, and death. He deserved better than me.

And I knew exactly where to hit. The blow to our relationship would be deep and lethal. A sob worked its way up my throat, and I tried to choke it down. He would hate me after all was said and done, but I was saving him. And I had the perfect ammunition.

Thirty-Four - Aiden

Where was she? It was almost time to go, and she'd completely disappeared. I was fine when she made up some lame excuse about running an errand. There were no errands to run on a cruise ship. But now, I was worried. *Had she fallen overboard?* As stupid as it was, the thought actually ran through my head. I made a quick stop and grabbed a takeout container for her, with blueberry muffins, banana bread, and a bottle of orange juice.

At ten, a voice came over the speaker, directing us all to the Lido deck.

Trisha met us there, and for once, didn't use a megaphone to tell us about our activity. "Parasailing."

Another one of my bucket-list items. I scanned the crew surrounding the stage. *Where's Dylan? She'd love parasailing. Was she feeling okay?* Maybe she'd gone back to the room and fallen asleep on the bed. That was as good an explanation as any.

While everyone else headed toward the ferry, I ran to the room. If she was still sick or asleep, time was of the essence. I burst through the door and scanned the room. Empty. *Darn it.* Unease filled me. Where'd she go? Could I even go without her? *Did I want to?*

Maybe someone knew where she was. I bolted to the elevator, still carrying her breakfast. As I waited for the elevator, I played worst case scenarios in my head. Dylan wouldn't just disappear without a good reason.

When I finally got to the ferry, she and Desiree were sitting in quiet conversation. She was a little pale, but otherwise looked fine. Dylan smiled at something the other woman said, her eyes glassy with unshed tears.

I walked down the gangplank carrying her breakfast, and she turned to me.

When she saw me, her smile wobbled, and she stood and met me half-way. *Something was wrong.* She wrapped her arms around my waist and buried her face in my chest. I rested my lips on top of her head and kissed her, her breakfast still in my hands. She sat close to Desiree, making room for me on the bench.

"Hey. You okay? I looked for you everywhere." I dropped onto the seat beside her and handed her the container of muffins and bread, then twisted the cap off the orange juice and held it for her until she was ready for a drink.

She shared a look with Desiree.

"I went to see the doctor this morning, since I haven't been feeling well." Dylan smiled and opened the container. "You brought me muffins and orange juice?" Her smile wobbled again, and she shook her head before grabbing a muffin and taking a bite.

"What did the doctor say? Is everything okay?" *Of course everything wasn't okay. She wasn't being herself.*

She nodded with her mouth full. "The flu. The test just took longer than I expected." She took the orange juice from my hand and held it out. I twisted the cap off the rest of the way, and she took a long drink, then held it out while I screwed the cap back on and took it from her so she could keep eating.

There was no effort, no coordinating, just us.

Maybe telling her about today's adventure would help her feel better. "Did you hear what the activity is?" I couldn't wait to tell her, watch her face light up, see the smile that stopped my heart and started it all at the same time.

Her hand came up to cover her mouth. "What?" The words were muffled by the huge bite of muffin in her mouth. She grabbed the orange juice, and we repeated the un-capping process.

I waited until her mouth was empty. "Parasailing."

Dylan's reaction did not disappoint. She laughed and a huge grin split her face as she leaned into me and squeezed my knee with her free hand. "I can't wait." A tiny squeak escaped her lips, and she put another bite of blueberry muffin in her mouth.

Her smile just did it for me. I loved being the one to put that joy in her eyes, that smile on her lips. The longer we were together, the more I wanted to be the man to do it forever. I unscrewed the lid on her orange juice and waited until she took it, our fingers brushing. We'd need to have a serious conversation sooner or later. Figure out our next steps.

The ferry dropped us at a dock where three separate boats and crews were ready. Desiree led us to one of the boats, and handed us our mics, another routine we'd grown accustomed to. As I put the one in my hands on Dylan, my hands brushed against her back and collar. Then, as she clipped hers on me, heat crept up her cheeks. With the back of my knuckles, I caressed her blush, then placed a kiss on her forehead.

Our boat would've been large enough for all three couples, but with the film crew, they split us up to make room, giving us the illusion of privacy. As we boarded the boat, we were handed bright orange life jackets. We put them on and headed to the bow.

The boat's engine revved, filling the air with exhaust and the smell of gasoline. As we bounced along the water, Dylan stared out at the ocean, her hair whipping in the wind. The boat rounded a peninsula and one of the parasailing crew came over with two harnesses. He gave us a brief explanation, then helped us each thread our legs through the contraption and secured the straps around our waist.

As we waited for them to finish their prep, I turned to Dylan and checked her straps. She was precious cargo, and I didn't want any accidents. I pulled her to a seat and wrapped my arm around her. She leaned on me with her eyes closed. I wished I could do something to help her feel better, but at least we knew what it was now. They'd be able to treat her, and she'd be better in no time.

A few minutes later, the crew got to work unfurling the yellow-and-blue-checkered parasail. I nudged Dylan and pointed to it. She turned and a small smile tilted her lips. Her fingers twined with mine, and she rested her head on my shoulder, our thighs pressed together.

"It's pretty."

I could barely hear her words over the purr of the engine. With her other

196

hand she caressed my forearm, her fingers tracing lines and connecting my freckles like a child's connect-the-dots picture. I placed a kiss in her hair, then laid my head on hers.

The boat slowed, and the same guy that helped us with our harness waved us to the back. Dylan went first, stepping onto a platform near the back. There was a bar about six feet long. Straps hung from it and the crewman hooked her to two of them. He said something I couldn't hear, and she smiled, but it didn't reach her eyes. *She must feel like garbage.*

When my turn came, I stood on the platform and the man latched me in, advised me to sit back, enjoy the view, and hold on to the straps below the carabiners. There was a camera attached to the pole that came out and pointed right at the two of us.

"Ready?" the crewman shouted.

Dylan gave him a thumbs up, and I nodded. The captain gunned it, the boat speeding forward. The winch began grinding, and just like that, my feet left the platform, and we swung back and forth like kids on a swing set.

I laughed, kicking my feet. A thrill shot through my stomach at the weightlessness. I glanced over at Dylan. She held the straps and looked down at the ocean. A tear dripped down her cheek, but she was smiling.

"You okay?" I reached a hand out and grabbed hers, linking our fingers together.

She glanced at me and nodded, but didn't speak.

The view was spectacular. The deep blue of the ocean blended with the light blue of the sky to the west. But it faded in comparison to the woman beside me. "It's beautiful up here."

Her hand squeezed mine, and she brushed another tear from her face. "It's really pretty." Her voice was rough with emotion, and she laughed. "Sorry, I don't know what's going on. I just think I'm overwhelmed by the view." Her last word squeaked out, and her shoulders shook. Her head dropped and she covered it with one hand.

I wanted to pull her into a hug, force her to tell me what was going on. The knot of worry expanded in my gut. "You know you can tell me anything, right?"

"There's nothing to tell, Aiden. I really am just overwhelmed by all this." She gestured to our surroundings. She gasped and pointed. "Look!"

I looked in the direction she pointed and saw the spray of a whale.

Seconds later, another whale surfaced, and Dylan laughed. "It's incredible!"

As I stared at Dylan, suspended in the air, surrounded by all this beauty, lyrics flowed through my head.

After a few minutes, the whales submerged and Dylan held the strap with one hand and rested her face against it as the wind pulled and tangled her hair. She was quiet, lost in her own thoughts. Our pinkies were linked between us, and I pulled her hand to my mouth and placed a kiss on the inside of her wrist over her tattoo. I loved that tattoo. Loved kissing it, loved kissing her.

Thirty-Five - Dylan

My heart was breaking and rejoicing at the same time. To share this moment with Aiden was like a dream. Tears trickled down my face, each one representing a different emotion. I closed my eyes so I could focus on the breeze pushing my hair out of my face and running across my body. Ocean air filled my lungs, clean and salty. There was nothing like being near the ocean. Was it being with Aiden that made me love the ocean so much, or was there more to it? I thought the mountains were my favorite, but after a month at sea, I might've changed my mind.

I looked over at Aiden. He was so different from the Aiden I met the first day. He seemed so carefree, so relaxed. *So happy.* His smile, that had been guarded and occasionally sardonic, had changed in the past month, and it appeared more frequently. Several times I'd caught him smiling at something, then he'd turn to me and his smile would transform, soften, just for me. My heart ached thinking about it, thinking about how much had changed for us.

"I love it up here," I said. There was blue in nearly every direction.

Aiden smiled at me, soft and sweet. "Me, too."

After a few more minutes, the rope vibrated as the winch worked to pull us safely into the boat. We landed on the deck of the ship, unscathed and completely dry. The crew unhooked us and drove us to the dock where we met the ferry and were taken to the cruise ship.

We didn't see either of the other two couples. They were already on board or hadn't gotten back yet.

I couldn't do it yet. I needed more time with him. Needed to touch him, be

199

with him. We went back to the room, kicked off our flip-flops, and dropped onto the bed. Exhaustion made my eyes heavy, and I curled into Aiden's side. He laid back, getting more comfortable, and I cuddled in tighter. I was going to savor every single minute. A tear spilled from my eye, and I discreetly wiped it away. *This is what I'd miss the most, laying in bed beside him, feeling his arms around me, hearing the beat of his heart.*

My eyes drifted closed as Aiden's fingers trailed up and down my arm. It would be the last time I ever fell asleep in his arms. I choked back a sob and clung to his shirt, inhaling his scent and committing it to memory.

When we woke, it was almost dinnertime. I slipped into the bathroom and took medicine to control the fever. *It had to be public. I can't believe I'm about to do this.* "Want to eat in the dining room tonight?" I stepped into the walk-in closet and rummaged through the drawers. *What did one wear to destroy their relationship in front of millions of viewers? What the heck was I doing?* I snagged a yellow sundress from the hangers and kicked the drawer closed.

"Sure." Aiden's voice was muffled by the closed door.

I stared at my reflection in the mirror. My eyes had dark circles that I didn't know how to fix. I dropped my robe and let my hand drift to the scar on my chest. The scar I'd been hiding from Aiden. The reason I never wore a two-piece. I called it my bullet hole. They'd cut it open to take a biopsy, but the chemo hadn't allowed it to heal properly. So now I had a crater just under my right breast beside my sternum.

It was a badge of honor, my proof of life. I survived. And hopefully, I'd do it again.

The lines I'd been practicing all day came back to me, and I mouthed them, unwilling, and unable to add any voice behind the hateful words, but I'd have to.

I pulled the sundress over my head and slid my feet into my favorite leather sandals. When I emerged into the bedroom, Aiden was laying across the lounge, his hands behind his head like a pillow. *Carefree.* He had no idea a storm was about to rage.

The butterflies in my stomach were back. Their erratic flight threatened to push my lunch back up. I took a shaky breath and retreated into the bathroom.

The smell of Aiden's cologne lingered in every corner of the room. I grabbed the bottle and brought it to my nose, inhaled a soft breath and stopped when the pain in my chest became too much. Citrus and woods. My throat tightened, and my chin trembled. I looked up and willed the air to dry the tears threatening to spill.

"You can do this." My voice cracked, and the words sounded less confident than I wanted. After I'd composed myself, I stepped out into the bedroom and plastered on my cheerful face. "Ready?"

Aiden sat up and took in my outfit, his eyes lingering on my legs and face. A slow smile spread across his lips, and I couldn't help my answering one. Pain speared through me, and I turned away from him before my smile drooped. Would that be the last time Aiden Miller smiled at me? Appreciated my outfit? *Made me melt with just one look?*

His hand slid from my elbow, down my arm, and his fingers laced with mine. His body heat warmed my side. He brought our hands to his mouth and placed a torturous kiss on my tattoo. *I almost lost it then, almost chickened out. Almost broke down crying. Almost told him I loved him, and to forgive me for what I was about to do.*

It had to be authentic. It had to look real. Heaven help me, I was about to break his heart. And mine.

As we waited for the elevator, Aiden trailed kisses along my jaw.

"Stop." I pulled away and tried to laugh it off. He was just making it worse, making it harder. *Making it impossible.*

"You okay?" He searched my face.

My chest ached; more than just the cancer. "I'm not feeling great." It wasn't a lie, and my heart raced. *I promised Desiree "epic." How was I going to pull it off?*

The elevator dinged, and we stepped in. As the doors slid shut, it felt like the closing of the doors on our relationship. Tears burned my eyes, and I turned away from Aiden to hide my face.

"You sure you're okay? We can take dinner in our room tonight." He rubbed his hand up and down my back.

No. "I'm sure."

When the elevator opened and we stepped out, my eyes darted down the hallway, searching for an escape, a diversion, anything to stop the runaway train.

As we entered the dining room, Desiree was there, Carlos beside her. She gave me a sad smile and nodded her encouragement. I wasn't just doing this for me; I was doing it for Aiden, for the heartache I'd be saving him. For the bonus Desiree would get if we had an epic breakup.

She came over and handed us mics. "Since we have fewer couples, we need more footage, so even if none of your dinner is usable, we want you mic'd, just in case."

My hands shook as I hooked the mic to Aiden's shirt. He didn't even question it, just attached the mic to my top, then helped me hook the battery pack to the back of my bodice. His hands grazed the bare skin in the middle of my back. *I can't do it. No. I can't do it.*

"I'll grab your dinner. Why don't you rest?" Aiden motioned to the table.

"No. I'm okay. I can do it."

"You sure?" His hand rested on the small of my back, and his fingers trailed a circular pattern on my skin.

"Yeah."

Aiden's gaze lingered on my face for a moment, as if assessing. Then he nodded and left to get in line for his dinner.

Breathing was suddenly impossible. My breaths came fast and shallow, and I dropped onto the chair, lightheaded.

Desiree strode over and crouched in front of me. "You alright?"

No. I nodded.

"Hey. Are you sure you want to do this?" She took my hand. "He'll understand if you tell him the truth."

That was exactly the problem. He would understand, and he'd stay for the wrong reasons. It was better this way. "No, it's okay. I'll do it."

Thirty-Six - Aiden

Dylan was already at the table when I sat down with my dinner. Her face was pale, and her eyes unfocused and aimed at some far off place.

"You alright?" Why had she insisted we ate here if she didn't feel well?

She blinked and shook her head before focusing on me, her brow creasing. "Yeah, fine." Her voice was rough, and she tucked a strand of loose hair behind her ear.

I studied her as I picked at my chicken. *What was going on in that head of hers?* As she pushed around the lettuce on her plate, I watched a myriad of emotions play across her face. The furrowed brows relaxed with a heavy sigh, and pursed lips turned to a frown.

Something was going on. She'd said it was the flu. That the doctor said she'd be fine. *This wasn't fine.* It was so far from fine, it was ridiculous. *To heck with the competition.* I needed her better, needed to see her smile, feel her fingers absently comb through my hair as we watched TV.

I wasn't just falling for her; I was gone. The feeling was better than my first view in the shark cage. My heart danced, lighter than I'd been in years.

"W-what's going to happen after this?" Her words tripped out of her mouth and a cute blush climbed her cheeks. She still wouldn't meet my eyes. Her gaze flitted from a spot over my shoulder, to her plate, and back. With each movement, she seemed more at war. As her gaze moved up, her lips set into a grim line and her jaw clenched intermittently, but as soon as she looked back down, the vacant sadness returned. She traced the lines of her tattoo, our tattoo, absently as she stared at her lap.

Had she forgotten our conversation? "We've talked about this. After this is over, I want to be with you. We'll make it work. I'll take some time off." Which would be nearly impossible with my new album. But I'd do it. "Maybe you can come with me on tour?"

Worry gnawed at me. She wasn't acting right. Wouldn't look at me, wasn't smiling. Was my fame that big a deal to her? I thought we'd moved past that. She was more comfortable in front of the cameras than she'd been four weeks ago. What was really going on? She wasn't usually this quiet. I thought we were beyond nerves, comfortable enough to talk about our concerns. I held my hand across the table to her, and she stared at it, but didn't take it.

Sad determination stole over her face, and her bottom lip trembled despite her tight jaw. "That's not what I meant." The first words cracked. Dylan cleared her throat and rubbed her wrist before her hands disappeared under the table. "I meant, publicity-wise." She stared down at her plate, then swallowed audibly as she looked over my shoulder again.

Why wouldn't she look at me? I got up and crouched in front of her, took her chin and gently turned her toward me, forcing myself into her line of sight. "We'll keep you away from the cameras." *Was that my voice?* I didn't know it could reach a pitch that high, but panic was rising like bile in my throat. I'd do whatever it took to convince her I could keep her safe and protected. "We can hire more security guards."

"That's not what I want." She jerked her chin out of my grasp and glanced over my shoulder. Her back went ramrod straight, and she exhaled, the breath hissing out between her lips. Her hands fisted in her lap, and despite the tears shimmering in her eyes, she met mine willingly for the first time.

I was losing her. No, I couldn't lose her. I had to make her see this could work, had to convince her the cameras would be gone as soon as we left the ship. "I have a cabin on Tahoe. We can disappear for a while. Or we can travel. See the world." *She'd love the cabin on Tahoe. I'd made the wooden swing on the front porch myself.*

"Aiden, no. This. This isn't what I want." There was venom in her voice. It laced through each letter and poisoned me more with each syllable. Her eyes were hard, though they still shined. She gestured between us, her brown eyes steely. "I can't do 'us.'"

No, she was not walking away. "Dylan, I'm in love with you." The words should have been freeing, but they tasted like ash. Bitter on my tongue.

As bad as I thought her reaction might be, I wasn't prepared for her laugh. No. Laugh wasn't the right word.

Cackle.

The talking in the dining room faded. I glanced around. People from the crew and wait staff stopped eating, their focus on us.

I sucked in a painful breath.

"Oh, Ace. Don't be naïve." The venom weaved itself into her gaze as well. Tears gone, her eyes were a dagger to my heart as she stood and looked down on me. Her lips twisted like the knife in my chest to drive the pain that much deeper. "Sheena had the right idea. Follow you to the top."

This wasn't Dylan. Those weren't her words. I stood and stepped close to her, my hands hovering beside her elbows, wanting to touch her, to pull her into me, but not knowing how she'd react. What possessed her to act this way? "Stop. This isn't you, Dylan." The words barely came out through the lump constricting my airway.

The tears were back, and she swallowed hard, shaking her head as she wrapped her arms around her waist. "The show has served its purpose. My name is going to be everywhere after this."

I had to touch her. I ran my thumb against her jaw, and she jerked away as if repulsed by my touch. "I know you, Dylan. You don't want the spotlight. Why are you doin' this?" I clenched my teeth in a bid to stop this from becoming a bigger scene than it already was.

She took several steps backward, her eyes flashing, her head slowly shook side to side as she spoke. "Don't touch me. And I've already got the spotlight." She flung her hand out behind me and I followed her gaze.

Carlos and Desiree were huddled twenty feet away. The red light on the camera was on and they were practically salivating over it.

"It's over. We're over. And I'm famous." She spun on her heel and I lunged for her, grasping her elbow and jerking her back against my chest.

"Why are you doin' this?" I spoke between gritted teeth. She knew Sheena crushed me, knew so much about me. Things I'd never told another living soul, and she was using them to hurt me, on TV.

"Because you've served your purpose." Her voice cracked, and she yanked her arm free and strode out of the dining room.

I stood frozen, staring at the door she disappeared through. It was so quiet I could've heard a pin drop. I blinked, and again, letting my eyes come back into focus. My chest was empty, numb. I looked around the dining room.

All eyes were on me.

What were they staring at? "Haven't you ever seen a breakup?" My tone started normal, but ended as a hoarse shout. I sat and picked up my fork, stabbing it into the chicken and bringing it to my mouth, tearing a bite off like a wild animal.

Still, they stared.

My hands shook as I sawed off my next bite with a knife.

And still. They stared.

I threw my silverware onto the table. They hit and bounced, echoing in the quiet dining room. *How could she do that to me in front of an audience? How could she so easily dismiss what we had? How could she use me like that?* I stood and grabbed the edge of the table, hurling it on its side.

The plates shattered on impact, the food splattering and sending salad dressing everywhere. "What are you lookin' at? What are you lookin' at!?" I kicked the chair and stormed out the door in the opposite direction Dylan went, out onto the back deck.

What now? Where was I gonna go? I couldn't go back to the room and didn't have anyone to stay with.

"Aiden." Desiree ran to catch up to me.

I clenched my teeth. She wasn't any better than Dylan; she captured every moment unapologetically on camera. The mic. I grabbed the mic and ripped it from my shirt, then hucked it into the ocean.

"Aiden, wait."

I spun on her. "Wait? *Wait!* You are unbelievable, you know that?"

"I—"

"No. I'm not done. I don't know how you convinced her to do that. What you promised her, what kind of deal you cut, but you don't talk to me anymore. I don't want to hear another word out of your mouth. In fact, I never want to see your face again." My chest heaved with my labored breaths, my voice growing more hoarse by the moment, the words strangled by emotion. "The same goes for Dylan. Tell her I never want to see her face. Ever. Again."

Whether or not she'd meant a word of it, she'd done it. She'd sold me, *us*, out and *nothing* she'd been promised would ever make that okay.

Tears stung the back of my eyes, and I stalked to the rail, leaving Desiree to disappear.

I ran a hand through my hair, tugging at the strands and trying to figure out why she'd do this to us. Why she'd end it like that. The lights of the bar caught my eye. The bartender was watching TV. A soccer game was playing. I stalked over and put my palms on the bar.

"Double shot of Jack, please." I shifted my weight from foot to foot as the bartender poured the drink. I needed it. Needed to numb the pain in my chest, the tightness in my throat. If I drank enough, I might even forget her for a minute.

He placed a napkin on the bar and put the glass on top of it. I brought the drink to my lips and dumped the contents down my throat. It burned, and the alcohol overwhelmed my senses. At least I couldn't smell her shampoo anymore.

I slammed the glass on the counter. "Just give me the bottle."

His nametag said Brad, and I stared daggers at the poor kid, standing between me and oblivion.

"The bottle." I tried smiling, but couldn't get my lips to make the movements. "Please."

Brad held the bottle close to his chest. He moved it toward the counter, then brought it back.

"Leave. The. Bottle," I seethed. I'd have his job if he didn't give me what I needed.

He slowly set the bottle on the counter beside my shot glass. I snapped it up and ripped the pour spout from the top, glugging the liquid into the cup and overflowing it onto the counter. I picked up the wet glass and tossed the contents into my mouth. The burning gave me something else to focus on, something besides Dylan's words. Her cackle. The way she'd flung her hand at the camera and gloried in the spotlight.

I repeated the process twice more, filling the glass and throwing back the liquid. I dropped onto the bar stool; the tension draining from me.

She dumped me.

On TV.

A hand clapped my shoulder, and I turned to see who it belonged to.

"Let's get you out of here." Carlos tapped his knuckles on the bar. "I need a new bottle of Jack, please."

Sonuva. It had to be Carlos. Had to be the man who had probably just broadcast the whole thing on TV.

The bartender seemed to waiver.

I slapped my hand on the bar. "Now, Brad."

He grabbed a new bottle from the shelf behind him and set it on the counter. Carlos scooped it up and grabbed my elbow, yanking me behind him.

"Where are we goin'?

"Just shut up." Carlos dragged me down a few flights of stairs to the gangplank, where a boat idled. He towed me behind him onboard and put an orange life jacket around my neck.

A few minutes later, we reached the shore. Carlos pulled off my life jacket and tossed it in the boat, then hauled me behind him over the dock, then onto the sand. The boat's engine cut, and the men aboard got off the ship, but didn't leave the dock.

There were two cabana chairs set up a few yards off the dock. He led us there, then dropped into one of the chairs. "Sit."

I turned and looked out over the water before lowering myself into the chair. The sun was starting its descent and would disappear behind the cruise ship before the horizon.

Carlos peeled the seal from the bottle and opened the lid, taking a long pull before handing me the bottle.

"What are you doin'?" I reached out a hand and took the bottle. Was he filming this? What were his motives? The whole thing was gonna blow up in my face.

His eyes were focused on the water. "Probably losing my job." Carlos reached out and took the bottle from my hand and took another drink before passing it back to me.

"Why?" I took a couple of swigs, letting the alcohol purge my emotions.

"I've been filming for *Couple's Cruise* for thirteen seasons. You and Dylan are the first contestants to ever treat me like a person."

At the mention of her name, I brought the bottle to my lips again. *What had Desiree promised her?* I took another drink. *Didn't want to know. Didn't want to think about it.* "I was in love with her."

He took the bottle from me. "I know."

Half of the sun was hidden behind the ship now. We passed the bottle back and forth in silence for a few minutes.

"I didn't like her the first day, face caked in makeup. She looked just like every other girl I'd ever dated." Another swig. "But there was something different about her. That night in our room, she changed into her pajamas."

Man, how I loved her pajamas. Her hair was wet, fresh from a shower, her face free of cosmetics. I could almost smell the scent of her shampoo on the pillow.

I brought the bottle to my lips to drink away the memory.

Thirty-Seven - Dylan

I rolled over and stared at the spot beside me. It was as empty as I felt. He didn't come back. Not that I expected him to, but a small part of me wanted him to. Wanted him not to leave me, not make me go through this alone. His pillow was still wet from my tears; I cuddled it last night as sobs wracked my body.

Aiden's cologne bottle was on the nightstand next to the bed where I'd left it. In a moment of complete self-destruction last night, I sprayed the pillow with it. I grabbed the bottle and brought it to my nose. It wasn't quite what he smelled like. It was missing that smell that was uniquely Aiden, the smell of his skin.

The clock said three. *Holy crap, I'd slept the day away, again.* My body ached, and pain lanced through my chest. Whether the broken heart or the cancer, I couldn't be sure. *I did this to myself. I didn't deserve my own sympathy.*

When someone knocked on the door, I almost had a stroke. *Was it Aiden?* I peeked through the peephole and had to conceal my disappointment as I pulled open the door.

"Hey, Desiree." I forced a smile.

Desiree gave me a closed lip smile and looked me up and down. "*Almost as bad as I was expecting.*"

"Sorry to disappoint." I wandered into the closet and put my suitcase on the floor in the center of the room. Most of my clothes were in there, but some clothes from the show were mixed in, too. I picked through my drawers as Desiree brought a chair into the closet and sat by the door.

"Whatcha doing?"

"Just getting all my clothes." I picked up the shirt I'd worn on my first excursion with Aiden. The memory of his arms wrapped around me as I reeled in the fish came with painful clarity. I pushed it away and dropped the shirt back into a drawer.

"You can keep them all, ya know?"

I shook my head. "No. I can't." I wouldn't need them, anyway. The gowns and fancy blouses, those weren't me. They belonged to a different Dylan. *Aiden's Dylan.*

Piece by piece, the clothing I'd brought with me made their way back into the suitcase and all the show's clothes were out until the two versions of me were separated once more.

"How are you feeling?" Desiree knelt and helped me scrunch everything into the case.

"Peachy." I zipped it closed and leaned back on my heels, closing my eyes. Memories swam behind my eyelids. *Aiden's hand caressing the back of my neck. The way his lips brushed my ear as he told me secrets. Talking about bucket list items, checking them off. The memory of our first real kiss and how he'd stopped me from going too far.* A tear dripped from my chin. I hadn't even realized I'd started crying or had I even stopped? "I'm in love with him."

Her hand grasped the back of my arm. "I know, sweetie." She grabbed my suitcase and wheeled it out of the closet.

I glanced over at Aiden's things, his guitar on the top shelf. His clothes hanging in neat rows, his boots dropped haphazardly in the corner. Another tear dropped, and I wiped my eyes, stood and reached for the guitar. I laid the case carefully on the floor and opened the lid. It meant so much to him, and he'd let me play it. He'd trusted me with it, with such an important thing in his life, and even more, he'd trusted me with his heart.

I'm in love with you.

A sob broke free, sending pain through my heart. I brought a shaking hand to my mouth to cover it.

Desiree came to the closet doorway, then rushed to my side, dropping to her knees. "Sweetie." She closed the lid on the guitar, buckling the latches.

211

"Where does this go?"

I bent over the case and pressed my forehead to it, inhaling the faint smell of him.

I love you, too.

He was better off without me. A painful breath hissed from my lips, the ache in my chest reminding me why I'd broken our hearts.

"Why don't you hop in the shower, and I'll stick around to help you with your makeup." Desiree rubbed her hand up and down my back.

By the time we had to head down for eliminations, I'd showered, put on a silver gown with jeweled straps, silver sling-back heels, and a layer of armor—er—makeup on my face. I had to sell it one more time. *Sell the lie and set him free.*

The last thing I did before leaving the room was grab the bottle of cologne from the nightstand. I unzipped my bag and put it right in the center of my clothes so it wouldn't get broken. I was a glutton for punishment.

Three couches were set up on the stage. Barbie and Jake were already seated, chatting animatedly. Desiree mic'd me up and directed me to the empty couch at the edge of the stage. Laura and Christian came in hand in hand, smiling and laughing.

My heart broke a little more.

Trisha's heels clacked on the wood floor as she climbed the steps to the stage. Crew members rushed around, getting into position.

No sign of Aiden.

Desiree made eye contact with me from behind the cameras and shrugged her shoulders.

The clock on the wall to the left of the stage said there were thirty seconds until we started the live broadcast. *Where was Aiden?*

Someone handed Trisha her sparkly microphone, and she positioned herself in front of the stage.

He wasn't going to show.

A hand behind the cameras held up five fingers.

Four.

Three.

Aiden's footsteps rushed onto the stage from the same side the couch was on, as if he'd been watching, waiting until the very last moment to make his appearance.

"Welcome to *Couple's Cruise—Celebrity Edition*."

I kept my eyes straight ahead. *Couldn't look at him. Didn't want to see either the hurt or lack of hurt on his face.*

The week's events, the shark tank and parasailing recapped on screen. My chin trembled, and I clenched my jaw. I couldn't sit here and torture myself, couldn't allow myself to break down in front of him. He needed to move on.

I stared down at my lap, unable to watch. My finger traced the notes on my tattoo. *No, I couldn't do that, either.* I clenched my hands in my lap and stared at the back of Trisha's head.

Barbie and Jake were safe.

How much of our fight did they air? How much damage had I done? His album was sure to get a lot of traction now. I'd made him a victim, and women everywhere would be looking to help him get over the wicked witch who'd broken him on national TV.

Trisha was beside our couch now, between us and Laura. We stood.

He'd get over me quickly. There'd be a line of women begging to replace me. And when his album came out, I'd buy the first copy. Tears blurred my vision, and I turned my head away from Aiden so he couldn't see them.

"Aiden and Dylan, I'm so sorry. It's time to say goodbye."

Numb.

In a blur, I hugged the two remaining couples, wished them well. I turned to say goodbye to Aiden, but he was gone.

Desiree escorted me to the top of the deck, where a helicopter pad was hidden away. My bags were already waiting for me. I wrapped my arms around her and cried into her shoulder.

"Thanks—" My voice cracked. "Thanks for everything."

"Thank you, Dylan. I'll miss you." She handed me a card with her name and phone number on it. I clutched it as I walked to the helicopter.

A crewman opened the door and helped me inside.

Aiden was pressed against the far door of the chopper, a headset on, his eyes glued to the seat in front of him. His hair was disheveled. His scruff looked especially messy, and he was wearing the same outfit he'd worn for dinner last night. Is that what he wore to eliminations?

He didn't even acknowledge my presence. There was a headset on my seat, and a crewman helped me buckle in and put it on my ears.

"Can you hear me?" The pilot's lips moved, but without the headset, I wouldn't have heard a word.

I nodded.

He checked my harness one more time. "Enjoy the ride."

The door closed, and I leaned over and rested my head against the warm glass.

Our pilot's voice sounded in the headset. "Did you enjoy the cruise?"

Please, no. I couldn't do the small talk. Not when I was barely keeping it together. Not when I couldn't trust myself to speak.

"It was a lot of fun." Aiden's voice tore at what was left of my heart. "We did a bunch of real fun things."

"What was your favorite part?"

I held my breath. Aiden was my favorite part. Every thought, every word, every breath revolved around him.

"The down time. The time between filmin' when we just got to relax, hang out in our room. Watchin' TV, playin' games, writin' songs."

My eyes closed as I listened to his words, memorizing the cadence and timbre of his voice as a tear trailed down my cheek.

214

Thirty-Eight - Aiden

My hand trembled as I brought the bottle to my lips and took a large gulp, some of it splashing onto my shirt as I searched the cabinets for a clean glass. None. They were all dirty. I didn't need one, anyway. I just needed to get her out of my head.

Her.

Why, after almost a month, was she still in my head? The girl I'd let in after I swore I wouldn't let anyone else. The girl who broke down my barriers one at a time. The girl who wiggled through the cracks in the walls I'd carefully erected without ever realizing what she was doing. Or maybe she did.

I tilted the bottle back. If I could still think, I hadn't had enough.

Twice I had let a girl in. Only twice in my entire life had I entertained the thought of love, of spending my life with someone. Both times I'd been burned. Both times I hadn't seen it coming. *Why was I so blind? So optimistic?* I knew better, and I gave in, anyway.

Another tilt of the bottle left me with nothing but glass against my lips. I pulled the bottle away and looked at it, squinting to clear the blurriness. As if staring at the bottle would somehow make it full again. *I needed more. I could still see her. Smell her.*

The floral scent of her shampoo. Blonde waves still damp from the shower. *What had I missed?*

I ran my fingers through my hair and one got stuck on something sticky. *Gross. When was the last time I'd showered?*

I glanced down at my clothes, trying to remember when I'd put them on, and lifted my arm to take a whiff of my armpit. An action I instantly regretted. How long had I been wearing that shirt? Taking up the half empty bottle on the counter, I unscrewed the cap and tilted it toward my lips; the burning pushed away the smell of heartbreak and worthlessness.

But not the memory of Dylan.

Another long swallow as I stumbled into the bathroom and set the bottle of Jack on the counter. My reflection spun, and I shook my head in a useless attempt to steady it. My hair was disheveled, my usual scruff had grown into a beard, and my eyes were bloodshot. I looked at the shower, but squashed that idea. Too much work, and I'd get water in my whiskey. *Couldn't have that.*

Dylan did this to me. It was her fault I was like this.

If I said it enough, it would be true.

Dylan agreed to be my girlfriend for cash. For fame.

Another drink.

Dylan played the game as well as Sheena had. Maybe better. Dylan fooled me when I was already jaded. Sheena, I could explain away by inexperience and blind love.

But Dylan?

I replayed our first day. Meeting her and her fake blonde hair. Wrapping my arms around her waist and lifting her off her feet, even then feeling like I'd known her.

Dragging her into a trailer to get to know her before we had to go on air and talk about our relationship.

Our relationship.

I scoffed and brought the bottle back to my lips.

The lie about how we'd met at Evan's birthday party.

What would've been different if we *had* met at Evan's birthday party? If I'd met her before the cameras, and the manipulative producers, and the makeovers. If I'd gotten to know the real her from the get-go.

Before the kale chip incident.

I closed my eyes against the burning pain in my chest at the memory. It was the start of my fall. The instant she'd found the first crack and began working her way in. She hadn't known it, hadn't been trying. One tiny near death experience, and I was lost.

Numb. I needed to be numb.

I tripped over a box on my way to the couch and caught myself on the coffee table. My hand landed on a fork handle sticking out of a half-eaten container of beef and broccoli, spattering the sauce against the wall.

Dylan loved Chinese food.

I wiped my hand on my boxers as I pushed myself onto the couch. *Oblivion. I needed oblivion.* No matter how I tried, I couldn't get there. No matter how much I drank, she haunted me. Taunted me with the knowledge I'd messed up.

Again.

I let out an exaggerated breath as I held the bottle away from my lips; the letters swirling together in a muted haze of earth tones. "You'll never leave me, will ya, Jack?"

But she had.

She'd left me. Hadn't even looked back. Walked away and left me standing there to gather the pieces of my heart.

Lyrics. Always about her. Why her? Every time, her. I struggled to sit so I could write them down. At least she had the decency to leave me with material for the album I needed to record. Isn't that what I'd wanted? Been angry about the cruise for taking time from? I needed to write lyrics, I'd said. Focus on my music. If I didn't have material, I was done.

Fate had a real sense of humor.

Where'd that notebook go? I put Jack down to move takeout containers, empty bottles, and pizza boxes.

My heart ached and my head pounded. I rubbed my temple and scooped up the bottle, bringing it to my lips.

I needed to get her out of my head, and if the bottle wasn't working, that left me with only one option. I scooped up my notepad and began writing, letting the memories drip from my pencil and the lyrics ease the pain.

Thirty-Nine - Dylan

Thursday, I sent Colby and Mom home so I could watch the *Couple's Cruise* finale by myself.

I hugged a kleenex box to my chest as I watched. Seeing Barbie, Jake, Laura, and Christian brought back so many memories. My chest ached, a self-inflicted wound that I wouldn't heal.

Even seeing Trisha was hard. She hadn't spoken a kind word to me the entire time we were on the cruise, but she'd become a staple in my daily life.

Since it was the finale, they played a recap of the entire show. The couples like Aiden and I who had made it so far into the season were in more clips than the others.

Aiden's arms wrapped around me as we reeled our marlin in. A brief flash of us in the ice cream shop with Carlos, laughing as we grilled him about his life. Carlos was a person that others would have overlooked, but not Aiden. He saw a person and treated him like an equal. I loved that about him.

They played a clip of one of the eliminations. I was red-faced in the background. Aiden's arm was around me, and he was suppressing a smile. It was the night I'd been so nervous, and he'd called me stegosaurus.

A sob caught in my throat, but I smiled through it. The memories were bittersweet. Where the show missed the highlights, my mind filled in.

The week we won immunity standing next to Barbie and Jake. *Our first kiss.* The fake one that I'd hated. Seeing it made me miss his lips on mine. The way he cupped my chin in his hands, the way his lips grazed mine. I placed a trembling hand over my lips, wishing I could still feel those lips, his hands, his breath scalding my skin. Tears overflowed from my eyes, and

I hugged the tissue box tighter and wiped my eyes.

Zip lining. How we'd raced during the rappel. None of that was shown, but I could still see the smile on Aiden's face when I'd challenged him to the race. *Hear his shout of victory. Feel his arms wrapped around me.* I squeezed my eyes closed.

It was torture of the sweetest kind.

The shark cage, parasailing.

Finally, Trisha came back on the screen, her flashy microphone in hand. She was flanked by each of the couples.

"The winner of *Couple's Cruise—Celebrity Edition* and two hundred thousand dollars going to the charity of their choice is..."

I hated her pauses. They had the desired effect, building up anticipation, but really, they made me just want to shake the answer out of her.

"Jake Donahue and Barbie Simpson!"

My shoulders shook, whether with laughter or tears, I couldn't be sure. A smile split my lips at the same time a weight crushed my chest. If I hadn't had the relapse, would Aiden's and my name have been announced? I flipped off the TV, turned out the lights, and held the tissue box to my chest, crying until I fell asleep.

Friday morning, I went in to see my oncologist. Later that morning, I had a CT, MRI, blood work, and a biopsy. The cancer was back, but we had to figure out to what extent.

By that evening, I had a PICC line placed on the inside of my upper arm, and my first round of chemo was complete.

~

Eight days after I was admitted, I was discharged.

Melissa, a patient advocate, wheeled me down to the lobby, and we waited for Mom to pull the car around. "It's been fun having you here, Dylan. You're the first celebrity I've ever met."

Pain radiated in my chest. I wasn't a celebrity. I was some girl who fell in love with a boy and dumped him on television.

"It's a shame what happened between you and Aiden." The way she said it made my teeth ache from clenching them so hard.

"Can I tell you a secret?" I wanted to tell someone, clear my conscience even if it was useless. I'd never forgive myself for the way I'd hurt Aiden, just like I never would've been able to forgive myself if I hadn't. "I only broke it off because of the cancer. I didn't want him to go through this."

She gasped. "So he doesn't know about the cancer?"

I shook my head, unable to speak.

"So the breakup?"

Emotion clogged my throat, and tears swam in my eyes. "I had to."

"That's so sad." Her voice sounded legitimately upset. I didn't have the strength to turn and look at her face.

The elevator door opened into the main lobby. She wheeled me out and to the front doors just as Mom pulled into the drive.

She parked and came around to the other side of the car and opened the passenger side door for me.

Once I was all situated in the car, Melissa handed me a blue barf-bag. "Just in case you feel nauseous."

I shot her a wobbly smile and pushed open the barf bag. I was totally gonna need it. "Thanks, Melissa. And thanks for actually talking to me." It'd been weird this time.

My last stay at the hospital, when I was seventeen, the nurses were always there, chatting with me, very friendly. This time, the nurses were quiet, in and out, not a lot of extra talking."

"Security, because you're a celebrity." She smiled and backed away.

Ugh. I hated that word. *Celebrity.* It might as well have been a swear word.

"And because of what you did to Aiden." Melissa cringed. "Sorry. I'll let them in on the secret."

I let my eyes fall closed. In my haste to spare Aiden from this, I hadn't considered the blow-back from people. If the situations were reversed, I'd probably hate me, too.

Mom leaned over and reclined my chair just a little bit so I didn't have to do all the work holding myself up. She buckled my seatbelt and planted a kiss on my forehead. "Let's get you home, sweetie."

I closed my eyes and focused on breathing as bile danced in my stomach, trying to keep the nausea at bay.

"Wanna stop at the bakery while we're in the city and get some blueberry muffins? I know they're your favorite." The crank of the engine filled the silence between us.

My throat tightened, and thoughts of Aiden surged through my mind. I turned to the side, and my head swam. A few seconds later, I emptied my stomach into the blue bag.

Mom put the car back into park. Her door slammed and she came around and opened mine, took the bag from me, and handed me a new one. She was so efficient, pulling a baby wipe from the passenger side door, and handing it to me to wipe my face. Then she held a bottle of water to my lips and let me swish my mouth clean before helping me sit. Mom held my hair back as I spit it onto the cement. *This was the crap I didn't need Aiden to see.* He'd never look at me the same again.

Tears burned my eyes. My first stint with cancer, I kept thinking I hadn't even had a chance to live yet. Cancer stole my senior year of high school. I hadn't been strong enough to walk down the aisle at graduation. They had to install a special ramp to the stage of the auditorium so Jenny could wheel me up to get my diploma. I couldn't even wheel myself, I was so weak.

This time was different. I'd lived. I'd tasted what life was like, and I wanted to keep living. Thoughts of death were never far from my mind, and they were always followed by thoughts of Aiden.

I cradled my wrist to my chest, staring at the bar of music. He'd played it on the guitar for me. I hummed the bar, trying to imagine him singing words to the line. What lyrics went with the notes? Would I hear it on the radio someday and recognize it?

"Will you turn the radio on, please?" It was too soon for it to be out yet, but suddenly just the thought of hearing his voice was enough to get me through this. The small sliver of hope that he'd forgive. That once this was over, I could find him. *Convince him. But what if I had another relapse?* I had almost reached my five-year mark before my relapse, almost considered cancer-free. I'd just started that clock over.

A sob caught in my throat, and I wiped away the stubborn tears that

221

had started to fall. He wouldn't want to see me, anyway. Desiree wanted epic, and, for better or worse, I'd given her epic. Regret was a bitter pill to swallow.

Mom reached out and rubbed my arm, and I flinched away.

"My arm is still tender." *The stupid PICC line.* I'd have another scar. Lots more scars, like another crater in my chest from the biopsy. Maybe I'd wear a bikini if I survived it. Tell people I'd survived a mafia hit. The five-year-old train-track scar from my port was a couple inches below and to the right of my breast, and now I'd have a nice crater to go with it. When all was said and done, my torso would be a mess of scars and bad memories.

"I watched the show, Dyl. You can talk to me." Mom's hand hovered over me as if she was unsure where she could touch without hurting me.

The sob squeaked out. "I'm in love with him."

Mom sat silent, something she'd mastered, listening, encouraging me to continue.

I dashed the tears from my eyes and curled my arms around myself, being careful of the PICC line. "I miss him."

"Why did you end it?" she asked, but kept her gaze straight ahead as we pulled onto the road.

"Nobody deserves this amount of worry." She wouldn't convince me that I'd done the wrong thing. I'd spared Aiden a huge amount of stress and heartache.

Before my initial diagnosis, we had family pictures taken. Then, when I finished my last round of chemo, I took a selfie with Mom and Dad. Even though it had only been two years, they looked ten years older. The worry, the stress, it aged people. Even Colby looked older, much older. Like he'd seen death and barely escaped. I couldn't do that to Aiden.

"No one deserves to go through this alone, Dyllie Bean." Mom held her hand out to me, and I placed mine in it.

My throat constricted. "That's why I have you." I squeezed her hand and dashed at the tears with the wrist of my other hand.

"You know the difference between you and me?" Mom asked.

"What?"

She lifted my hand to her lips and kissed the back of it. "We both miss the men we love, but yours is still alive. You're choosing to miss him."

"Mom. Can we please not do this? I don't have the energy. Let's change the subject." I flopped my head to the side.

"Something came for you in the mail." Mom's voice was light, as if she didn't know how much to tell me.

I was instantly suspicious, but feigned nonchalance. "What?"

"A check for twenty thousand dollars." Her voice was an octave higher than usual.

"Put it toward medical bills. The money was the whole reason I decided to do the show." I turned my face away and let the tears stream down my cheeks.

Dad's truck was as good as gone.

Forty - Aiden

Forged in fire had seven seasons, one hundred forty-one episodes, and I'd seen every one. Or slept through them, anyway. Turned out that our local liquor store delivered. Which meant I didn't even have to leave the house.

At least I'd quit thinking about Dylan all the time. She was never on my mind. I never thought about how much I hurt or how upset I was at her for selling me out. Never thought I smelled her shampoo, or felt her curled into my side as I slept. I closed my eyes and let myself imagine her beside me.

Oof. Something solid dropped on my stomach. "What the heck?" I picked up the magazine and glared at Evan.

He looked around the house, disgust etched in every feature. "Get it together, Aiden. I've been calling you for weeks." He pointed at the magazine, then spun on his heels and left.

That was it?

I rubbed my eyes and grabbed the bottle of Jack. *Empty, dang it.* The bottle slipped from my fingers and clunked to the floor. *What was so important that he had to wake me up?* I lifted the magazine and mumbled the headline, "*Couple's Cruise* Contestant's Cancer Relapse." The picture was blurry, and I brought the magazine closer to my face.

Would've known that blonde hair anywhere. It plagued my best dreams and worst nightmares. My blood ran cold, and my whole body went numb, except for my heart. My heart beat an increasingly painful rhythm. I was instantly sober, dropped my feet to the ground, and flipped through the magazine, searching for the story that went along with the cover picture.

There. A picture of the two of us sitting on one of the elimination couches.

224

My throat closed, and I had to force myself to read the words.

"I only broke it off because of the cancer. Didn't want him to go through this."

Tears gathered in my eyes, and I cried like a baby. My chest constricted, crushing my heart and making it impossible to breathe. I dropped the magazine and gripped the edge of the coffee table.

Cancer.

It was a death sentence, and she'd broken up with me because she knew it. *I was a fool.* I should have gone after her, made her explain.

What had I done? What made her think that I couldn't handle it? Why did she run from me instead of turning to me for help?

How could I have missed the signs? The fever, the pain.

On our last day together, she'd taken every opportunity to touch me. Trailing her fingers along my arm, linking our pinkies together, sitting close. *She knew.* She knew, and she was saying goodbye. How could I have overlooked it? She was trying to spare me.

The sadness in her eyes as we parasailed, I knew something was off, why didn't I ask her? Press her for answers?

I had to fix it.

Fix us.

Forty-One - Dylan

"Does it hurt?" Jenny wrinkled her nose and stared uneasily at the dressing over the freshly placed port above my right breast. She wasn't good with medical stuff.

I dragged my eyes open and flopped my head toward her. "Yeah." I grimaced through another wave of pain centered in my chest, then sucked in a few shallow breaths until the worst had passed. "Thanks for coming. It means a lot."

The first time I had cancer, she didn't come to the hospital at all. Waited until I was home to visit. Taking me to the hospital was a big step for her.

She came to the bed and stood with her hands out to her sides, as if trying to figure out how to lift me. "How does this work? Do I carry you like a baby or something?" She smiled and forced a laugh, but it fell flat.

"You can't carry me like a baby. Just help me up." I smiled to put her at ease and reached weakly toward her. That was my life now. I had to smile. I was the one going through cancer, but I had to comfort the people around me. Make *them* feel comfortable with the weird things happening to *my* body. If I died, I'd do it lying to my family and friends. Death was its own release. I wasn't afraid.

Lies. All of it.

The truth was, I wasn't ready to die.

Jenny helped me sit, and I grabbed the scarf on the bed beside me. My hair was already starting to come out. I held it out to her, and she tied it around my head. It was probably time to just shave it off. A month into chemo was about when I lost it all last time. I wasn't quite ready to shave it off yet, though. Part of me still hoped it wouldn't all come out, but when I was brushing it after my shower today, that telltale sound of velcro being ripped open told me I was fighting a losing battle. It was coming out.

She pulled me up and slung my arm over her shoulder. "I forgot how awkward you are when you have no strength."

Together, we stumbled out to her convertible, and she helped me into the front seat. My abs were already sore from my shower earlier. My bones ached, and my head pounded. I hadn't even put my own pants on. My throat tightened. *When did putting on my own pants become the sign that I was doing okay?*

"No barfing in my car." She smiled again, and I knew her well enough to know it was fake. She reclined my chair and buckled the seatbelt across my lap.

The door slammed and Jenny went around to her side, turned the car on and kicked it into reverse. A few minutes later, as we were driving to the hospital, Aiden's voice rang out over the radio. I closed my eyes and let it wash over me. It was like sewing closed a stab wound while the knife was still in it. A tear escaped my eye and trickled into the hair at my temple.

"What's wrong? Are you in pain? What's happening? Where does it hurt?" The car started to slow.

"Don't pull over, I'm fine." My words croaked out through the emotions clogging my throat. *I missed him, missed how he would order my favorite Chinese dishes without having to ask. Missed watching the corners of his eyes crinkle as we laughed over our favorite episodes of* The Office. *The way we geeked out over* Forged in Fire, *and how we both added knife making to our bucket list.* I choked on a sob and clutched my hands in my lap. *The way his face lit up when I came out of the bathroom in my pajamas and makeup free face. The way he accepted me for who I was, and not the person I was pretending to be. The way he'd stare at me, his eyes narrowed, a small smile parting his lips, then lift his notebook and jot something in it. The way he kissed my tattoo. Our tattoo.* I turned my wrist and stared down at it. The notes he'd drawn. Were those all the proof I'd have of our relationship? A couple bars of music on my arm?

Jenny gasped. "Oh Dylan, the song. I'm so sorry." The sound cut off.

As much as it hurt, I welcomed the pain. Pain meant I was alive. And the heartache was proof I'd done more than just live. I'd *lived*. Falling in love was one more item to check off my bucket list.

"You should just call him." She was so matter-of-fact about it.

"I don't have his number." The words were barely a whisper. I wouldn't call him even if I did. I cleared my throat. "Besides, you're one to talk. Just call Evan." Those words were barely louder, despite my efforts to force them to be.

"Things with Evan aren't that simple." Her tone was short and made me crack open my eyes. She had a stranglehold on the steering wheel, her knuckles white from the effort.

"Why not? You love him. He loves you. Sounds pretty simple to me." I let my head fall to the side so I could see her better.

She shook her head and visibly relaxed, flexing her fingers, but her tone remained clipped. "Trust me. It's complicated."

Something was going on. Jenny had been super withdrawn since I got back from *Couple's Cruise*. She wasn't herself. We never kept things from each other, but I had a feeling she had a secret. "I'm here when you're ready to talk, Jen." My eyes drifted closed.

The song turned back on, and we listened to it in silence.

As the final chord played, Jenny turned off the radio. "I'm pregnant." She whispered the words, and my eyes snapped open. Her chin trembled and tears swam in her eyes. "I'm so scared."

My knee jerk reaction was to point out that was why we'd made the pact, but she didn't deserve my anger. She needed compassion. "Oh, Jenny." My hand twitched as I tried to reach toward her.

"I feel so stupid. I'm so worried about this, and you're over here fighting for your life. My problems feel so insignificant compared to yours." The tears broke free and trailed down her cheeks. She turned on her signal and pulled into a parking lot.

"Don't compare our problems. Having a baby is a huge deal. Life changing. Does Evan know?"

She shook her head. "I don't want to tell him." Her words squeaked out, and she grabbed a tissue from the console between us.

What? "Why not?"

Jenny wiped her eyes and blew her nose, shaking her head. "There are so many reasons. You wouldn't understand."

It was like a punch in the gut. We shared everything and had always been there for each other. But it wasn't about me. It was about her, about what she needed from me as a friend. "Jenny, it's me. Tell me. I might not understand, but I will always listen. And I'll always care."

She blew her nose again, her shoulders shaking. "Dads leave." Jenny's dad left when she was ten. Went to the grocery store for ice cream and never came back; until she'd won *Singing Sensation.* Then he showed up every time he ran out of money.

I couldn't even imagine what brought her to that conclusion. But telling her it was unreasonable wouldn't do any good. My heart ached for her, and I tugged her toward me. Or, I tried. It was more like an ant trying to move a semi-truck. She leaned over the console and wrapped her arms around me.

"I'm so sorry." I did my best to hug her while I reclined in the chair, my arms not wanting to work, but I forced them to, anyway. *Bone tired was an expression I knew all too well.*

A few minutes later, Jenny sat back and wiped her eyes, resolve clear in her expression. What she'd decided was a mystery, but she had my sympathy. She wiped under her eyes and buckled her seatbelt, then gripped the steering wheel while she stared out the window.

"I'm okay." She seemed to be talking more to herself than to me, so I didn't respond. Jenny put the car in gear, and off we went.

Too soon, we pulled into the hospital parking lot. Jenny pulled a baseball cap low over her face and disappeared into the building. She came out a minute later with a wheelchair and a nurse to boost me in.

Jenny pushed on the back of the chair while the nurse pulled the lever to sit it up. The weakness was one of the worst things about cancer.

We rolled into the hospital and up to the cancer floor. My hospital visits were an all-day event. Jenny checked me in while I transferred to the couch in the waiting room. A few minutes later, they pulled me back to draw my blood.

When I came out, Jenny clutched a magazine to her chest, her brows drawn. "Dyl. Sit."

I grabbed the handles of the chair across from her and eased into the seat. "What's up?"

She stood and moved to the seat beside me. "Don't freak out, but remember how weird it was when you saw my face on the cover of a magazine for the first time?

I nodded.

"Well, this is so surreal." She held the magazine in front of me.

Across the top, read the headline, "*Couple's Cruise* Contestant's Cancer Relapse." Below it was a blurry picture of me in a hospital bed.

How the heck had they gotten that? I closed my eyes and let my head fall back against the wall. "I don't care." *Which was a lie*. I didn't have the energy to care. Maybe I could worry about it later, but now, I just wanted to sleep.

I stretched my legs out and put them on the coffee table in front of me and folded my arms across my chest. It was shaping up to be a long day.

"Dylan Kennedy." A nurse stopped in front of me with a wheelchair. "Ready for your MRI?"

Did it matter? We were doing it either way.

Jenny stood and held a hand out to me and pulled me to my feet, then braced me as I spun to drop into the wheelchair.

The nurse turned to Jenny. "We'll be right back."

Jenny nodded and sat, opening the magazine.

An hour later, they brought me back to see my oncologist.

"Hey, Dylan. How're you feeling today?" Dr. Brandon sat on his rolly stool and wheeled it in front of me.

Dr. Brandon was one of the few people who actually wanted an honest answer to that question. Everyone else always wanted to hear how well I was handling my diagnosis with death. Wanted to hear how brave I was being. Didn't care to know I ached deep in my bones, or that every time I washed my hair, more and more of it was coming out. Didn't care that I was mourning the possibility of death.

I smiled and gave him a thumbs up, knowing he wouldn't believe me.

He raised an eyebrow, one corner of his mouth tipping up into a sardonic smile. "Tell me."

"My bones hurt." I leaned back in the chair and yawned.

"What else?" He nodded, his mouth in a line. "I see you've already lost fifteen pounds. Are you eating okay?"

"I'm not hungry, and when I do eat, it doesn't stay down." *I popped nausea pills like Tic Tacs.*

"Well, I've looked over your MRI, young lady, and your tumor doesn't seem to be responding to this round of treatment. I'd like to up your dosage, if that's alright with you?"

My tumor hadn't changed. "What does that mean?"

"We'll have to be a little more aggressive. There's a drug I'd like to try, if you're amenable." He went into an explanation, and I tried to listen, but lost track of what he was saying with the tumult of my thoughts.

Treatment isn't working. I'm too young to die, have too much I still want to do. I had a bucket list, and I'd need years still to complete it. Tears stung my eyes, and I blinked them away.

Dr. Brandon patted my hand and pushed away from my chair. "Try to eat more, okay? We'll run some fluid with your chemo again today."

"You got it." I forced the response out through the emotion.

We had another hour before my next appointment, so Jenny wheeled me down to the cafeteria. I was being especially lazy. I could walk, but the thought of standing for that long was enough to make me want another nap. That, and my eyes refused to focus. *Treatment wasn't working.* I was grateful my mom had to work today; that I wasn't that seventeen-year-old girl who needed her parents' permission to switch treatment. If Mom knew, she'd age another decade. She'd worry, and for all her worry, there was nothing she could do.

"What do you want to eat?" Jenny parked my chair at a table, bringing me out of my thoughts.

Nothing sounded good anymore. "Just nothing spicy." Spicy burned coming back up, and I could almost guarantee it would come back up, especially right after chemo.

She waggled her eyebrows at me, but her smile didn't reach her eyes. Jenny was terrible at medical stuff, and my heart swelled at her attempt to treat me like the old Dylan. The Dylan that wasn't dying.

She crouched beside the chair and rested her hand on my armrest. "They have Chinese. You want Sweet and Sour chicken?"

My throat closed at the reminder of Aiden. *Dang it. Would it ever stop hurting when I thought of him? Would Chinese food forever make me think of Aiden Miller?* I turned my hand over and stared at the tattoo on my wrist. At least I was able to do a few things on my bucket list before I died. "Sure."

Jenny disappeared into the crowd while I traced the notes and hummed the tune.

A while later, she placed a styrofoam container in front of me and opened it. *"Bon appétit."*

I picked up the fork and stabbed a piece of chicken, rolled it around in the rice and nibbled a piece off the end. *It was tangy and warm and tasted like regret.*

My stomach turned. *Nope, couldn't do it.* There was no way I could eat that. It'd ruin Sweet and Sour for me forever. *Well, more than he already had.*

Jenny sat across from me, keeping up a stream of chatter about her album. She reached across the table, stuck her fork into my chicken, then popped the piece in her mouth. "How are you feeling?"

Like death warmed over. "Good, considering the circumstances." I forced a smile. "Think that hair stylist from *Couple's Cruise* would cry if she saw my hair?" I bawled my eyes out when I saw it.

She laughed and speared another bite of chicken. "You're cute with a pixie cut. Do you want to do something about it? We can stop at a salon, and you can wear a mask or something."

"I'm going to be exhausted after this. I won't be able to sit for that long. Maybe another day." I dropped my fork on the table and slid the container toward her.

"Sounds good." Jenny shoveled another bite into her mouth, making appreciative noises as she chewed. "This is so good."

"At least one of us can enjoy it." I leaned back and took measured breaths through my mouth so I couldn't smell it.

Jenny polished off my lunch, then wheeled me back to the cancer floor, and I slept through chemo.

Forty-Two - Aiden

Garbage was everywhere.

I looked around the room for the first time. Really looked. Whiskey bottles littered every surface, including one wedged in the crack between sofa cushions. I waded through the piles of filth to the kitchen and grabbed the roll of garbage bags, I'd definitely need more than one and set to work cleaning.

The first thing on the to-do list was to find my cell phone.

I opened the first garbage bag and began filling it with takeout containers. Each time I pushed one into the bag, the rotted stench from the others would resurface, gagging me. Normally, I'd just call a cleaning company, but this was a new low for me. A new level of filth that I'd be embarrassed to present, even if just to a group of strangers paid to clean it.

Two hours later, my cell phone was charging, the garbage was cleaned, and I was loading the dishwasher.

My first call was to Peggy.

"I need Dylan's phone number."

"Aiden, good to know you're alive. I've left you several messages. Don't suppose you've bothered to listen to any of them, have you?" Her sarcasm was thick and grated on my nerves.

"Her number, Peggy, or I'll find a new manager." I ground my teeth and squeezed my cell phone, daring her to push me on it. She was the reason I'd met Dylan, which meant she was also the reason I lost her.

"I'll see what I can do." She ended the call before I could respond.

The second call was to my record producer.

"Aiden Miller. Heard you fell off the planet," Don said.

"I need to record. Can you come to me?"

"Always. When do you want to start?"

"As soon as you get here."

The third call was to the only pawn shop I could find in Clearwater, Montana.

"Pawn shop, this is Jeff."

"Hey Jeff. I'm looking for a '48 Army green Chevy 3800. I'm willing to pay thirty-grand, cash."

"Who is this?" Jeff asked.

"Aiden Miller, Dylan Kennedy's boyfriend." Okay, that was a stretch, but he didn't need to know that.

"Y-yes, sir, Mr. Miller."

The fourth item on the agenda was to finish Dylan's song. The lyrics for the final verse had been evading me for weeks.

My notebook was wrinkled with water damage, or whiskey damage. Most of the pages were stuck together, but her song was still there.

I picked up the pen and began writing on a blank sheet of paper.

The phone buzzed a minute later. A text from Peggy. She'd sent me several pictures, a copy of Dylan's contract. Her name scrolled across the bottom in a looping script.

Near the bottom, where the name of the charity was, I read the name Huntington Cancer Institute. That was where she wanted to send the money if we won; to cancer research. If it were possible, my heart ached more. A cause so close to her.

An idea formed in my mind, an idea that she would absolutely love. My only regret was that I wouldn't be there to see her face when she got it.

Forty-Three - Dylan

I squeezed the pillow to my chest and inhaled Aiden's cologne. When I'd first taken it from his nightstand on the ship, I felt a little guilty, but the more his scent clung to my bed and clothes, the more that guilt faded.

Mom knocked on my door. "Hey, sweetie. You need any help getting ready?"

My jammies were at the foot of my bed, waiting to suck the rest of my energy. I pushed up, bringing my pillow with me. Did I want to do it myself, or act like a toddler and have Mommy put them on for me? *Definitely a toddler.* "Please."

She perched on the bed beside me and put her arm around my waist.

I laid my head on her shoulder. "I think it's time, Mom."

"Time for what? We still have a half hour before we have to go." She glanced at her watch.

"The hair." I made a buzzing sound with my mouth and mimed shaving it off. It'd been coming out all week, and Mom had basically followed me around with a vacuum cleaner. A lump formed in my throat, and I held the pillow tighter. They'd have to bury me in a wig.

"Oh, Dylie Bean." Mom rubbed my back with one hand and tucked the remaining strands behind my ear with the other, her smile tinged with sadness. "We don't have to do it now."

"Let's just get it over with before I change my mind." *Not that going bald was something someone could change their mind about. Millions of men across the world would have full heads of hair if that were the case.*

She helped me to my feet and into the hallway bathroom. "Are you sure?"

Mom dug around under the sink and produced a haircutting cape.

No. I nodded.

Ten minutes later, I stared at my bald head in the mirror. How did men do it? I'd kept my wigs from last time, but I couldn't bring myself to wear one. They were so hot and hard to make look nice, and I was always worried it'd shift and people would be able to tell it was a wig.

Mom helped me back to my room and into my jammie pants. They slid on way too easily. She pulled on the waistline, then cinched the drawstrings snug.

Would her smile ever reach her eyes again? She always looked so sad. The dark circles under her eyes and the wrinkles that bracketed her smile seemed more pronounced. It'd only get worse if I didn't pull through. My stomach was tied in knots. Today was the day, the moment of truth. If my tumor hadn't responded, it wouldn't be the end of the world, but it would mean more treatments, and the possibility that they wouldn't work at all. That it really was the end. I'd die and Aiden would never know how I felt.

The drive to the hospital was uneventful. I made Mom sit in the waiting room while I went back for my appointment. They did another MRI and more bloodwork. It'd been eating me all week, knowing it wasn't getting better. The tumor wasn't responding to treatments. I'd almost broke down and told her once, but I was waiting. Waiting to see how Dr. Brandon's new treatment was working. If it *was* working.

Dr. Brandon strode into the exam room and sat on his rolly stool. "Morning, Dylan. How are you feeling today?"

I shrugged. "That all depends on what you have to tell me about my MRI." I forced a smile. I wasn't looking forward to that conversation with Mom. *Let her think that I was getting better, that the treatments were working. It was the least I could do.*

He smiled and put on his stethoscope, quiet as he listened to my heart and lungs. "Everything sounds good. Your tumor looks to be responding to this treatment." He patted my shoulder, and I sagged in relief, tears stinging my eyes, then dripping down my cheeks without warning.

"You're doing well, Dylan. I have every reason to be hopeful." He pushed away from me and went to the small desk in the corner of the room and typed on his laptop. "We'll keep up this phase of treatment until I'm satisfied, then we'll move into the maintenance phase. I'm glad we tried that other drug."

Me, too. "Yeah, losing my hair faster is fine, as long as it's working."

He glanced at the scarf wrapped around my head. "It'll come back in no time. The important thing is, I'm optimistic. Let's beat it."

When I joined mom in the waiting room, I couldn't help the smile that overtook my face.

"Good news?" She half stood, as if she was afraid to hope, afraid if I told her no, the chair would be too far away to catch her fall.

"Yes, the tumor is responding to treatments."

Mom pulled me into a hug, wrapping her arms around my waist.

"I'm so relieved." She laughed.

A weight lifted from my shoulders, and I joined in. "Me, too." There would be no conversation where I told Mom I was dying. No comforting her while I fought an internal battle, while I came to grips with my fate.

A short time later, they took me back for my next round of poison. *I mean, treatment.* With the new round, they were keeping me overnight to monitor me.

Mom plopped into the chair next to my bed and pulled out a book as the nurse bustled around me, getting things set up and layering me in heated blankets.

"Just go to a hotel. I promise it'll be okay. I won't be offended." I raised an eyebrow at her, daring her to disagree. She never slept well in the chair, then complained about it on the hour-long drive back home.

"You sure?" Mom hadn't even tried to resist. *She was learning.*

"Yeah."

She planted a kiss on my forehead and gathered her stuff. "Call me if anything changes, or if you just need me. I'll be here, okay? I'm just a few minutes away."

"Go." I waved a hand as the nurse hooked me up to Satan's urine. *I mean poison—I mean chemo.*

It was making me better, so the medicine was welcomed, but as it began flowing into my veins, I could almost feel my energy seeping out. Sleep came in lazy, disjointed sections, accompanied by strange, nonsensical dreams.

"Dylan?" Becky, my nurse, walked in carrying a gift basket with mylar balloons floating from the handle. "This came for you."

That's weird. "Here?" Why would anyone send anything to me here? I was only here six hours a week.

She brought it in and set it on my tray, then wheeled it beside me.

"Need me to help?" She scooted a stool over and perched on the edge. "I can be your hands. You just rest." She grabbed the card and opened it.

"A special thank you." She flipped the card open. "Thank you so much for your recent donation to the Huntington Cancer Institute. Your contribution of two-hundred thousand dollars—"

A sob caught in my throat. There had to be a mistake. "We didn't win. We didn't get to decide where the money went."

"Let's just see what they said, shall we?" She skimmed the card. "Your contribution. Yada yada yada. Help with the research. That's it." She turned to the basket and untied the ribbon, then opened the cellophane. She held up a pair of leather jeweled flip-flops, identical to the pair I wore on the cruise.

My breath caught.

"Flip-flops?" Becky's eyebrow raised. "Is there a story here?"

I nodded, unable to speak. I'd have to return it all. It was a mistake, but part of me hoped it wasn't.

The next item sent goosebumps all over my body. A flat jewelry case. Becky flipped the top open and turned the box for me to see. A black and pink pearl necklace. Aiden bought it the day we were in Rio. *The basket was from Aiden? What did that mean?* My breath squeaked out. I brought a trembling hand to my mouth and reached for the box with the other. My vision blurred with tears, and hope bloomed in my chest.

The bag of kale chips made me burst out with laughter. "You have to watch the show. I almost choked on kale chips."

"Reeses." She pulled out a big package of the chocolate bars.

239

He remembered. I wiped my eyes on the pillow in my lap.

"What's this?" She held a small black device in her hand and pulled a pair of headphones from the basket. "An MP3 player?" Becky placed the headphones over her ears and pressed a button. A second later, she smiled, pulled the headphones off, and held them out to me.

I studied her face as I slowly reached for the headphones, searching for some clue as to what I was about to hear. "What is it?"

"Just put them on. You'll see." I took them from her hand and slid them over my ears, then nodded for her to start the audio.

A guitar strummed, and Aiden's voice came over the speakers. "Test, test. This is a rough cut of Every Breath, written for Dylan Kennedy, performed by Aiden Miller."

Hope was a dangerous thing. My lip began to tremble and tears stung my eyes anew. *He wrote me a song? And sent it to me?*

Aiden cleared his throat and began to play. As he started, I recognized the melody as the notes on my tattoo.

"This wasn't what I was expecting
Then again you never are
You've been shakin' things up, girl
Right from the start.

You laughed when the ocean kissed your face
And it caught me by surprise
'Cause then I wanted to be the waves
And bring that smile to your eyes

Every Breath
Since we met
I have spent
Tryin' to figure out these feelings
They weren't part of the agreement
But now every breath
I have left

240

Will be spent
Telling you
No one takes away my breath like you do

I'd been looking for a muse
  From the Rockies to the Gulf Coast
  Then you got under my skin like a tattoo
  Now your touch is the one I crave the most
  I don't know how,
  But baby you've found a way
  Over my walls
  With every smile of your unpainted face

Every Breath
  Since we met
  I have spent
  Tryin' to figure out these feelings
  They weren't part of the agreement
  But now every breath
  I have left
  Will be spent
  Telling you
  No one takes away my breath like you do

You play my heart strings
  Just like you played my guitar
  So tender and careful
  I forgot to be afraid and fell hard

Every Breath
  Since we met
  I have spent
  Tryin' to figure out these feelings

They weren't part of the agreement
But now every breath
I have left
Will be spent
Telling you
No one takes away my breath like you do"

As the words played, my hope bubbled. But could I trust it? And what did it mean? Did he want to get back together? Did he forgive me?

I glanced at the array of items on my bed, and my heart swelled with love. I had to talk to him.

After Becky left, I called Jenny.

"I need Aiden's number." Just the thought of talking to him made my voice squeak.

"What? What's going on, Dylan?" Jenny was all concern and understanding.

I smothered myself in the pillow covered with Aiden's cologne. I didn't want to tell her too much if it didn't mean anything, or if it wasn't anything more than a thank you. "He sent me something. I need to talk to him."

"What did he send you?"

I rubbed a hand over my head and down my face. "It doesn't matter. Do you have his number or not?"

"No."

"Can you get it?" It would require her to talk to Evan, and I wasn't sure she'd be willing to do it.

"I'm not calling Evan," she snapped.

After a beat, I heard her exhale.

"But I'll put out some feelers."

"Thank you." She was going through her own stuff right now, and I didn't want to push her. Yet. "Talk to you later."

"If I get his number, you owe me."

"Deal."

Forty-Four - Aiden

My hands were slick with sweat. I'd performed a thousand times, but it was different this time. Dylan would be there. It'd been a week since I sent the basket. A week of wondering if I was doing the right thing, a week of second guessing myself. A week of worry, and one secret phone call to her mom.

I'd flown in early this morning and went to the pawnshop to pick up Dylan's truck. An hour later, I was parked at the hospital and pulled a baseball cap lower over my eyes before stepping onto the elevator, guitar in tow. I pressed the button for the cancer floor and scooted to the back as more people loaded on. It wasn't quite how I'd imagined it going; a crowd of people crammed against me with their sweaty bodies, but no one recognized me.

The door opened on the cancer floor, and I pushed to the front and exited into the lobby.

Antiseptic assaulted my nose. And my heart pounded in my chest. It was show time. I took a big breath and let it out slowly. The nurses' station was directly in front of me, and I set my guitar case on the ground and folded my arms on the counter while I waited for someone.

Emotion clogged my throat as I looked at the pictures and letters hanging on the wall. Cancer didn't care how old someone was, how much life they had left to live, whether the victim was five years old, or fifty.

A nurse came up from behind me. "Can I help you?"

I pulled off my cap and ran a hand through my hair. "I'm here to visit a patient."

She put a hand to her chest. "Bless my soul, it's Aiden Miller."

"It's a surprise." I put a finger over my lips, hushing her.

She mimed zipping her lips shut and locking them with a key. "Who are you here to see?"

Another nurse popped her head out of one of the rooms and gasped. "Oh, my gosh."

It was gonna be a thing. But what better way to calm my nerves than cheering up people in the same situation as Dylan? I lifted my guitar case and set it on the counter, unlatched it, then pulled out my baby.

"Which room is Dylan's?"

The nurse pointed to a closed door near the end of the hall.

"Is there anyone who you think might enjoy a song?" I asked. Dylan was behind that door. In that room fighting for her life.

"Everyone." She led me to the opposite end of the hall and knocked softly on a door, then slipped inside, leaving me in the hallway.

The other nurse hovered behind me.

"What's your name?"

She looked down at the badge clipped to her shirt, then turned it around to face me. "I'm Becky, and I'm so glad you're here. Dylan is going to freak."

In a good way, hopefully. Did Becky have some insider information that was causing her to smile with her entire being?

"That basket you sent her." She clasped her hands beside her face and nearly swooned. "Oh, it was so romantic."

She did have inside information.

"She's probably got those headphones on right now listening to that song you sang for her." Becky fanned herself, her cheeks turning red.

I'd gotten her nice headphones. Maybe that was arrogant of me, but I wanted her to hear me how I sounded, not some tinny version of my voice.

The other nurse came out a second later, and I glanced at her nametag, Sophie. She nodded and waved me into the room. The man laying on the bed looked ageless. No hair or eyebrows. My heart ached for him. He struggled to sit and gave me an encouraging smile, waving his hand in an inviting motion.

"Can I sit on the edge of your bed?" I walked to the bed and waited for his reply at the foot.

"Yeah, man. Have a seat." *Young. He was young. Too young for cancer to be eating him alive.*

I slunk onto the edge of the bed. "What's your name?"

"Tyler."

"Nice to meet ya, Tyler I'm Aiden Miller." I shook his hand. "You have any requests?" I strummed a chord.

He shook his head.

My eyes closed, I took a deep breath and played the intro to one of my favorite songs. "This one is called, *Bucket List.*"

Never too young to start a list of things to do before you die.

Never too old to check them off, never too proud to cry.

Oh, I'd jump from a plane with a parachute, even sport a fu manchu.

Get a tattoo or try something new, dye my hair a neon blue.

As long as I could do them with you.

The next few verses almost caught in my throat as I sang, the reminder of the song more powerful than ever as I sat here in a room of people also fighting for their lives.

Tyler wiped his face with his palms and smiled at me. "Thanks, man. I haven't heard that one on the radio."

"You're the first person I've played it for besides my producer." I shrugged. It was one more song inspired by Dylan. The entire album was a soundtrack for our relationship.

"Awesome. Any chance I can get a selfie with you?"

"You bet." I shifted beside him on the bed and put my arm behind his shoulder. He held his phone out, and we smiled for a selfie.

On the way to the second patient, Nurse Becky brought a crying woman to me in the hall. "This is Kathy, Dylan's mom."

I handed my guitar to Becky and wrapped Kathy in a hug.

"Thank you for being here," she whispered. When she pulled back, she wiped her eyes. "Sorry, I was trying not to cry."

"It's alright. Dylan's an amazing woman. Thanks for raisin' her right."

The entire entourage followed me into the next room, where I sang for an older gentleman.

It can burn like honey on fire
Sweet but dangerous
It can be real smooth
Or make you choke on the truth
Whiskey's just like love
You can sip it slow
And stop when you've had enough
Or just let go
And deal with the hurt of having too much
It's hard to give up nippin' on the good stuff
Whiskey's just like love

Each verse brought a wave of memories. It was a song I'd written right after Evan threw the magazine on my stomach, and I'd found out about Dylan's diagnosis.

I sang to four patients and all the nursing staff before, finally, we approached Dylan's door. A lump had already formed in my throat. In my mind, I'd come, and she'd jumped up and been happy to see me. Had taken me back with open arms. This wasn't a fantasy though, this was real. My hands, which had gradually relaxed, were sweaty once again. There were too many "what ifs" and if I stood there going over them all, I'd never get the courage to go in.

Here goes nothing. I opened the door and took a quick breath. The curtain was drawn, blocking her from view, but her sleepy voice was singing my song. I glanced behind me and Kathy had her phone out, filming.

A grin stretched across my face as I recognized the lyrics. "She's singing my song." I barely put any voice behind the words, trying to keep my presence a secret. But the sound of my lyrics on her lips warmed my soul.

I inched the curtain open, and my stomach plummeted.

Dylan hugged a pillow to her chest as she leaned back in a chair with her eyes closed. Her lips moved, and the words of *Every Breath* croaked out on a whisper. The headphones covered her ears, and I took time to just study her. She had a bandana over her head, a tube ran from a spot above her collarbone to a machine dripping yellow liquid. Her cheeks were sallow, and the tan she had on the cruise nearly two months ago was almost gone.

She sang the chorus slightly louder. Her normally pure voice was slightly throaty.

She looked so weak, so frail. The fantasies I'd entertained of her jumping up and hugging me shattered. She'd be more likely to fall asleep from exhaustion. My love for her crescendoed, and I wanted nothing more than to hold her in my arms. To promise her I'd be here for her. To prove to her that I could handle all that life threw at us.

As she sang the chorus, I picked up where she was and played my guitar with the recording I couldn't hear. A second later, I joined her in singing the next verse.

Forty-Five - Dylan

I drifted in and out of sleep, my eyes closed as I listened to *Every Breath*. Before we left home, I'd sprayed my pillow with his cologne and brought it with me. It was currently clutched to my chest. The ache and hope mingled in my chest to make a heartbreak concoction.

Why had he sent me the song? The question had been plaguing me, even as I listened to the song for the thousandth time.

The song ended, and I waited for it to start at the beginning. Only there was no pause in the music. It took me a minute to realize it wasn't coming from the headphones.

My eyes snapped open, and I tore the headphones from my ears. Aiden stood at the foot of my bed, a hopeful smile on his face as he strummed a familiar guitar, making butterflies dance in my stomach again, a sensation I wasn't sure I'd ever feel again. But one look from Aiden brought them all back.

My breath caught in my throat. Holy crap. He was here! I brought a hand to my hair to make sure the bandana was covering it.

Aiden's voice was a little wobbly as he began singing another verse. One I hadn't heard.

"Now every line I sing, every breath I breathe
Begins and ends with you
You've forever beautifully ruined me
'Cause no one will ever take away my breath like you do
Every Breath
Since we met

I have spent
Tryin' to figure out these feelings
They weren't part of the agreement
But now every breath
I have left
Will be spent
Telling you
No one takes away my breath like you do."

He never broke eye contact, his gaze holding me a willing hostage. As he finished the song and his lips quit moving, his chin trembled and tears swam in his eyes. He shook his head and laughed, wiping them with the back of his hand. Becky came in and held her hand out, and he pulled the guitar strap over his head and handed her his baby without a second thought.

His image was blurry as he dropped to his knees beside my chair. He brushed my cheeks with his fingertips, then held my hand and brought my wrist to his lips.

"Aiden." His name barely escaped my lips. "I'm so sorry. I couldn't see another way. I didn't want you to go through all this."

He brought my hand to his cheek. It was wet with tears and scratchy from his scruff. "Don't. I'm sorry I wasn't here for you. Sorry it took me so long to come." He planted several kisses on my palm. "I'm in love with you."

My stomach dipped and my heart soared. I leaned forward, and he seemed to read my mind, meeting me halfway. Our foreheads met, and he placed a soft kiss on my lips.

"I love you, too."

Forty-Six - Aiden

Dylan rested with her hand in mine while the chemo dripped into her body. Her face was relaxed, and she hugged a pillow to her chest.

I replayed our kiss in my head, and leaned forward to touch her cheek, to reassure myself that she was really here with me again. When I did, I caught a familiar scent wafting from the pillow. "Wait a minute." Had she done what I thought she did? A smile crept to my lips. "That pillow smells familiar."

That beautiful blush crept up her cheeks, and I congratulated myself for still being able to make her do it. She held still and pretended to be asleep, but I knew better.

"I know you're awake, Dyl. I can see you blushing."

She buried her face in the pillow. "I don't know what you're talking about."

"Oh, ho ho." *She knew.* I stood and leaned beside her, inhaling the familiar scent of citrus and woods on the pillow. "Definitely my cologne."

"I don't need it anymore. I've got the real thing." She lifted her head and smiled a sleepy smile. "I can't be held responsible for anything I say while I'm getting chemo. It's all one big dream. So if I wake up tomorrow and you're not here, I'm going to be very disappointed."

My heart warmed, and I brought her wrist to my lips, planting a kiss over our tattoo.

"Dylan?" I waited until she pried her eyes open. "I almost forgot." I pulled the leather watch band from my left wrist and flipped it over so she could see the inside of my wrist.

Tears gathered in her eyes, and her hands shook as her fingers traced the tiny notes. "You got a matching tattoo?" Love shone in her eyes and a smile lit her face.

That smile right there was why I'd done it. That brilliant, breathtaking smile.

She lifted my hand to her lips and placed a kiss on my tattoo.

Warmth enveloped me as I traced a finger from her temple down her cheek. "That's not all I got."

Her eyes had already drifted closed, and I released her hand and walked to the window. I'd given Kathy the keys to the truck, and we'd figured out the perfect spot to park it so Dylan could see. I opened the blinds, and light streamed in through the window. After a second, I found the truck. The cars that had been parked around it had all left, and its location was fairly obvious.

"What are you doing?"

I walked over to her and hit the nurse button.

Moments later, the nurse came in. "Do you need something?"

I smiled my most charming smile. "Dylan would like to look outside for a minute. Do you think you can help us?"

The nurse gave me a confused look, but nodded. She disappeared, then came back with a wheelchair, and together we helped Dylan into it.

"What's going on?" Dylan asked.

"You'll see."

The nurse grabbed all the IVs and wheeled the pole with us as I pushed the chair to the window. I crouched until I was Dylan's height, then pointed in the direction of the truck.

"Oh." Her voice came out a squeak, and she lifted a trembling hand to her mouth. "My dad's truck?"

She reacted just as I hoped she would.

"You got it for me?"

I grabbed her hand and kissed the back of it. "Yes."

Dylan shook her head. "I can't accept that."

I laughed. Deep down, I knew she wouldn't let it be that easy. "Dylan?"

She looked up at me.

"I'm in love with you. Will you be my girlfriend?"

Despite the bags under her eyes, and the gauntness of her cheeks, when she smiled, my heart swelled. She was the most beautiful woman I'd ever known, inside and out.

She nodded.

"To make up for missing our two-month anniversary, I've bought you a gift."

Tears welled in her eyes, and she shook her head.

"And it would really mean a lot to me if you would accept this truck as a gift." I knelt in front of her and clasped her hands between mine in her lap. I looked up at her with puppy-dog eyes.

She laughed, and the sound was better than any song I'd ever written. "Okay."

Forty-Seven - Dylan

~Four Months Later~

Jenny towed me behind her as she waddled to the car.

"Where are we going? Just tell me." I clomped behind, trying not to fall over or sprain my ankle.

She'd spent way too long getting me ready, and my Spidey-Sense told me she was up to no good. We'd road-tripped eight hours to Salt Lake City, stayed in a hotel, and she'd even styled a wig for me.

"You'll see. Quit asking." She pulled a little harder, almost jerking me over in my high heels.

"You're going to break me if you aren't careful." I tried getting my arm free, but she just tightened her hold on my wrist.

She man-handled me all the way to the car, then started to buckle me.

"Whoa. I know you're practicing to be a mom and all, but you need to chill. I can do it." I took the seat belt from her and buckled it. "See? Easy peasy."

Her eyes narrowed, and she grinned. "Just buckle and quit asking questions."

"Yes, mom." I forced as much sass into those two words as humanly possible.

Jenny slammed the door in my face and went around to the driver's side.

Traffic was insane. The entire city seemed to be going in the same direction we were. "Why are we doing this?"

She didn't answer, just kept her eyes on the road.

"Are we there yet?" I debated repeating the question a million times just to get her used to a six-year-old, but refrained. *I'm such a good friend.*

"Shut your mouth." She held her hand in front of my face and closed her fingers like a mouth closing.

"Is that what you're going to say to your kid?"

"I'm about to just drop you off and call it good."

"Oh, good. The 'don't make me pull this car over.' You're learning."

"Dylan. Stop."

"Are you going to count to three? That's another good mom move."

She shook her head, her lips tipped up in an amused smile.

When the arena came into view, all other questions died on my lips. "Is Aiden here tonight?" He'd been touring for almost two months. We'd spent nearly every minute together after his appearance at the hospital, but eventually, Peggy had stolen him to go on tour. I'd talked to him every day but hadn't seen him.

Jenny smiled and shrugged her shoulders. "Maybe."

My heart picked up the pace, dancing in my chest, and my stomach decided now was the perfect time to drop out of my body completely. *I was going to see Aiden!*

We pulled up to the building and were admitted to VIP parking. Jenny signed autographs and took some photos with the security staff as we were escorted backstage. Bass thumped through me from the opening act.

The security guy stopped at Aiden's door that had a white star with his name engraved on it, hanging from a hook. My hands were clammy, and I wiped them on my jeans. *Why was I so nervous?*

I lifted a hand and knocked, my insides doing jumping jacks.

The door swung open, and Aiden greeted us. His dark hair looked damp, and he ran a hand through it. When his gaze met mine, his smile transformed, his eyes crinkling as he strode forward and scooped me into his arms, lifting me off my feet.

I wrapped my arms around him and laughed as emotion overwhelmed me. Being in this moment was a dream come true. His chest shook against me and when I pulled back, he walked us into the room and kicked the door shut, leaving Jenny in the hall. His eyes were red with unshed tears, and he held my face in his hands and brought his lips to mine.

The kiss wasn't gentle like the one he'd given me in the hospital. That one had said he was afraid to hurt me. This kiss was demanding. *Searing into my memory. Scalding me with its passion.*

He broke the kiss and pressed his forehead to mine, and his arms wrapped around my biceps. "I missed you so bad."

I nipped at his bottom lip, and my hands dug into his hair. "I missed you, too."

Someone knocked on the door and, a feminine voice called through it. "Five minutes."

We broke apart, and Aiden grabbed his cowboy hat from the couch and dusted it on his pants. "I've gotta get ready. I'll see you after the show?"

"Yeah." I nodded, and he leaned in for one more quick peck.

Aiden opened the door, and Jenny peeked in. Aiden paused and did a double take. "Wow."

"I know, I'm huge." She patted her belly, then brushed past Aiden into the room. "We'll see you out there."

He put the cowboy hat on his head and winked at me. "See ya soon."

Jenny fussed with my hair, making sure everything was in place. "How was it?"

"So good. I'm so in love with him." I took a deep breath, relieved when it didn't hurt. I felt lighter, like I could do anything. Must've been the adrenaline.

"Let's get out there. We're gonna watch from the side of the stage. It's pretty fun."

Security guys waited for us and escorted us to the side of the stage where some producers chairs were set up. *It was the best kind of déjà vu.*

The openers came running offstage, and the stage crew went to work setting up new instruments and getting ready for the main event.

Jenny turned to me. "Dyl, because I love you, I'm telling you that Aiden is going to bring you out on stage during the concert while he sings your song, even though he told me not to."

Oh, my gosh. I thought my body was freaking out before, but this was a whole new type of freak out.

"Calm down, spaz pants. You'll be fine. Take a few deep breaths, and just enjoy the fact that Aiden wants to bring you on stage to show the world he's in love. It's sweet."

Sweet. Yes, it was sweet, but that didn't mean I liked it. That was the type of thing that happened in the movies, not real life.

A guitar chord strummed through the stadium, vibrating me to the core. After the chord faded, another began. The crowd went crazy. A few seconds later, the drummer's stand rose from the floor of the stage, and he hit his sticks together in a slow rhythm that the crowd copied with claps. The crowd screamed, and another chord rang through the arena.

The main guitarist entered the stage from one side, and the bass guitarist came in from the side we were on. Fog filled the arena and Aiden and his guitar slowly rose from a hole in the stage, much as his drummer had. The roar from the crowd was deafening.

A guitar started the beginning of one of Aiden's old songs and the crowd went crazy. Aiden strutted to the microphone and sang.

He kept his eyes on the crowd, but occasionally, he'd look at me and wink. My heart stuttered each time, and I loved that he was singing for the crowd, but somehow made it feel so intimate. Like we were the only two people in the room.

A stagehand ran a stool from the opposite side of the stage and set it beside Aiden.

"Before I play this next song, I want to introduce someone to y'all." As he spoke, he switched guitars, then strummed the opening chord for *Every Breath.*

The crowd screamed, and my heart forgot to beat for a second.

"Dylan Kennedy, would you please join me on stage?" He held a hand out toward me and waved his fingers, motioning me to him.

Holy crapoly, he was actually doing it. My butt might as well have been glued to the seat.

Jenny nudged me. "Go."

Aiden turned to the crowd. "She's a little shy. Help me get her out here.

Let's give her a round of applause."

Another roar from the crowd. Aiden turned to me and waved me out.

Nope. I shook my head. My hands shook, and my stomach was wound tighter than my Great Aunt Julie's girdle.

He jogged toward me, stopping just shy of leaving the stage. As he got to me, he pulled his hat off and put it over his heart. "Please, Dylan, go out there with me?" He reached out a hand and waited for me to take his.

Jenny nudged me again, jerking her head toward the stage.

I stood, putting my hand in his. He laced our fingers together in a familiar gesture, and I took a deep breath before stepping out with him.

The crowd went nuts.

He led me to the stool and helped me sit on it. That's when I noticed another microphone set up in front of the stool, right at my mouth height. *What the heck?*

"Y'all, since the first day I met this woman, I've been tryin' to come up with the perfect nickname for her. I tried kitten, kangaroo, and even stegosaurus."

The crowd laughed and cat-called. I felt my blush all the way to my hairline.

"But I think I've finally found the perfect one." Aiden looked over at me and grinned.

I tilted my head to the side and suppressed a smile as he moseyed toward me.

"You see, Dylan and I both share a deep appreciation for Chinese food." He spoke to the crowd, but kept his gaze on me.

My mind went through all the things he could settle on. Sweet and Sour, Egg Roll. If he called me Egg Roll, I'd never forgive him. Porcupine? I'd taught him how to coat his chicken in rice like one.

"Dumplin'."

I laughed, but my heart expanded at the name.

"You see, dumplin's are delicious, and addictive, and they remind me of home. Just like Dylan."

Oohs and aahs filled the stadium.

Aiden came over and wrapped me in a hug and placed a kiss on my forehead.

"Speakin' of my Dumplin', I wrote a song for her." He stood behind me and put his hands on my shoulders. "I'm gonna sing it for ya, Dylan, and if you want to join in, I'm sure the world would love to hear your voice." He raised his brows and nodded his encouragement.

Aiden turned to the drummer, who smashed his sticks together, counting them off.

I let Aiden sing the first verse alone, but I joined him for the chorus. The next few I sang harmony for both the verse and chorus. I expected him to stop after that, but the band kept playing.

He turned to me and waggled his eyebrows. "There's a secret verse."

Heat crept up my cheeks. It was my verse.

The crowd cheered.

Aiden closed the space between us and pulled me to my feet, wrapping an arm around my waist. Citrus and woods, the real thing, wrapped around me. He sang the final verse while staring directly into my eyes, his blue ones pools of emotion.

When he finished, the crowd went insane.

He pushed his guitar over his shoulder, dipped me, and planted a chaste kiss on my lips, sending my stomach into my throat.

As he steadied me, he turned back to the fans. "Doesn't she have an amazing voice?"

Another moment of insanity from the crowd.

He kissed me again, and I was liable to melt on the floor in a puddle of gooey Dylan. Hearing the crowd cheering for me was exhilarating. I raised my hand and waved to the crowd, and they erupted again.

"They love you." Aiden pulled me to his side and planted a kiss on my temple. He brought the mic back to his mouth. "They aren't the only ones who love you, Dylan."

"Aww!" the crowd seemed to say as one.

Aiden dug in his pocket and then dropped down onto one knee. "Dylan Kennedy, I loved you almost from the first moment I saw you, and I promise to love you with every breath I have. Will you marry me?"

I froze, my hand covering my mouth and my eyes welling with tears. Love swamped me for the man kneeling in front of me. I'd put him through so much, so much hurt and heartache, and he wanted more.

"Yes."

The word echoed through the nearly silent arena, followed by a huge roar from the crowd.

"She said yes!"

I was going to be Mrs. Aiden *Freaking* Miller.

Forty-Eight - Aiden

My heart was like a machine gun in my chest, and I stared at the door, waiting for Dylan to emerge. Nerves bundled in my stomach, a weird mix of excitement and disbelief.

I adjusted my suit again and smoothed a hand over my hair.

Dylan's door opened, and as she stepped out and met my gaze, my breath caught. She was the most amazing, beautiful woman on the planet, and she was all mine.

A breathtaking smile lit her face, and she exhaled visibly, then slowly walked toward me. Her hand came up, and she patted her chest, right over her heart. Dylan shook her head and laughed.

I couldn't tear my gaze from her. When she finally reached me, I held my hands out to hers.

"I can't believe you talked me into this," she whispered.

I grinned. "Are you ready to bungee jump, Dumplin'?"

Epilogue - Jenny

A bridesmaid's dress at nine months pregnant. *They're killing me!* I yanked the top up, dropping the girls down where they belonged. The only benefit of pregnancy was these amazing boobs.

Desiree, the only other bridesmaid, zipped my dress up, tucking in my extra rolls.

"Thanks. As far as bridesmaid dresses go, these aren't bad." I stared at myself in the mirror and swooped my hair to one side.

"Didn't you pick them out?" Desiree twisted a couple of my curls around her finger and laid them in place.

I grinned at her. "Yeah. I told her I wouldn't be a bridesmaid unless I could."

We finished primping, and I slipped my feet into my silver heels. Now to hope Evan didn't show up. I'd forced Dylan to lie to Aiden about the whole thing. The poor guy thought I was six months pregnant with a rebound's baby.

Dylan knocked on the door, then peeked her head in without waiting for an answer. She swept into the room in her simple white gown and closed the door behind her. "I'm gonna barf!"

"What? Are you having second thoughts?"

"No! I snuck into the kitchen and ate a bazillion of those little eclair things." She grinned, but put a hand to her stomach.

"Cream puffs." I'd taken a few myself. "You'll be fine. You need the extra calories, anyway." She'd lost so much weight during the last round of treatments that I was starting to feel self-conscious about my own ballooning waistline. *Okay, she didn't have to lose any weight to make me feel like a cow.*

"What if I throw up on Aiden? He'll think it's because I don't want to marry him."

I grabbed Dylan's shoulders and spun her to face me. "Look. You love him, right?"

She nodded.

"He loves you, right?"

Another nod.

"I didn't squeeze my fat butt into this dress to watch you ruin your wedding. Have I ever steered you wrong?"

She scoffed.

"Lately! Have I ever steered you wrong in the last week?"

Dylan hesitated again.

"Okay! This pep talk is going well." I dropped Dylan's shoulders and faced Desiree. "Whatcha got chika? She's not getting anything good from me." I gestured to Dylan and took a couple of steps back, letting Desiree take my spot.

She tossed her beautifully styled blonde hair over one shoulder and slunk forward. "What Jenny is trying to say is, you're going to be just fine. You can do hard things. Look at *Couple's Cruise.* You didn't think you'd be able to do that, and you nailed it! After you and Aiden announced your engagement, you were a champ dealing with all the press. This is easy. This is just showing Aiden how much you love him. Forget the cameras, the press, everyone else. This day is about the two of you and how much you love each other."

There was a tap on the door, and Mrs. Kennedy poked her head in. "Oh good, you're here." She slipped in and closed the door behind her, then wrapped Dylan in a hug. "You ready, sweetheart?"

Dylan's whole body seemed to let out a relieved breath. "Ready."

A thought occurred to me. "You made sure I was walking down the aisle with Colby, right?"

A blush crept up Dylan's cheeks.

"Dylan Kennedy, soon to be Miller. I am *not* walking down the aisle with

262

Evan. I refuse." How could I walk down the aisle with the father of my child? He didn't even want to be a dad.

The music started out on the back lawn, and the wedding planner rushed into the room. "It's time, ladies."

She ushered us down the stairs and behind the partition draped with flowers that stood behind the guest seating. She shuffled us into our order.

"Switch me spots." I grabbed Desiree's arm and widened my eyes at her meaningfully.

The wedding planner shushed me and sent Desiree down the aisle.

Desiree met with Colby, and the two walked down arm in arm.

I moved to the front of the line. Looking across the aisle, I made eye contact with Evan. His eyes bulged, then went to my stomach. I straightened, giving myself every possible inch my five-foot frame could manage, and lifted my chin. My OB said I was lucky. This, being my first baby, meant I didn't get as big as a second-time mother, so I still looked like I had some time before my due date.

But I wasn't ready for this conversation. Wasn't ready to face Evan. Would never be ready to face him.

"Don't ruin my wedding," Dylan murmured from behind me.

The wedding planner nudged me forward, and I realized Evan was already standing at the center of the aisle, waiting for me.

I'd always been able to read him, but his expression gave away nothing. Someone shoved me from behind, and I stumbled forward. Evan lunged, catching my arm and steadying me.

"Thank you," I said between clenched teeth.

"Mmhmm."

His cologne hit my nose, and I was transported back in time. I'd met him at a party. The music was loud, and I had a headache, so I'd gone out to the balcony to get some air. As I sat on the patio chair doing breathing exercises, Evan had come out, lighting a cigarette.

"Don't light that," I'd snapped.

He paused with the flame a half-inch from the end and studied me. Then he'd pulled the cigarette from his mouth, and tossed it over the edge.

"Jen," he whispered. He pulled on his arm again, and I blinked back into the here-and-now.

We'd made it to the other end of the aisle.

I released my death-grip and stepped to my side of the wedding party.

The bride's music started, and Dylan and Mrs. Kennedy, both gorgeous in white dresses, appeared at the start of the aisle.

Tears filled my eyes, and a sob broke from my throat. *I can't help it people, I'm pregnant!*

As Dylan walked down the aisle, I glanced at Aiden, who was almost as emotional as I was. He wiped a hand over his eyes, and his smile was tight, but I saw his chin tremble under all that scruff.

I knew Dylan was wishing it was her dad walking her down the aisle right now, but her mom looked so perfect. They reached Aiden, and he wiped tears from his eyes as he accepted Dylan's hand from Mrs. Kennedy.

"Dearly beloved, we are gathered here today..."

That was all I heard before I either peed my pants or my water broke.

Dearest Reader,

It's me, Dylan. Thank you for attending my wedding and reading my story. I hope you enjoyed it as much as I did. I'm the luckiest girl in the world, even if my best friend did steal the spotlight on my wedding day. In lieu of wedding gifts, Aiden and I would love it if you would leave a review for the author of our lovely story. Thanks a bunch! I have to get going. The mountains of Hawaii are calling my name. And don't tell Aiden... We're going skydiving!

Also, don't forget to sign up for Sally O'Keef's newsletter!

Whiskey's Like Love by Riley Moore:

It can burn like honey on fire
   Sweet but dangerous
   It can be real smooth
   Or make you choke on the truth
   Whiskey's just like love
   CHORUS:
   You can sip it slow
   And stop when you've had enough
   Or just let go
   And deal with the hurt of having too much
   It's hard to give up nippin' on the good stuff
   Whiskey's just like love

Every Breath by Riley Moore:

This wasn't what I was expecting
   Then again you never are
   You've been shakin' things up, girl
   Right from the start
   ~

   You laughed when the ocean kissed your face
   And it caught me by surprise
   'Cause then I wanted to be the waves
   And bring that smile to your eyes
   ~

   CHORUS:
   Every Breath
   Since we met
   I have spent
   Tryin' to figure out these feelings
   They weren't part of the agreement
   But now every breath
   I have left
   Will be spent
   Telling you
   No one takes away my breath like you do
   ~

   I'd been looking for a muse
   From the Rockies to the Gulf Coast

Then you got under my skin like a tattoo
Now your touch is the one I crave the most
I don't know how,
But baby you've found a way
Over my walls
With every smile of your unpainted face
~CHORUS~
You play my heart strings
Just like you played my guitar
So tender and careful
I forgot to be afraid and fell hard
~

Now every line I sing, every breath i breathe
Begins and ends with you
You've forever beautifully ruined me
'Cause no one will ever take away my breath like you do

About the Author

Sally O'Keef was born in Canada, but moved to the US when she was a wee babe. She's been married to the love of her life for fifteen years, and has six wonderful children and a huge dog who snores in the background as she writes. When she's not writing, she loves reading, volleyball, and watching her children achieve their dreams.

You can connect with me on:
🌐 https://booksbysally.com
🔲 https://www.facebook.com/booksbysally

Subscribe to my newsletter:
✉ https://booksbysally.com/lead-collection

Made in the USA
Las Vegas, NV
06 February 2024

85398259R00163